Dolly Waggler

Lesley St. James

Death of a Dolly Waggler is a work of fiction. Names, characters, places, and incidents either are products of the author's imagination or are used fictitiously. Any resemblance to actual events or locales or persons, living or dead, is entirely coincidental.

Madcap Mystery

Mechanicsville, Virginia

ISBN-978-1-7361855-5-1 (trade paperback)

ISBN-978-1-7361855-4-4 (ebook)

Library of Congress Control Number: 2021911030

For Matthew

CHAPTER 1

"Under my lederhosen, I'm anatomically correct," said the squirrel, and then he felt me up.

Alas, I wasn't dreaming. I was on the set of *The Mr. Snicklefritz Show*, and the beloved puppet Squirrelly-Joe was putting the moves on me. For the umpteenth time in two days, I wondered why I was there. Oh yeah, money.

"I highly doubt that," I replied as I swatted the plush paw that was attempting to cop a feel. "Your butt is slit open, and a three-hundred-pound man has his fist shoved all the way up to your head."

"I don't know what you're talking about," sniffed Squirrelly-Joe. With a "Humph!" he turned and stormed off.

"You're a puppet! Deal with it!" I called after him. It was the third time in two days that the squirrel had hit on me—correction—that the puppeteer had hit on me, at least I thought it was the puppeteer. Larry Stubbins seemed like a nice, normal guy. He didn't leer at me. He made polite conversation at lunch. He was kind and caring to the kids who visited the set. But that Squirrelly-Joe was a lecher.

I shook my head to clear the fog.

"You're doing it again, Jill," I told myself. "The puppets aren't real. The puppets aren't real." I wasn't convinced. The puppets on *The Mr. Snicklefritz Show* seemed very real indeed. The set of the show was a wacky world where anything was possible. It was a place that I never expected to visit and that I was looking forward to leaving. Unfortunately, it was only Tuesday. I still had over a week and a half to go.

Was it only last Friday that I'd accepted the job out of desperation? At the time, it seemed like an answer to my prayers. I was back home in Luthersburg, Virginia, for Thanksgiving, sitting on my bed in my childhood bedroom with a stack of bills and a calculator. I added and re-added the numbers, but nothing changed. The bills still tallied up to more than my salary that month. Considerably more. Somebody wasn't going to get paid. Somebody was going to be unhappy.

"Oh, well," I thought. "Can't be helped." The money fairy wasn't going to suddenly pop up with a wad of cash. She'd lost my address years ago. I picked up the stack of bills and flipped through them again, trying to decide who to shaft that month.

Power bill? Nope.

Cell phone? Too necessary.

Amex? Still ticked off at me about stiffing them last month, as they'd informed me many times via telephone. If I did it again, they might hire a hitman.

Visa? I hadn't missed a payment in a year and a half. I had a contender.

Gym? I credited my Zumba class for the fact that I'd remained the same size despite Halloween and Thanksgiving, but the price was pretty steep. I laid it on top of the Visa as a maybe.

Cable and internet bill? Two hundred channels. All the entertainment a single, dateless girl could want on a Friday night, but it cost me big time. Another maybe.

I added up the Visa, the cable, and the gym, but it still

wasn't enough. I needed to forego one more bill if I wanted to eat that month. I couldn't take any more phone calls from Amex, and I needed lights in my apartment. I was going to have to take a chance on the cell phone bill. I'd been a good customer. They'd probably send me lots of notices before turning off my phone.

Decision made, I sat back and pondered how I'd come to this place of financial desperation. Was I trying to keep up with the Joneses? Hardly. My neighbors had squeezed four people into a studio apartment the same size as mine, so I wasn't keeping up with them—I was lapping them. Was my cash-strapped status instead the result of too many nights out with the Posse, my group of best friends who also worked in public relations? Maybe. Too many trips to the movies? Definitely.

And the cherry on top of this poverty sundae of my own making was that I had to forego my vacation to Bali. In what delusional state had I ever thought I might afford such a vacation? I'll tell you what state—a state of heartbreak.

Heartbreak is what makes you do crazy things like plan a vacation that costs half your yearly salary. It also makes you put purple streaks in your hair, adopt puppies, and give your number to guys you'd never consider dating if you weren't insane from heartbreak. Luckily, the vacation had never been paid for, my hairdresser removed the streaks, and the SPCA rep decided he wouldn't give me a puppy after he saw my apartment. I was, however, still dodging calls from dodgy men I'd met in dodgy places. Lesson learned.

If there was a silver lining to my current financial predicament, it was that poverty had put heartbreak on the back burner. I needed an infusion of cash and fast. I needed a second job. I was already Jill Cooksey, Senior Account Executive at the boutique PR firm of Waverly Communications. Now I needed another gig to hopefully put me back in the black.

On cue, my phone rang, and it wasn't American Express or

a dodgy male. (Massive sigh of relief.) It was my good friend Kate Vogel, an entertainment PR specialist, with an offer of two weeks of freelance work at *The Mr. Snicklefritz Show* that coincided with the time I had taken off for my doomed trip to Bali.

"It'll be a piece of cake," Kate had assured me. It was the thirtieth anniversary of the show, and my job was to organize and chaperone visits to the set by network executives, families, and the press. "Basically, you'll be babysitting."

I was used to babysitting clients. No big deal. Plus, the idea of working on a TV show had a certain cachet. Most importantly, I was going to make two thousand dollars that a certain credit card company was clamoring for.

Kate had failed to mention, however, that the puppet world was weird, something I hadn't expected. I'd grown up on Mr. Snicklefritz and his cuddly companions Squirrelly-Joe, Moose the Moose, and Martin the Marten. As a small child, I enjoyed entering the Snicklefritz world full of funny characters, fairy tales, and silly songs. Mr. Snicklefritz was a kindly woodcutter who lived in Gingerbread Cottage somewhere deep in the forest. His everyday companions were the aforementioned animals. Squirrelly-Joe was a hyperactive squirrel who liked to bring strange objects to Mr. Snicklefritz for identification. Moose was the exact opposite of Squirrelly-Joe. He was sleepy and slow-moving and always asking for a story, but he invariably fell asleep before it was over. Martin was a musician who sang songs while strumming a cigar box banjo, that is until protests over the presence of smoking paraphernalia on a children's TV show forced the switch to a ukulele. Mr. Snicklefritz's only human companion was the beautiful Princess Gretel, who visited him once in each episode. When I was a kid, she used to teach manners, but they were out of fashion nowadays.

The whole Snicklefritz gang lived in harmony and spent

their days acting silly—at least, that's what millions of kids thought. On my first day on the set, I learned otherwise. Kate was showing me around, and we entered the set between takes. She was introducing me to some of the crew when the catcalls, or rather squirrelcalls, began.

"Well, well, well. What do we have here? Hey Mama, why don't you come over here and tickle my tail?"

The rest of the crew giggled, but I was outraged. Sexually harassed on my first day of work, and in front of witnesses? This guy, whoever he was, was out of line. I turned around to tell him so, but no one was there—just the beloved puppets of my childhood, Joe, Martin, and Moose. Immediately I forgot the catcalling caveman. My childhood pals were real and right in front of me. A wave of nostalgia gripped me hard, but it was soon to be replaced with a wave of nausea.

"Take a picture. It'll last longer," Squirrelly-Joe spat in my direction. "Hey fellas, she wants me! When it comes to Joe, they never say no! You know what I'm going to do to you, Mama?" And then he started…er…accosting a tree stump made of Styrofoam. "Oh yeah! Oh yeah!"

And thus all my childhood illusions were swept away. Around me, the crew erupted into laughter, but I just wanted to hurl.

"Oh, for heaven's sake," whined Martin. "Must you do that here?"

"You're just wishing you could trade places with the stump," retorted Joe.

"Could you hurry up so we can get back to work?" yelled Moose.

"This is horrible," I whispered.

"Perhaps I should have warned you," said Kate. "Sorry."

"You know, when the dog acts like that back home, we put him in the smokehouse until he recollects himself," I said, looking everywhere except at the libidinous squirrel.

"I would think the smell of ham would excite him even more."

"Gives him different priorities."

When Joe requested a cigarette, a grip, one of those handy folks who wait around on the set to move whatever needs moving, actually brought him one, which he pretended to puff. I was struggling to make sense of what I'd just witnessed when Joe looked me straight in the eye.

"Meet me behind the set when we break for lunch. I have an appetite, and it ain't for food."

The crew, mostly male, were all laughing hysterically.

"So," I said to Kate, "TV is like high school."

"Exactly."

The rest of the day I avoided the set as much as possible. When I toured guests around, the puppets were warned ahead of time and were on their best behavior, mostly. At lunch, the puppeteers made polite conversation and seemed like nice people, but between takes, puppets had potty mouths.

Today, however, I had sent Squirrelly-Joe packing. Score one for Jill. Thankfully, it was early in the morning, and none of the other puppets were on the set yet. I just needed to speak to the floor director, the person in charge of the set who relayed all the instructions from the director in the control booth. Our floor director was a tall, slim woman named Flavia Gomez. I found her talking to some of the grips behind the set.

Flavia was one of those gorgeous people who have no idea that they're gorgeous. Her mass of long brown curls framed a spotless complexion and a pair of eyes the color of milk chocolate. On her model-like bod, she sported the latest in on-set apparel: jeans, a long-sleeved flannel shirt, and steel-toed boots. She was a grip's dream girl, and the grips certainly weren't happy with me when I pulled her away to tell her about the on-set visits scheduled for that day.

"Sounds like a 'rainbow' morning," she said. "We might actually get some work done."

"Rainbow" was the code word used whenever children or important visitors were on the set. It meant "keep it clean," and keeping it clean meant fewer hijinks and more filming.

I left Flavia to the grips and headed back to my cubicle in the production office. On the way, I cruised by the craft services table, affectionately known as "The Trough." Craft services was supposed to provide energy to people who worked a long day, many of them on their feet. The reality was that craft services pushed carbs that did get you through the day but that also added pounds over the course of a television season. I'd been warned to avoid the peanut butter cups that appeared by the bowlful magically every day, but I just couldn't help myself. Hands full of chocolate, I made it back to my cubicle just as the phone started ringing. It was my mother.

"Jilly! So glad I caught you." She might not have if I'd seen the caller ID before I picked up. Thanksgiving had been only the week before, but my frighteningly efficient parent, Loretta Cooksey, was now in full-on Christmas mode and had been peppering me with questions about gift ideas and decorating schemes since I boarded the train back to New York on Sunday. She hadn't asked me about food yet, but I figured this call would strike it off the list. I couldn't blame her. Without my dad, who had passed a couple of years before, the holidays were a hard time for her, and she dealt with it through elaborate planning and preparation.

"Now I know we always have ham at Christmas," Mom rolled on, "but I thought about shaking things up a bit. I have a recipe for chateaubriand that I'm dying to try."

"Sounds wonderful, Mama," I encouraged. Ham was always Dad's favorite anyway.

"Now, about your present. I'm sending you an email right

now with a selection, and I want you to pick one out. Let me know soon, okay, so I can tell Santa in time."

Before I could suggest that maybe we should skip presents this year due to my lack of funds, I heard shouting and thumps and crashes.

"Mama, I gotta go. It sounds like the end of the world is happening." I hung up and hustled down the hall toward the studio, ground zero for Armageddon. I arrived just as Carl Biersdorf, also known as Mr. Snicklefritz, came barreling off the set followed by the executive producer Marcus Sanderson.

"Don't forget, you were just a dolly waggler when I met you, Carl, and you're still just a dolly waggler! You'd still be playing with sock puppets in Cincinnati if it weren't for me!" Marcus was a tall, slim man with salt and pepper hair and, at this moment, a face the same color as the raspberry gumdrops that decorated Gingerbread Cottage. Carl, in a similar state, was the color of a cinnamon red-hot.

"Get outta my way!" bellowed Carl. Shorter and stockier than Marcus, he plowed like an offensive lineman through a wall of cast and crew who had materialized out of nowhere. As he passed, Larry Stubbins (a.k.a. Squirrelly-Joe), Bryce Camplen (a.k.a. Martin the Marten), and Phil Rainey (a.k.a. Moose the Moose) closed ranks and prevented Marcus from following. The standoff that followed was straight out of a spaghetti western. Sweat glistened on Marcus's brow as he faced the puppeteers' stony expressions. Their eyes narrowed further, daring Marcus to make a move. His eyebrow twitched, but he held firm. The tension was palpable.

"Okay, everyone, back to work," called Flavia, and she clapped her hands, breaking the tension and effectively calling cut on the scene. "There's nothing to see here. Just a little disagreement. Everything's fine. Chicken parmigiana for lunch today, guys, so you got something to look forward to."

Everyone started to shuffle back to their jobs. The

puppeteers and the producer held their stance for a moment more before going their separate ways. Soon Marcus was back in the control room with the door shut, and the puppeteers were back on the set, donning their puppets.

I approached Flavia.

"What on earth just happened?"

"Marcus just shot himself in the foot," said Flavia. "That's what happened."

"Come again?"

"The worst thing you can ever call a puppeteer is a d-dolly waggler." Flavia stumbled over the word like it was *Voldemort*. "It's the greatest insult in the industry. It implies that puppeteers are simply playing with toys instead of perfecting their craft. You might hear puppeteers call each other dolly wagglers when they're joking around, but if you aren't a puppeteer, you don't say that word." She sighed and raked a hand through her curls. "We won't get a thing done today."

She was right. When I brought kids through for set visits later that morning, the puppets, while watching their language, were not cooperating with the director. They cracked jokes, performed an amazingly detailed hula dance, and had long conversations with each of the children.

There was no sign of Mr. Snicklefritz.

By the time the set visit was over, it was lunchtime.

When I exited the lunch line with my tray laden with chicken parmigiana, salad, and more of those darn peanut butter cups, the studio cafeteria was eerily quiet. I scanned the room looking for a place to sit and for a glimpse of Marcus Sanderson or the puppeteers.

"They won't show," said a deep baritone voice behind me. I turned to see Devon Cauthorne, a tall forty-something man with cropped, black, curly hair graying at the temples. He also carried a lunch tray, although his looked much healthier than mine.

"They're all having a closed-door lunch meeting to clear the air and mend fences," he continued. "No dramatics over lunch. Everyone's going to be very disappointed." I knew Devon worked with the puppeteers, so he should know. His cool brown skin crinkled around his eyes as he grinned at me, and I smiled back.

Devon led me to a table in the corner, and we sat. I had been introduced to him on my first day (was that only yesterday?), but this was my first chance to really talk to him.

"Is today typical of life in television production?"

Devon laughed.

"Every season has its highs and lows. Puppeteers, directors, producers, heck, even editors can act like prima donnas from time to time. Tempers heat up, especially when we're behind schedule. I've been with the show for twenty years, so I've seen some things."

"Saving all the stories for your memoirs?"

"Something like that."

Because I didn't really understand Devon's job and because he seemed like such a nice guy, I asked him about it.

"I'm a right hand," he replied.

"So am I," I joked, "but what's your job?" Devon rolled his eyes.

"A right hand performs a puppet's right hand."

I was utterly confused.

"Why doesn't the puppeteer just do the right hand himself?"

Devon patiently explained that most puppeteers were right-handed, which meant their right hands were controlling the mouths of the puppets. They could control a puppet's left hand with a little stick, but the puppet's right hand would just flop around without someone to control it. That was his job.

"Without the right hand, a puppet looks lopsided and out of control."

It finally made sense, yet I wondered what it would be like

to spend twenty years being a puppet's right hand. Devon read my mind with his next remark and almost made me blush in embarrassment.

"But I won't always be a right hand." He smiled at me knowingly. "Don't get me wrong; I'm glad for the work. Puppetry isn't an easy game, and the gig has put my kid through college. But I won't be a right hand for too much longer."

He leaned in conspiratorially, and I followed suit.

"My ship is about to come in." His eyes practically glowed as he said it. I arched an inquiring eyebrow. "I'm up for a very big role. The role of a lifetime."

I arched my eyebrow even higher, hoping he would say more, but Devon just smiled like the cat who swallowed the canary.

"Well, congratulations, and good luck," I said and meant it. After twenty years of being a right hand, it seemed to me that Devon deserved all the luck in the world. He thanked me with a wink, and we went back to eating. For the rest of lunch, I peppered him with questions about the technical side of puppetry and TV production, and he was very patient and answered all my questions. By the end, I didn't feel quite so lost in my new environment.

After lunch, the set was a very different place. In fact, it seemed like the puppeteers were falling all over themselves trying to be gracious to each other, to Carl, and to Marcus. He was stationed in the control room watching the filming, and the puppets on the set were seriously kissing his butt.

"Shout out to Marcus!" chirped an overly chipper Squirrelly-Joe.

"Yeah, Marcus is the greatest!" proclaimed Martin. "He's my best friend."

"No he's my best friend!" countered Moose, and a nauseating fight over Marcus's best friend status ensued. The crew ate it up. I wanted to vomit. Suck up city! I caught Devon's eye at one point, and he mimed vomiting onto the set. Now that made me chuckle.

The only person not chuckling was Mr. Snicklefritz. Carl was performing his lines and doing his job, but he was certainly not sucking up to the producer. In fact, between takes, Carl made a point to look anywhere but at the control room. As I watched the children's television icon during the times when he didn't have to smile and act lovable, I realized that Carl Biersdorf was barely holding it together.

CHAPTER 2

When my alarm sounded at five the next morning, I contemplated not showing up for work. The television production workday started much earlier than my normal PR day, and I was having trouble adjusting. I let myself linger in bed for a few more minutes before I threw back the covers and forced myself to get up. The first thing I did was walk six feet to the "kitchen" of my studio apartment to procure coffee. Having to get up before most civilized people had forced me to start using the timer function on my coffee pot, and I was hooked. Day three of waking up to freshly brewed coffee had me convinced it wouldn't take twenty-one days to make this a habit. I settled back on my bed with my coffee and looked at the day's headlines on my phone. Then I checked my voicemail and found two messages from unknown numbers. I played the first.

"Uh, hi. This is Terrence. We met at that all-night felafel stand a couple of weeks ago. Just wondering if you want to hang out sometime. Call me."

I racked my brain for any memory of Terrence. After the boyfriend fled our relationship, my friend Anupa decided the best thing for me was to go dancing—every night. She dragged me to one club after another usually followed by a twenty-four-hour eatery where we would invariably get hit on and I would invariably hand out my number as a form of revenge against the reporter-who-shall-not-be-named. (I have a theory that men position themselves by the food trucks, waiting for women to emerge from dance clubs hungry and vulnerable. Actually, it's not unintelligent.) I remembered the all-night Indian restaurant (George), the all-night diner (Raphael), and the all-night pizza place (Mark), but the felafel stand? Then I remembered. It was the very first night out with Anupa, almost a month ago! Terrence was certainly playing it cool by waiting that long to call. Oh, well. It didn't matter. I blocked his number and erased the message. Bye-bye, Terrence.

Then I played the other message—silence followed by a hang-up. Someone must have lost his nerve, thank goodness.

By this time, the coffee had kicked in, so I got up and transformed my bed back into a futon sofa before I continued with my morning routine. I surveyed the shoebox apartment, looking for messes that needed straightening. My desk was clean and organized. The sink was clear of dirty dishes. The place was pretty orderly, so I headed for the shower.

Cleaning my apartment at five thirty in the morning before I'd even had a shower might seem like neat-freak craziness, but I was attempting to turn over a new leaf. Until recently, my apartment had resembled a Superfund site, but clutter and filth were now things of the past. Thanks to a certain organizational guru who had urged me to purge everything that didn't bring me joy *and* the aforementioned boyfriend who dropped out of my life with absolutely no warning, leaving me with a surplus of emotional energy that had to be channeled, I was a new and improved and spotlessly clean Jill Cooksey.

By six thirty, I was ready for work. Despite having to get up at the crack of dawn, the TV gig was a bit of a vacation simply because I got to wear jeans and sneakers to work. TV was a far more relaxed environment than beauty PR, my specialty. Even so, I did tend to dress up my jeans with blouses, cardigans, and jewelry, but old habits die hard. Today I was wearing pearls with an Oxford cloth shirt and a jaunty red cardigan, and my straight blond hair was swept back in a ponytail secured with a red scrunchie. I was going for casual but classy. Satisfied with the effect, I slung on my parka, wrapped a chunky scarf around my neck several times, and freed my ponytail. Then I checked for the apartment key that I wore on a chain around my neck, grabbed my Behemoth Black Bag (which held all my city-dweller essentials), and sallied forth into Queens.

The other thing that made this gig a vacation was that I didn't have to get on the subway. I had learned since starting the job that Queens had been ground zero for the fledgling film industry in the early twentieth century. Before the studios decamped for the palm trees, orange groves, and ample sunshine of California, many had called Queens home. Now the motion picture companies were gone, but the studio space remained. *The Mr. Snicklefritz Show* was produced in one of these historic buildings. For a film buff like me, it was a dream come true. Even better, the studio was only a twenty-minute walk from my apartment—twenty bracing minutes. The cold, dry air slapped me in the face as I exited my building. As it filled my lungs and stung my cheeks, it finished the job the coffee started. Invigorated, by the time I reached the studio, I felt lighter than I had in several weeks.

In the foyer, I waved hello to Stan the security guard and pushed through the double doors to enter the world of television. When I got to my cubicle, I divested myself of outerwear and headed to the cafeteria for breakfast.

I was standing at the buffet, trying to choose between muffins and croissants, when Bryce Camplen, also known as Martin the Marten, sidled up to me.

"Jill, right?" he asked as he reached for a chocolate chip muffin.

"That's right," I said, choosing a chocolate croissant. I picked up my plate and my coffee and headed for a table, and Bryce followed and sat down beside me. Someone wanted a breakfast buddy.

"I'm surprised that you're here so early." I tried to make conversation. "Doesn't the talent usually show up about eight?"

"Usually," he said as he broke his muffin open and began spreading it with butter, "but I wanted a chance to talk with Marcus today."

I thought back to yesterday's performance when all of the puppets were kissing up to the producer. I was surprised that any more kissing up needed to be done.

"So, what's going on there?" I asked. "You guys were really mad yesterday, and then it seemed to blow over pretty quickly."

"Oh, you know," said Bryce. "Tempers flare. It's no big deal. Marcus was out of line, and he totally admitted it, which was really big of him. Carl, on the other hand..." He paused and took a sip of his coffee. It didn't seem like he was going to say anything else.

"What about Carl?" I probed.

"Carl's stubborn. Always has been."

"Well, he's been doing this job a long time, hasn't he?"

"Over thirty years," said Bryce.

"I'm surprised he's not thinking about retirement."

Bryce gave me a conspiratorial side-eye.

"Who said he isn't?"

"Oh! So Mr. Snicklefritz may be leaving Gingerbread Cottage and decamping to Boca."

Bryce snorted. "I can't imagine Carl Biersdorf in sunny Florida. More like Vegas."

"Has the retirement been announced?" I hadn't read any press materials about it, and what with the thirtieth anniversary of the show coming up, it seemed like an appropriate time to announce a changing of the guard.

"I don't know," said Bryce. "I know he's supposed to retire, but no one's really saying anything yet."

"Then how come you know about it?"

That conspiratorial look was back.

"Well, you know when Carl leaves, *Mr. Snicklefritz* will continue on. This show isn't going anywhere. It's a children's television staple."

"That's true," I said, not quite following where he was going.

"Sooooo, they'll need a new Mr. Snicklefritz." Bryce connected the dots for me.

"Oh! But wait a minute," I said. "Who will play Martin the Marten?" Bryce Camplen had been Martin the Marten for the last fifteen years.

"Don't you worry. We've always got understudies waiting in the wings. There's a whole line of puppeteers who have perfected our voices. It's kind of spooky actually. One thing we all need to remember is that we can always be replaced."

"So there is somebody poised to take over the role of Martin if you move into the role of Mr. Snicklefritz?"

"Oh sure. We always have backup plans and backups of backups."

I thought of Devon Cauthorne. Was he hoping to move up to the Martin role?

"Wow! Does everyone know that you'll be the new Mr. Snicklefritz?"

Bryce took on a wary look. "You know, I probably shouldn't have said anything to you. Nobody really knows about this. I mean, I've talked about it with Carl. I'm actually Carl's choice for his replacement. He and I have talked about it a lot, but you know, it's the sort of thing you just don't talk about until it's a done deal. I mean, there are a lot of people who would like to be Mr. Snicklefritz. We wouldn't want any more scenes like we had yesterday. If you could keep it to yourself, I'd really appreciate it."

"Oh, that's not a problem," I assured him. "I work in PR. Keeping people's secrets is what I do."

He smiled. "I probably wouldn't have told you except that I just feel so comfortable with you."

What a nice thing to say, I thought, and I smiled at him. Mistake.

"You know," he continued, "I didn't just happen to bump into you. I've actually been looking for a minute to talk to you and see if maybe you'd like to go out sometime."

Bryce must have interpreted the dismay in my facial expression as surprise because he grinned at me. He had a stunner of a smile which prompted me to look at the rest of Bryce Camplen. He was certainly a good-looking man. In fact, with red hair, green eyes, and a hint of freckles, he was very striking.

And he was a puppeteer.

I'd never dated a puppeteer. Actually, I didn't know anybody who had dated a puppeteer. You don't run into puppeteers too terribly often, do you? I supposed it was a career like any other career. Lawyer, doctor, puppeteer? Sure.

Bryce had been more successful than most with his solid gig on *The Mr. Snicklefritz Show*, and he was about to become even more successful when he took on the title role. But his success wasn't really my concern. Puppeteers were a new breed for me. Some of them were, well, odd, but Bryce didn't seem to be. This was his calling, and he was good at it. Better yet, he didn't sexually harass people with his puppet.

Yes, there were a lot of checks in Bryce's "Pros" column, but none of them outweighed the giant "Con"—I was a woman with a broken heart, and I had firmly resolved to take a break from the male species.

When my now ex-boyfriend Mike McCall ghosted me, as in suddenly he just wasn't there, I hadn't seen it coming. Together we had taken on a murder investigation and managed to start dating along the way. He was a reporter; I was in PR. While the relationship wasn't without its little bumps, I thought we complemented each other perfectly.

I thought.

Now I was severely gun-shy. I didn't need any more hurt, any more unanswered questions, and that's what men left you with.

Jill Cooksey is an island.

Yeah, a gorgeous tropical island in the south Pacific where no men were allowed. That island Wonder Woman came from.

But Bryce wasn't really a man, I reasoned with clearly flawed logic. He was a puppeteer, and he was smiling eagerly at me—a man (correction, puppeteer) who spent all his time trying to make children happy. How awful could he be?

"I'd love to go out with you," I said forcing a smile.

"Great! Are you free for dinner tonight?"

Whoa! Fast mover. The polar opposite of Terrence. But I didn't have any plans, and I wasn't going to be working on the show for too much longer. It made sense except for the part where I didn't want to date anyone.

"I don't have any plans except, you know, to collapse from fatigue at the end of the day."

Bryce laughed. "Yeah, it's a grueling day around here, isn't it? But we don't work all year round. The season only lasts about nine months, and then we're off for three. You work really hard, but then you get some time off."

"Not a bad gig."

"Not at all."

We made plans to meet for dinner at a local Greek restaurant.

Jill Cooksey is a peninsula?

"Well, I've got to get to my dressing room and get ready for the day," he said. "I'll see you later, Jill."

"Bye, Bryce."

I took my chocolate croissant, my cup of coffee, and my feeling of dread back to my cubicle and threw myself into my to-do list to avoid thinking about the date I had just agreed to. If I thought about it too much, I'd probably have a panic attack, so I started printing out the list of the day's visitors. Today's group was made up of some past employees of the show and their kids and grandkids. It was going to be an easy morning full of reunions and swapping stories. I wouldn't have to do much except show them around, and then as they recognized people they knew, they'd probably take it from there.

As I worked, my email pinged, and I saw it was from my mother.

Jill,

You have not responded to my email about your Christmas present. Please respond as soon as possible as some of the gift choices are time-sensitive.

Thank you,
Your mother.

Leave it to Mom to write a Christmas email that was all business. She had attached a list to the new email, so I opened it up and took a look. Then my jaw dropped. What was my mother thinking? The email was full of photographs of guns, handguns to be more precise, of every shape, size, and color. There were Glocks. There were revolvers. There were tiny little guns that looked like toys, but the prices were astronomical. The cheapest thing on the list was five hundred dollars and the most expensive was two thousand. Time-sensitive? Was there a gun show coming to town?

Undoubtedly, our adventures earlier in the fall had left an

indelible mark on my mother. When a PR campaign for a fragrance had been sabotaged by murder, it had been my job to figure out who had done it and why. My mother clearly was remembering the standoff during which she was armed but I was not.

A handgun, I thought. Do I want a handgun? I wasn't averse to guns. I was from a small town in Virginia, and my dad had taught me how to shoot. But did I want a handgun? In New York City?

"Oof." Unable to process my mother's bizarre choice in Christmas present, I closed her email and turned my attention back to work, which was always the antidote when the world became too crazy.

When eight o'clock rolled around, I knew that all the performers should have been in the building, probably in their dressing rooms. I needed to have a quick word with each of them ahead of time to let them know who was coming to visit. I made my way to the dressing rooms and started knocking on doors.

Bryce wasn't in his, but as he'd arrived early, he was probably already on the set. I hesitated outside of Larry Stubbins's dressing room because, frankly, I didn't want another encounter with Squirrelly-Joe. But I told myself that I had to be professional and I had to let him know. We would see what happened. I knocked on the door.

"Come in," said Stubbins, so I did.

Larry's dressing room, after thirty years, was an extension of its occupant. A recliner had pride of place facing a huge television and a gaming system. The walls were either covered by posters for *Dungeons and Dragons* and *Warhammer* or by shelves lined with row upon row of small figurines that I was pretty sure Larry had painted himself. An entire army of orcs, dwarves, and elves stared down at me. The only exceptions were the shelves on the back wall which supported nothing less than an armory. I saw a Samurai katana, several shuriken, and, I was pretty sure, replicas of Bilbo's sword Sting and the Morgul blade from *The Lord of the Rings* films. They all looked wickedly sharp.

"Hey, Jill," Larry said from the lounger without taking his eyes off the game he was playing. "How's it going?"

"Fine," I mumbled. I gave the short, rotund puppeteer a piercing look. "How are you?"

"Good! Excited about today."

"Why is that?" I was afraid to ask.

"Well, we're recording a new song today. It's going to be a really fun number."

"That's cool," I said cautiously.

"Hey, did you get any of those chocolate croissants from the buffet this morning? They were outstanding. They got a new baker or something."

"Yeah, I managed to snag one."

Larry was his normal, affable self. I couldn't understand the difference between him and Squirrelly-Joe, but I didn't want to bring it up either because what if it changed him? What if mentioning it brought the Squirrelly-Joe out in him, and then I'd have to deal with the randy rodent making the moves on me? I decided to just play it cool. I went over the guest list with him and then moved on to Phil Rainey's dressing room.

As I entered Phil's inner sanctum, I could feel the stress leaving my body. Incense wafted about the room while a Himalayan salt lamp burned soothingly in the corner. Phil, a hippie from way back, sat in the lotus position in a papasan chair. Statues of various deities were secreted in the corners of the room. One wall was draped with rich eastern fabrics in deep orange and maroon. Another wall was covered with rock-n-roll concert posters that appeared to be originals, including Fairport Convention, Muddy Waters, and Janis Joplin. A record player sat on a small table with a huge stack of LPs. The well-worn covers suggested frequent listening. Scattered across the remaining two walls were framed photos of Phil with some of his music icons and other heavy hitters in the world of puppetry. There was a picture of him at the White House wearing a suit but no tie, his hair pulled back in his trademark sleek ponytail, which was at that time either dark brown or black. There were also portrait-style photos of Moose the Moose wearing various costumes: in a smoking jacket with a Meerschaum pipe while sitting in a wingback chair; sporting dreads and a knitted Rastafarian cap while playing steel drums on a beach; driving a Volkswagen Beetle and throwing up a peace sign.

"Hey, Jill. How's it hanging?" asked Phil.

"Can't complain, Phil. Just wanted to go over the guest list with you for today."

"Perfect timing. I just finished aligning my chakras."

Phil had taken over the role of Moose the Moose when Carl Biersdorf took *The Mr. Snicklefritz Show* national. Before that, Carl had actually done both roles. When the show went national and the budget increased, Carl and Marcus decided that somebody else should perform the puppet, and Phil fit the bill. He could do the Moose voice perfectly, and over the last thirty years, he had become synonymous with the character. In fact, hardly anyone remembered that Moose was actually originated by Carl. I only knew this because I'd read all the press materials

Phil was very go-with-the-flow, thanks to those aligned chakras, so briefing him took no time at all. My next stop was Carl Biersdorf's dressing room. I hadn't had much interaction with Carl, who was moody and mercurial. He kept to himself a lot, and most of what I'd seen of him involved temper tantrums and sulking, except for his performances, which were always great. Carl was a terrific actor who could really convince you that he was full of sweetness and light even when he was full of bile and shadow. I knocked on his door.

"Enter."

If Phil's dressing room was a temple to zen, Carl's was the exact opposite. At some point, it had started out homey with a sofa and coffee table, a mini-fridge, and a microwave. Framed photos of Carl as Mr. Snicklefritz posing with celebrities and politicians graced the walls. Award statues were arranged on glass shelves. The Daytime Emmy collection rivaled the terra cotta army of Emperor Qin Shi Huang and seemed to go on forever. A long time ago, this dressing room was tasteful and well-appointed, but now it looked like some frat boys had moved in and made themselves at home. Several ashtrays overflowed with cigarette butts. A nearly full bottle of O'Sullivan's whiskey sat on the coffee table, but empties littered the floor and the top of the mini-fridge. Most of the photos hung askew, and the award statuary was arranged in some interesting tableaux that had me blushing. A crack in one of the glass shelves foreshadowed disaster.

And yet there were also photos of Mr. Snicklefritz as a goodwill ambassador, maybe for the United Nations or the United States, on the great wall of China, in front of the pyramids in Egypt, by a well somewhere in Africa. There seemed to be pictures of him with children of all nationalities in very exotic locales, and in every photo, the kids were looking at him adoringly and he was looking the same way right back. Clearly Carl Biersdorf, despite his crusty "get off my lawn" exterior, had a heart for children.

He did not, however, have a heart for me.

"What?" He asked from the couch where he was sprawled, a glass of whiskey in hand. He was not alone. The current Princess Gretel, Britney, was snuggled up to him, and the hand not holding the whiskey was holding part of her anatomy.

Keeping my eyes glued to my clipboard, I started going through the day's guest list, but he cut me off quickly.

"Yeah, yeah. I got it. Keep it clean. Play nice. Yada yada yada. Was there anything else? I got my hands full right now, as you can see." At this, Britney snorted.

"Nope," I mumbled. "See you on set." I fled.

Back in my cubicle, I took some deep breaths and recited my mantra: "Two thousand dollars. Two thousand dollars."

AN HOUR LATER, before my first group of visitors, I took a trip to the set just to see how things were going and to make sure everybody in the crew also knew it was a rainbow morning. Martin and Moose were already on set and seemed to be whispering to each other over by the tree stump, their backs turned towards the crew. When Joe appeared, they suddenly started whistling and acting nonchalant. I wondered what was going on.

"Good morning, everybody," called out Squirrelly-Joe. "Did everybody get a good night's sleep? Because I didn't, if you know what I mean. She kept me up ALL night."

Then Martin stepped aside to reveal what he and Moose had been doing—affixing a sticky note to the poor tree stump that had been the victim of Joe's lust the day before. The sticky note read "#MeToo." Joe was unfazed.

"Badge of honor!" He was repellent, but the crew laughed anyway.

Then the director came on set, and they started blocking out the new musical number which I had heard was titled "The Booger Song." Oh boy. Out of the gross frying pan and into the even grosser fire. I had a quiet word with Flavia, who interrupted blocking for a moment to remind everyone that it was a rainbow morning. A production assistant hastily took down the #MeToo sticky, and everyone put on their happy faces.

An hour later, I brought my first tour through the studio. I waited until the on-air light was off to open the door and let everyone in. We found the cast and crew rehearsing a particular part of "The Booger Song." Carl was on the set now, and there was also a disembodied nose puppet with fuzzy green boogers coming out of the nostrils. It was thoroughly disgusting.

"How on earth is this educational?" I asked aloud to no one in particular.

"Well, this song reminds children that bodily functions are normal and everyone has them, so they shouldn't be ashamed." The voice belonged to a woman who stepped from the shadows on the periphery of the studio. She was in her fifties, tall and slim with hair pulled back in a severe bun. Tortoise-shell-rimmed glasses sat on her nose. She wore a blouse, a pencil skirt, pumps, and a strand of pearls. Considering my outfit, we could have been a mother-daughter shoot for a catalog.

"I'm sorry. I didn't see you there."

With incredible poise, the lady extended her hand and smiled at me.

"I'm Patricia Miller-Sanderson." Of course. She was the educational advisor to the show, had been for decades, with PhDs and EdDs from Ivy League institutions. She was also married to executive producer Marcus Sanderson. Very convenient. If he ever had any questions about the show, he could just ask across the breakfast table.

I introduced myself and explained my temporary role during the thirtieth-anniversary celebration. "And please forgive me. It's just that . . ."

"A plush nose with fluffy boogers streaming out of it

doesn't on the surface seem educational? Without a bigger context, it's really hard to see." Gracious indeed.

The cast was finished rehearsing and was ready to record the section of the song. The director decamped to the control room where he could watch everything as it would appear on television. Flavia called quiet on the set. The pre-recorded audio, which included the song and the puppet singing, began to roll, and the denizens of Gingerbread Cottage put on a show.

"If you sneeze into your hanky,
don't be troubled by the green.
They're just boogers.
They're just boogers.
They catch germs but you can't see them.
Just be careful not to eat them.
That's disgusting.
That's disgusting.
Forget to cover your nose,
A booger lands on your toes,
just wipe it off and sanitize.
Throw your tissue in the trash,
to the doctor make a dash."

The portion of the song finished, and the puppets were frozen in place in their final positions. Flavia called cut, and everyone on set started clapping. I turned to Patricia, who was looking at me expectantly.

"Oh yeah," I said. "I can really see the messages for kids." Ah, PR.

Just then Flavia called a fifteen-minute break, and Patricia headed off to the control room. Meanwhile, it was time for me to introduce the visitors to the cast.

By the time I got them up on the set, by a system of steps that were hidden from camera view, and warned them about the gaps in the flooring through which the puppeteers performed, Carl Biersdorf had disappeared.

"Where is Mr. Snicklefritz?" whined one little boy. "I wanted to shake his hand. Daddy, you said we could shake his hand."

"I don't know. I don't know," said Daddy.

"Maybe he had to go wee-wee," said a little girl. "When you gotta go, you gotta go."

"Excuse me for just a moment," I said. "I'm going to go see where Mr. Biersdorf went."

"Who is Mr. Biersdorf?" asked another little girl.

"Mr. Snicklefritz, I mean."

"Well, hello kids," said Moose as I started to leave to find Carl. I turned back to the puppets and gave Squirrelly-Joe a gimlet eye.

"Best behavior, Joe."

"I don't know what you're talking about."

I left the set through a door that led to a hallway that in turn led towards the dressing rooms. Shouts greeted my ears before I was halfway down the hall. Carl and Marcus were at it again.

"It's my decision!" yelled Carl.

"Except you've already made the decision!" boomed Marcus. "You've set things in motion."

"I don't care!"

I paused to listen—and to avoid walking into a war zone.

"I can't believe you're taking his side!" yelled Marcus at someone else.

"Well, I can't believe you want to leave me after twenty-five years of marriage." That was Patricia's voice.

Right there and then, I decided that Mr. Snicklefritz did not need to visit the set that day. Something was going down, and I needed to stay out of the middle of it. Trying to be as silent as a ninja, I retraced my steps to the set, where I made my apologies to the kids. Mr. Snicklefritz was not feeling well. Ten seconds later he made me out to be a liar by bursting onto the set, and he wasn't alone. His best friend by the name of O'Sullivan was tagging along.

"Let's get this stupid booger song done. Clearly this is Emmy-winning material!"

My little tour group froze in their tracks, and then the puppeteers picked that untimely moment to pop up from under the stage to show the kids that the puppets were really attached to people. The startled children screamed, and wee-wee girl fainted.

"Okay, everyone, the tour's over. They need to get back to work. Let's go visit the candy table." I did my best to usher the traumatized families off the set.

All the peanut butter cups the kids could eat calmed them down quickly, but their parents were less than pleased.

"I think they forgot what a rainbow morning is," said one former production assistant.

"That's just par for the course with Carl," said a former writer's assistant. "He's always been a—"

"Rainbow morning," I reminded her.

"A character, I was going to say."

I followed up the candy fest with Gingerbread Cottage tote bags filled with plush toys, books, and other merchandise. By the time everybody left, they were so excited about their swag that the unpleasantness was forgotten, I hoped.

But it wasn't forgotten by me. I returned to the set hopping mad. I was only going to be there for two weeks, and it wasn't my show, but it had a legacy. It was important. And it actually was my show in that I'd grown up on it. I had loved it. Now, between sexual harassment and drunkenness, these people were giving the show a bad name.

I approached the set intent on giving everyone involved a tongue-lashing, but by the time I got there, my temper had cooled slightly, especially because I remembered the two thousand dollars I was making and the impact it would have on my life and my credit score.

This is not your real job, Jill. This is not your real job. I repeated the mantra silently to myself.

Jill Cooksey is an island.

I just needed to do my job and get out with the cash. Still, if the talent kept acting up, my job was going to get harder and harder, so I approached the one person everyone seemed to listen to—the floor director. Flavia was standing at a podium going over the script and making some notations.

"Excuse me, Flavia," I said.

"Hey, Jill. What can I do you for?"

"So what do you think can be done...how do we prevent what just happened from happening again?"

Flavia laughed bitterly. "When you figure that out, let me know."

"So this happens a lot?"

"Oh yeah. Carl's an ass. Always has been from what I hear."

"But he *is* the show. Can no one have a talk with him?"

"You think we haven't tried? I think that's what really developed the rift between Marcus and him. They used to be thick as thieves, but I think Marcus has tried to caution him about the drinking and the explosions on the set and the bad publicity. And that's just made Carl angrier."

"So there's no way around it."

"Nope. Not if the set visitors want to meet Mr. Snicklefritz."

Hmm. Maybe I would try to discourage that. It would be hard with the thirtieth anniversary. The fact that Kate's company had issued invitations to past cast and crew, educators, and some carefully selected families to come and meet Mr. Snicklefritz and friends was problematic and shortsighted.

"Just do the best you can," Flavia reassured me. "No one is

expecting you to work wonders. This isn't a new situation. We're just trying to maintain the status quo."

I thanked Flavia for her insight and went back to my cubicle via the craft services table for some more peanut butter cups. The sugar fairy had been by (curse her!) and had left the gift of Twizzlers. I scooped up a few. They were good for gnawing while one contemplated.

I turned to my computer. One thing Flavia said stuck in my brain: bad publicity. I was just an on-the-scene body to help wrangle visitors, so I didn't know the ins and outs of Mr. Snicklefritz's publicity situation. But a quick Google search stirred that hornet's nest for me. In the interest of not burying the lede, the worst thing I saw was a *Gotcha! Magazine* article in which a very drunken Carl, with Britney on his arm, had been confronted by some angry adults outside a bar in Tribeca. He had carried his drink outside the bar and was standing in the street with it, a legal no-no. The adults, perhaps parents of small children, remonstrated with him. I quickly scanned the text. One passerby reportedly overheard one of the adults say, "You're a disgrace. You're supposed to be a role model. Look what you're doing!" to which Carl replied, "It's just TV. It's just TV."

I moved on from the top headline to some other stories. More sightings of a drunken Carl. TV critics asking if Mr. Snicklefritz's time had come and gone.

Tearing my eyes from the screen, I glanced at the clock. I needed to get ready for the Princess Gretels, but I wanted to know more.

Another headline asked the question "How Educational is Kids' TV?" Not, I thought, based on what I'd seen that day. I quickly opened that article. *The Mr. Snicklefritz Show* was not the focus of the piece, but it was mentioned among several shows that were only marginally educational in that critic's opinion and not worth kids' time. A quote from Patricia Miller-Sanderson caught my eye.

"You have to remember that we are speaking to kids using *their* language at *their* level. If you can't code-switch to kid talk, then you're not going to see how utterly educational shows like *Mr. Snicklefritz* are."

Sounded like a PhD to me. I closed the browser and considered what I'd seen. According to Bryce Camplen, *Mr. Snicklefritz* was a children's television staple, but the nation went off staples all the time. Look at white flour and white sugar, which currently were the Hitler and Stalin of the food pyramid. Anything could be brought low by shifting public opinion.

Glancing again at the clock (where had the time gone?), I snapped myself out of my reverie, shoved another Twizzler in my mouth, and attacked the next thing on my to-do list. A Princess Gretel invasion was scheduled for that afternoon, and I had to be ready.

AT LUNCH I avoided as many people as possible. I came in late after everyone else had gone through the line and took my tray to the farthest corner of the cafeteria. I'd already had a tête-à-tête with Bryce that morning, and I would be spending a lot of time with him that evening, so I didn't feel the need to be chatty. Plus, I wasn't sure if he or I wanted anyone to know we were going on a date. I was also just kind of disgusted with the people around me. I know that's a little judgmental, but lascivious puppet behavior and drunken temper tantrums were not part of my normal workday. Some vacation.

I had to stop calling it that. Maybe if I called it a *paycation* like some people called staying home a *staycation*, it would keep me in the right frame of mind to do my job, and I wouldn't feel bitter.

The puppet crew, including Devon, who I assumed had played the role of Disembodied Nose with Boogers, were all sitting together laughing and yukking it up. They seemed to be getting along very well, and that was nice to see. For the first time, I noticed how everyone arranged themselves in the cafeteria in cliques: the puppeteers; the producers and production coordinators; the camera operators and grips; the art department; the writers; and the production assistants. Just like in high school, everyone was segregated. The puppeteers' table was certainly the loudest, but the camera people and grips were giving them a run for their money. The quietest group of all was made up of the production assistants, also known as PAs. The lowest people on the totem pole, they seemed to be trying to fly under the radar. I got that. When I started in PR as an account assistant, I was the dogs-body. I had to impress and at the same time try to stay out of the line of fire.

As I watched those underdogs of TV production, one person stood out. I couldn't remember his name even though I'd been introduced to him once. He sat at the end of the table away from everybody else and was reading a book while he ate his lunch. I recognized a fellow introvert. Usually, when I was trying to get away from everyone, I climbed out the window of my office onto the flat roof of the building next door. Around a little corner was an overturned bucket where I could sit and read or ponder the universe. I didn't have that sort of place here, but I could always escape into a book if I wanted to get away. With all the drama on the set and off, escape seemed a necessary part of the TV workday.

Speaking of drama, Carl hadn't made an appearance at lunch, and I assumed he was enjoying a liquid repast in his dressing room. I also didn't see Patricia or Marcus. Either they were all still fighting or licking their wounds. As far as I could tell, nobody else knew about the argument because the rest of the cast and crew were on the set when it happened. I thought I was the only one who had ventured to the dressing rooms, but there was always a chance that someone else had heard and that the three were feeling a little embarrassed. Surprisingly, Marcus showed up a few minutes later. He skipped the lunch line (I'd heard through the grapevine that he was notorious for ordering takeout) and headed straight for the puppeteer table where he slapped Devon on the back.

"Nice work today," he proclaimed for everyone in the room to hear. It seemed overly loud actually, like a performance. "You really brought that nose to life. It was so funny. Really well done."

He was laying it on pretty thick. Yes, the nose was a central figure in "The Booger Song," but it had no face and was basically a nose on a stick that danced around. Marcus was definitely trying too hard, but he did get everyone's attention. As the de facto leader of the production, when he spoke, people shut up and listened. I looked at Devon. He was beaming.

"Thanks, man. That means a lot."

"I mean it," said Marcus. "Really good job. And good job everybody." He turned to the rest of the table and included them in his praise, which warmed them all up because I could see they were slightly taken aback by Marcus's effusive praise of the right hand.

So as not to appear completely awkward, I surmised, Marcus quickly made the rounds, pausing at the PA table to say a brief hello and at the writers' table for a slightly longer chat, and then he was gone. From where I sat in my quiet little corner surveying the room, Marcus had just given his best performance and an Emmy-worthy one at that.

CHAPTER 3

After lunch, I went straight back to my cubicle because the Princess Gretel invasion was imminent. Kate had briefed me on "The Princess Gretel situation" as she called it, and it was quite a hoot. Princess Gretel was a supporting character on *The Mr. Snicklefritz Show*. She showed up once an episode for a brief segment, which meant Princess Gretel wasn't supposed to be on the set every day. According to Kate, that was a good thing. The first Princess Gretel was a raven-haired beauty named Dominique Dillard. She originated the role when Carl started the show back in Cincinnati. When the show went national, she went with it. She also happened to be Carl's wife at the time. When the marriage ended, so did her time as Princess Gretel, and a new Princess Gretel was cast.

The Princess Gretels (PGs for short), according to Kate, didn't last very long, never more than one or two seasons.

"Shouldn't it be Princesses Gretel?" I asked Kate.

"You're going to get beat up," she replied.

Considering the show had been on for thirty years, there were a lot of PGs, and that day they would all be having a reunion, which was odd because they'd never actually worked together. A smaller studio space had been converted into a Princess Gretel museum with poster-sized photos of each of the PGs in costume and in action on the set, along with the props they'd used. In the middle of the room, fourteen thrones had been constructed for the Princess Gretel roundtable. It was kind of like one of those reality TV shows where they gathered all the characters together to talk and reminisce while a Steadicam moved around the room capturing each of them. It wouldn't be a formal interview since it was supposed to be a conversation between the Gretels looking back on old times, comparing their experiences, and talking about what Princess Gretel had brought to the show over the years.

During my time watching *The Mr. Snicklefritz Show*, from about age two to age seven, I'd witnessed three different PGs, and I'd loved all of them and wanted to be them, mostly because of the gown. The gown was clutch. Princess Gretel wore an over-the-top ball gown reminiscent of Glinda, the good witch in *The Wizard of Oz*. Poofy and airy and glittering, the gown was silver with gemstones crusted around the hem, the neckline, and the sleeves. She also wore a tall silver crown with more glittering gemstones. To preschool girls, she was a thing of beauty. As the years passed, the design of her costume changed slightly with the times, but it was always a spun silver confection.

I remember telling my mother that I wanted to be Princess Gretel for Halloween. There was a costume at the local department store, but Mama said it cost a mint, so she would make one for me. I was dubious, but Mama always did what she put her mind to. A fabulous seamstress, she worked on that costume for two straight weeks, and when it was done the day before Halloween, it was impressive. My six-year-old self exploded with happiness when I stepped into that dress and Mama fastened up the Velcro in the back. The skirt was super poofy with loads of tulle overlaid with silver satin. She had bought up all the fake jewels at the local Ben Franklin to create my gown, and it was stunning. As far as I knew, it was still at home tucked away in tissue paper, a thing of beauty and a joy forever. I even had a picture of myself in that gown to share with my Princess Gretels, the three that formed my childhood and taught me important lessons on manners and decorum, such as always say please and thank you, eat with your mouth closed, and try to include everyone in the fun.

Just thinking about meeting Princess Gretel was making me giddy and nervous. Butterflies careened around my stomach. How silly, I thought, to be getting giddy over meeting a character from a children's TV show. I'd met plenty of celebrities in my PR work, but I'd never been nervous about meeting one until that day. The Princess Gretels were scheduled to arrive at two, and we were set to film from three until six. That meant when the afternoon shooting on the main set finished at five, the executive producer and the director could come in and have eyes on the filming in the smaller space just to make sure it was going the way they intended and would be usable for the thirtieth-anniversary special.

I had about an hour until the princesses arrived and a little bit of prep work to do. I had put together more Gingerbread Cottage goody bags, this time with more grown-up fare. There were still a couple of plush toys, especially a plush Princess Gretel. She didn't look like any of the actual PGs on the show, but she was wearing a silver satin gown crusted with jewels. To these bags I had added a bottle of champagne and two crystal champagne flutes etched with the *Mr. Snicklefritz* logo and the words "30 years." I had also put in framed cast photos from each of their tenures on the show.

I walked over to the large cubicle that we called The Pen where the PAs would hang out when there was nothing else for them to do. (The barnyard imagery of The Trough and The Pen was not lost on me.) The Pen was empty except for one PA, the loner that I had seen reading a book in the cafeteria. I tried to remember his name but came up short.

"Hi," I said. "I'm Jill, the public relations coordinator. I'm sorry, but I've forgotten your name."

He gave me a little smile. "That happens a lot," he said. "My name is Chuck."

"Hi, Chuck. I need some help. I have some tote bags that need to be moved to the small studio space for the Princess Gretel reunion. Could you give me a hand?"

He nodded and followed me back to my cubicle where we loaded up a flatbed dolly with ten tote bags. Then Chuck slung the remaining four on his arms, a significant accomplishment considering each held a champagne bottle and crystal stemware.

"Just a heads up, Chuck," I said. "There's a bottle of champagne and two crystal champagne flutes in each one of these bags, so we need to be careful."

"Roger that," he said, and I led the way to the small production studio.

The art department had finished with the space earlier that morning, and it was really something. The huge posters of the Princess Gretels would have been eye-catching enough, but the thrones the art department had made for each of them were really quite adorable. Silver and encrusted with jewels, like the dresses, the thrones sparkled and shimmered thanks to lights on a grid system overhead that were positioned strategically. Also in the room were several museum-style plexiglass cases filled with props from the Princess Gretel segments, such as her book of manners, her white party gloves, and her wand, which she used to turn poorly behaved little children into angels. We placed a tote bag behind each of the thrones, matching a label inside the tote bag with a label hidden on the back of each throne. The art department assured me that the bags wouldn't be seen during filming, which would mostly take place from the waist up.

I thanked Chuck for his help.

"No problem."

Chuck was a PA of few words, so I decided to try to draw him out.

"So, I saw you in the cafeteria," I said. "What were you reading?"

"A book."

"Right," I said, trying not to roll my eyes. "What book?"

"Nothing special."

"Oh, okay." I wasn't going to press, and he clearly didn't want to tell me. Maybe it was something embarrassing like a romance novel. The cast and crew would never let him live that down, so I let it go.

"So is this your first time working on a television show," I asked.

"No." He sounded like a surly teenager. He must've seen the look of annoyance that crossed my face because he added quickly, "I've worked on a few shows." Then he rattled off a list of public television heavy hitters that I recognized.

"Wow. That's pretty cool." I decided to work with his ego instead of against it. "You must know a lot more about television than I do. This is my first time working on a show."

"Really? How did you get the gig?" Bait taken.

"A friend. It's just a short-term gig. I actually have a real job."

"And they let you come work here?"

"No," I said. "I'm on vacation."

That made him laugh. "Some vacation! Long hours. Same food over and over."

"Don't forget the temper tantrums and public drunkenness," I added. "Let me ask you a question, Chuck. Are all TV shows like this?"

He thought about it for a minute, the space between his green eyes wrinkling in concentration. "No. Not at all. I mean, there are always egos. That just comes with the territory if you're dealing with performers and creative people. And everyone's in competition with everyone else, so that creates tension. But no, they're not all like this."

"That's good to hear."

"Do you need anything else?" Chuck had spoken to me more than he spoke to anyone else all day, and I think the little introvert was getting tired. Still, we weren't done.

"The Princess Gretels will be arriving soon. Do you think you could help me welcome them and guide them to the green room?"

The green room was where the PGs would hang out until it was time to film. While they were waiting, hairdressers and make-up artists would touch up their hair and faces, and a costumer would look for any wardrobe disasters and try to avert them. All Chuck had to do was escort the PGs to the green room and hand them off to the other professionals, yet he seemed to hesitate.

"Is something the matter?" I asked.

"No," he said finally. "I'll do it. No problem."

"Great! I'll meet you at reception." I just had to stop by the green room to make sure craft services had stocked it with what I'd requested. Craft services was notorious for its generosity with chocolate, but healthy treats were usually in short supply. I had asked for fruit and veggie trays, sparkling water, stuff like that for the PGs to snack on. When I got there, I was both delighted and utterly dismayed with what I found. A gorgeous buffet was set up on one side of the room with a tower of gourmet cupcakes, another of French macarons, adorable little glass bottles of Italian sodas, an elaborate tray of cookies, and, all the way at the end, a small fruit tray and a small veggie tray.

Well, they'd done as I'd asked, sort of. Considering the elaborate nature of the sugary end, the fruit and vegetable offerings didn't stand a chance. I myself couldn't resist stealing a macaron from the back of the tray where it wouldn't be noticed. I popped it into my mouth and moaned. Ladurée! Craft services had certainly spared no expense. The lack of healthy options notwithstanding, I was pretty certain anybody would be happy with a tower of Ladurée macarons, so I headed for the lobby.

I got there just as the first of the PGs was arriving. Chuck was already there and holding the door as Princess Gretel Number One, Dominique Dillard, entered the building. Her raven hair may have been streaked with silver, but Dominique was still the stunning princess from the photos. Logically, she had to be in her sixties, but she looked a good decade or so younger than my mother, who I hoped wasn't reading my mind at that moment. Her silver fox fur coat was open at the front to reveal a sleek gray pantsuit accessorized with a chunky jewel-toned beaded necklace and matching bracelet. A large garment bag was slung over her shoulder.

"Ms. Dillard." I extended my hand, and she took it. "I'm Jill, the PR liaison. It's such an honor to welcome you back to *The Mr. Snicklefritz Show*."

Dominique gave me a tight smile and looked around the lobby.

"You're the first to arrive," I chirped.

"How appropriate," was all she said. After an awkward moment, I filled the silence.

"This is Chuck. He will escort you to the green room."

She took a long look at Chuck and pursed her lips. "Don't bother. I know the way." With that, she turned on her heel and pushed through the double doors.

"Ice, ice, baby," muttered Chuck.

Indeed.

Just then, a flurry of movement caught my eye as another princess entered the lobby. My heart stopped. Princess Gretel Number Three, a PG of my childhood, was standing before me. Like a little kid again, I ran up to her and began gushing. So uncool of me!

"Welcome back to *The Mr. Snicklefritz Show*. I'm Jill, and this is Chuck, and we'll be taking care of you today. It's just such an honor to meet you."

"Oh, thanks." Number Three seemed taken aback, and then I noticed what she was wearing. PG Number Three had arrived in her PG gown. The silvery sartorial confection of my dreams was standing right in front of me. Little did she know, I had an exact duplicate in a trunk in my mother's house. She must have noticed me ogling the gown because she added hastily, "You know, it just seemed like the right thing to do. Relive the glory days. Put on the old dress. I hope that's okay. I hadn't put it on in years, but it still fits like a glove."

"You look beautiful. I'm sure that's fine," I said while mentally asking myself if it really was okay. She was going to stand out like a sore thumb. I hoped wardrobe would have some street clothes in her size that she could change into should the director object.

"Oh good," she said. "It feels good to be back in the old gown."

I asked Chuck to show her to the green room, and they had just turned to go when a huge black airport-style shuttle glided to a stop at the curb out front and let loose a blare of horn in the form of *La Cucaracha* that sounded ominously familiar. Oh dear, I thought. What was happening?

I ran out of the glass doors to the front sidewalk. The large black bus had black tinted windows, and it was impossible to see what was happening inside, but my curiosity was satisfied in a hot second when the doors flew open and I was met with a wall of sound, sparkling lights, and, I believe, a disco ball. The inside of the bus was configured as a miniature nightclub on wheels. I got just a glimpse of the driver. Lush black pompadour, luchador mask air freshener on the dash. Could it be my old friend Jorge?

Before I could inquire further, a wave of silver tulle crashed over me as nearly a dozen Princess Gretel's spilled out of what was clearly a party bus.

"Princess Gretel in the house!" yelled one while raising the roof. Several more clinked champagne glasses while another swigged bubbly straight from the bottle. All was noise and confusion. The flash of fake gemstones. The sparkle of silver sequins. They were laughing and drinking and taking selfies and drinking and singing and drinking. Then, like a hive of silver honeybees obeying some direction only they could hear, they magically coalesced into a conga line and danced toward the building chanting, "I like to move it, move it! I like to move it, move it!" The hair was wild; the tulle was everywhere; the Princess Gretels were having a blast. In their wake, the PG who was clearly in charge descended from the van looking very pleased.

"I'm Number Nine. I organized this little party. You're welcome. All right, ladies!" she yelled over my head. "Time to tear up the Gingerbread Cottage!" The PGs responded with screams of delight.

An hour later, the Princess Gretels were ready for the reunion, sort of. Upon arriving at the green room, the intoxicated Princesses had fallen on the craft services table, devouring every cupcake, every cookie, every macaron like a horde of silvery locusts who didn't like vegetables and fruit. Then the champagne ran out, and, replete with alcohol and carbs, several of them took on a mile-long stare as they entered a sugar coma. A couple of them settled down for a nap, to sleep off the champagne I hoped, while a couple of others, Number Nine included, seemed unfazed. They were the youngest

Princess Gretels and seemed accustomed to partying. They began touching up their makeup and their hair. Even though some of the PGs were slightly comatose, I still had the makeup artist and the hairdresser touch them up, but half of them didn't even notice.

At three, it was time to start filming. I woke up the napping PGs, and Chuck and I, with Number Nine's help, managed to herd them into the studio. We got them onto their thrones, and that's when I noticed that two were missing: the reigning PG, Britney, and PG Number Six. I knew Britney was probably still filming in the main studio, but I hadn't a clue where Number Six was.

"We're missing Number Six," I whispered to Chuck. "Was she in the green room?"

"Nope." I looked at my monosyllabic coworker. His shoulders were hunched up to his ears, and his eyes were cast down. He looked miserable. A herd of drunken princesses can have that effect.

I was fixing to ask why he was so glum, but the art department chose that moment to descend. The art director and her assistants flitted about arranging the princesses' gowns to make them look as regal as possible while makeup and hair did some last-minute touch-ups. PG Number Six's throne and artifacts were removed from the set, and lighting techs tweaked a few of the lights on the overhead grid to make sure that everyone was looking good. After that, many of the women raised their hands to shield their eyes.

"You're going to need to put your hands down," said a gaffer. "They're casting shadows, plus you can't sit through the whole taping with your hands up."

"But the lights are hurting my eyes!"

"Can we wear sunglasses?"

"I think that light is giving me a migraine."

Against the litany of complaints, the gaffer had little choice but to adjust some of the lights, bringing down the glare. The effect was less dazzling, but at least the hungover PGs didn't appear to be in pain anymore.

Then the director bounced into the room along with two camera operators with Steadicams strapped to their bodies.

"Good afternoon, your highnesses," said the director, or rather the assistant director, AD for short. He had been tasked with starting the interview process which the director of the show would join in on once the regular filming for the day had ended.

"Are you ready for a fun afternoon of reminiscing and telling stories?"

"Oh yeah," said Number Nine. "I think we're all ready." The mischievous glint in her eye had me worried.

Before the AD could offer further instructions, Britney sailed into the room, her enormous silver gown, the newest iteration, billowing about her.

"I'm so sorry I'm late! Hello, girls!" Britney bobbed about the room, greeting each of the PGs with an air kiss on the cheek. I knew she was from New Jersey, but her fake-friendly was Scarlett O'Hara thick. She was just doing it to show off her dress, the newest and shiniest of them all. The PGs, even Number Nine, endured it with good grace and the occasional eye roll, but Britney was brought up short by Dominique. By simply raising her hand to signal "stop," Dominique brought Britney to a halt faster than a traffic cop.

"Hello, Britney." Dominique's face showed neither regard nor disdain. She was indifferent, a much more devastating emotion.

That's when I noticed that Dominique was wearing her Princess Gretel gown. It must have been in the garment bag. The heavy, silver silk-satin was of a quality rarely seen nowadays. The puffed sleeves and sweetheart neckline were edged with gems that looked more real than paste. Her waist was cinched to such a degree that I had a hard time breathing when I looked at it, and I couldn't begin to imagine the yardage in that impossible skirt, which spilled over and around her throne regally. Her black and silver tresses were swept up in an elegant twist atop which perched a silver crown. What looked like a costume on everyone else, looked like her natural plumage. The others may have been princesses, but Dominique was a queen.

Britney, denied the tribute she thought was her due, flounced over to her throne and tried to arrange her skirts to outshine Dominique. It didn't work.

The AD expelled a loud breath, which he must have been holding while the drama played out, and flushed slightly.

"Okay, the two cameras are going to be moving around, but you should just ignore them. Have a conversation. It's not supposed to be scripted. I'll start you off with some questions to get the ball rolling, but we really want this to be casual, fun, a reminiscence."

Being directed snapped some of the more comatose Gretels out of their fog, and they all seemed to be paying attention, which I was glad to see.

The AD started with a simple question. "Can you share your stories of how you came to the role of Princess Gretel? What led you to the Gingerbread Cottage?"

There was silence for a time while the princesses processed the question and began formulating their answers. At least, that's what I thought was going on, until Princess Gretel Number Four spoke up.

"All right, I'll start. I met Carl at CBGB. Green Day was playing. I had no idea who he was or that he was on kids' TV. I mean, he offered me a joint, so kids' TV was the farthest thing from my mind." She laughed. "And the next morning, when we woke up, he offered me the Gretel gig. I was an art student at NYU. I didn't have a pot to piss in, so I said sure. Why not?"

"I met Carl at a dance club," said Princess Gretel Number Ten. "It was eighties night, and I was dancing with all my girlfriends, and then suddenly there's this guy all over me trying to do the Lambada, and I'm like 'What's going on?' But then I thought, just go with it, so I stuck my tongue down his throat. The next thing I know, we're making out in the bathroom, and the next day I'm being fitted for this gown. No lie. It happened like that."

"I was in the gown the same day," said Number Nine. "I was minding my own business working on Coney Island running the Himalaya. Carl got on, and he stared at me the entire ride. When his ride was over, I went on break, and he found me. We got to know each other under the boardwalk. I didn't go back for my second shift. Instead, we ended up in wardrobe."

A choking sound erupted from the AD, and his eyes bugged out of his head. This gossip-fest wasn't what he'd intended, I was certain.

"Okay, let's move on to another question," he croaked while shaking his head vehemently at his camera people and me as if to say "We're not using that."

No kidding we weren't using that!

"So next question," he went on. "What did you enjoy most about being part of *The Mr. Snicklefritz Show?*"

"I love being a role model for children, someone they can look up to and admire," cooed Britney with saccharine sweetness.

"You didn't say how you and Carl met," challenged Number Nine. The twinkle in her eye was extra sparkly. Britney's eyes, on the other hand, were wide with fear.

"It's not really important—"

"Wasn't it in Panama City? Spring Break? I heard something about Girls Gone—"

The AD broke in. "Let's try to stay on topic. The question is, what did you enjoy most about being part of the show?"

"Respect," said Number Two bitterly. All eyes turned to her. "I was a secretary in an advertising firm. It was all 'Fetch me a coffee' and 'Pick up my dry cleaning.' And all those ad guys had wandering hands. It was awful. So I complained to my then-boyfriend, Carl, who I didn't know was married at the time." She gave Dominique a significant look. "And he said, 'I've got a job for you where you'll be treated like a princess.' And I was. People respected me. Nobody asked me to fetch coffee. They fetched *me* coffee. And I only had to work one day a week, and I made more than I did at my secretarial job. I got to practice my music. Princess Gretel was the best thing that ever happened to me. It changed my life."

Now that was an interesting story and mostly useable. I wondered if they would be able to edit out the part about the married boyfriend, but it was interesting to hear how a rather simple role in a children's television show could elevate someone's life.

"It was the best thing that ever happened to me too," said Number Seven.

"Me too," echoed many of the others. Only Dominique stayed silent watching everyone's reactions.

"Yeah, it was fantastic," said Number Eight, "until it wasn't."

All the PGs nodded.

"You lived a charmed life as Princess Gretel until Carl moved on," continued Eight bitterly.

"Same story every time," said Number Eleven. "PG was the flavor of the month. Well, at least a season. Sometimes two."

"Yeah, one minute you're getting frisky behind the grandfather clock in Gingerbread Cottage—"

"Oh yeah!" shouted one PG.

"And the next minute your replacement is walking through the door, and Marcus is giving you walking papers."

"Yes. Carl liked to give gifts, but he also liked to take them away," Dominique Dillard finally put in.

"How long have you been Princess Gretel, Britney?" asked Number Nine again. "Two years?"

"Tick tock!" yelled Number Five, and everyone laughed, except Britney, who looked stricken, and Dominique, who was stoic.

"So what happened *after*?" I asked. As PR coordinator, it wasn't my job to direct, but the AD wasn't making a move. Something had to be done.

"I joined a symphony," said Number Two. "I'd had a lot of time to practice, and I got really good."

"I went back to Coney Island," said Number Nine. "Sugar Plum Fairy never really suited me."

Some of the PGs told stories of great success and contentment. Even if their stories weren't all sunshine and rainbows, at least the show had given them some financial stability.

"Those royalty checks!" exclaimed Number Four. "They're the best! Am I right?" This statement was met with a roar of applause.

"Hey! There are goody bags behind the chairs!" piped up Number Ten. Squeals of delight replaced the applause. I looked to the assistant director, but he clearly had no idea what to do with these women who were snatching up the goody bags and rifling through them. Then I remembered the champagne.

Oh snap!

Pretty soon the corks were popping and the bubbly was flowing. Reminiscences became bawdier and more detailed, and I learned a lot about Carl that I never wanted to know. At around four o'clock, the champagne started moving through their systems, and suddenly every princess needed a potty break. They also wanted someone to hold their gowns. Lord, have mercy! I sent Chuck to the pen for some female PAs because I had to draw a line somewhere.

At five o'clock, the party was still going, and that's when the door quietly opened and the director of the show walked in. He was stopped in his tracks by the sight that met his eyes, and I started to chuckle. I couldn't help myself. The whole thing was so absurd. Then the cherry on top of the sundae was the arrival of Carl, who practically danced into the room with a huge grin on his face.

"Afternoon, ladies!" he taunted the Princesses with a twinkle in his eye to rival Number Nine's. For a moment, the room was silent. And then one of the PGs yelled, "Get 'em girls!" That Princess Gretel hive mind took over, and they all, except for Britney, Dominique, and Number Nine launched their champagne flutes at Carl. Britney and Dominique abstained, while Number Nine threw the bottle. Carl, who could move really fast for an old guy, darted out the door and slammed it behind him in the nick of time. A hailstorm of crystal stemware exploded against the door and ended up a heap of shards in a puddle of champagne.

The segment was very much over, and Chuck, the other PAs, and I managed to herd the Princess Gretels back to the lobby, where I was relieved to see the party bus was still parked. I walked over to the passenger door and slapped it with the flat of my hand. With a hiss and a pop it opened, and I was met by the grinning visage of my good friend Jorge, proprietor of the Guadala-Car-a car service of Astoria, Queens.

"Hola, señora Jill."

"Jorge." I shook my head. "I should have known."

He winked at me and tapped the horn, which resulted in an ear-shattering rendition of *La Cucaracha*. Jorge and I went way back. He was the owner and my favorite driver. Whenever I needed a ride somewhere fast, Jorge and Guadala-Car-a always came through for me.

"How do you like my sweet new whip?"

"Can you call what is essentially an airport shuttle a whip?"

"Don't diss my girl!" Jorge feigned indignation. "She's a real moneymaker. You and your friends should hire it sometime. Have a night out on the town!"

"Does it have a karaoke machine?"

"No." Concern wrinkled Jorge's brow. "But I can get one!"

Party bus rental was not currently in my budget, but I had to admit it sounded fun, especially with a karaoke machine.

It took a few minutes, but we got the Princess Gretels situated in the party bus, including Number Three, who was in no condition now to find her own way home. Jorge assured me he would get all the ladies to their respective abodes, and I was relieved and utterly wiped out when the door to the party bus finally closed and it took off.

CHAPTER 4

"We're not having dinner alone tonight."

"What?" I replied, a little confused.

"A very special friend of mine will be joining us."

Bryce and I were seated at a table for two at Uncle Nick's, my favorite Greek restaurant in Astoria. Our walk from the studio to the restaurant had been pleasant, if a little cold, and I was feeling optimistic about the evening, until this moment. It was more than a little odd that Bryce should bring a friend along to our first date. Then I wondered if maybe he didn't think this was a date? Was this not a date? I thought it was a date. I had psyched myself up for this date. It had been kind of hard, but I'd done it. *Hmm.* I was a little disappointed. Maybe this wasn't a date after all.

"Oh, who is your friend?" I asked mildly, trying not to give away my consternation.

"Well," said Bryce, "you'll meet him in just a moment."

And suddenly Bryce was gone. What the—?

He had bent over and was rummaging under the table in the black duffel bag he had carried from the studio. What was he doing? A strange foreboding gripped me. I suddenly had an idea of what he was up to.

Not that. Please. Not here.

When he popped back up, he was indeed not alone, and my fear was realized. He had a puppet with him.

"Hi, I'm Jim-Bob," squeaked a puppet voice.

"Er, hi," I managed. Jim-Bob reached out a soft, plush hand for a shake. Without thinking, I took the hand and shook it. Was this really happening?

"Bryce has told me a lot about you. Do you like Greek food? I like Greek food. At least I think I like Greek food. I've never actually tasted Greek food. But Bryce likes Greek food, so probably that means I like Greek food too."

I was struggling to make sense of what I was seeing. I looked from Bryce to Jim-Bob and back to Bryce.

"Why do you keep looking at him? Hello? I'm talking to you. Why do you keep looking at him?"

With effort, I focused on the puppet.

"Cat got your tongue?" asked Jim-Bob.

"Um, it's nice to meet you," I croaked. Was this normal behavior for puppeteers? I didn't want to embarrass Bryce, but people in the restaurant were starting to stare, and it was making me uncomfortable. Finally, Bryce spoke, and as he did, Jim-Bob turned his head to listen to Bryce.

"Jim-Bob is one of my oldest and dearest friends."

"Thank you," said Jim-Bob graciously. "I love you too, man."

"H-how did you two meet?" I asked, not knowing what else to say.

Jim-Bob cocked his head at me as if confused by the question, but Bryce jumped in. "Jim-Bob and I worked on a little kid's show together back in Grand Rapids a long time ago."

"So long ago," said Jim-Bob. "*Jim-Bob's Jamboree*. Whew! Those were the days."

As my initial shock began to subside, I took a good look at Jim-Bob. He seemed to be made primarily of yellow wool, and his hair was curly and brown and made of yarn. Closer inspection revealed that he was wearing cowboy clothes: a checkered shirt, a vest, some jeans and chaps, and little cowboy boots that looked like they'd been made for an infant. He was a cute puppet if you like that sort of thing. His face was benign, although it seemed that Bryce, by manipulating his hand, could give Jim-Bob a wide range of expressions from affable to disgusted.

"So," I said to Bryce, "do you take Jim-Bob out to dinner much?"

"Of course he takes me out to dinner," said Jim-Bob. "I have to get out of this duffel bag sometimes. Imagine if you had to spend as much time in a duffel bag as I do. It's murder in there. And I'm pretty sure he used to use this as a gym bag. It smells. His socks are appalling. You need to know that before this relationship goes any farther."

That made me giggle, and Bryce smiled.

I was aware of people near us whispering, but I forced myself not to look around. I only glanced up when our waiter approached the table.

"Are you ready to...?" Then he saw Jim-Bob and was struck dumb.

The puppet ordered first.

"I'll have the souvlaki with some lemon potatoes. I don't want those green beans though. And extra feta, please."

Then Bryce ordered, which had the waiter completely confused. I felt bad for him, and I could practically read his mind: "Is the puppet's order for real? Do I bring the puppet an entree? Will they be offended if I don't? Will they complain about the bill if I do?" I smiled apologetically at the waiter and gave him my order. Slightly dazed, he hustled back to the kitchen to alert the staff that crazy people were dining in the restaurant that night, I'm sure.

Meanwhile, in my own private drama, it seemed like Jim-Bob was going to be a fixture of the date, so I resolved to make the best of it, knowing that it would at least give me a good story to share with my PR Posse. They were my best friends who all worked in public relations and helped each other out from time to time with their careers. They were my tribe, and I told them pretty much everything. This story was going to be epic.

"So Jim-Bob," I said, "do you often accompany Bryce on dates?"

"Oh yeah. Bryce likes to get it all out in the open right away."

"Get what out in the open?"

"Me. His family. He wants people to know right away that we are a package deal. Bryce and Jim-Bob together forever. Best friends."

"How sweet."

The puppet gave me the side-eye.

"Yeah, you don't really think it's sweet."

"I do." I was working my poker face hard.

"No, you don't. You think it's weird. You think I'm weird."

"Jim-Bob," Bryce soothed, "I'm sure she doesn't think you're weird."

"Look at her eyes. It's written all over her face. This girl thinks I'm odd."

"I'm sure that's not true," said Bryce more firmly. "Please excuse him. He doesn't always have the best manners."

Watching Bryce essentially have an argument with himself was giving me a headache, but I tried to smile winningly at Jim-Bob, hoping that might soothe him.

"I'll only believe that Jill likes me if she tells me so!"

"I'm sure she'll tell you—"

"She has to tell me that she thinks I'm cool."

"Jill will—"

"And she has to give me a hug."

I felt my smile become brittle.

"Bryce," I pleaded. I was reaching the limit of my patience, and I hoped he could hear it in my voice.

Bryce and Jim-Bob just looked at me expectantly.

I'd had enough.

Bryce seemed like a nice, normal guy back at the studio, but this date was proving otherwise. And I didn't even want to be on this date. I had sworn off men! I was too nice—that was my problem. Now my niceness was being exploited by what? A puppet? Bryce? Bryce's other personality? Were there more of them? I wasn't going to wait around to find out.

"I have to go."

"Don't go! Jim-Bob will behave himself!"

"She's just a coward, Bryce! Let her go. She's not for us."

"You shut your mouth, Jim-Bob! Don't be rude to my date. You say you're sorry or I'll . . . I'll . . ."

"You'll what? Put me back in the duffel bag?"

"Yes, and I'll leave you there for a month!"

"Noooooooo!!!!!" Jim-Bob collapsed in sobs on Bryce's shoulder while Bryce begged me with his eyes not to leave. I looked around at the other patrons, none of whom were eating their dinners. They were transfixed by the scene playing out before them. We were much more entertaining than poorly behaved children and probably a lot more horrifying. To preserve my dignity, I calmly stood and gathered my belongings. Before I left, I looked back at Bryce and Jim-Bob one last time.

"All you had to do was put the puppet away."

Their twin expressions of horror sealed the deal. I turned on my heel and headed for the door. The waiter met me there with a takeout bag.

"It's on the house."

Thirty minutes later, I was sitting on my futon eating

moussaka and looking forward to the slice of baklava that I'd caught a glimpse of at the bottom of the sack. I was not, however, looking forward to the next day. Facing Bryce wouldn't be pleasant, but I would get through it. I would make my money and pay my credit card bill and remain single because men were too much trouble. I had my friends. I had my job. I had quite enough, thank you very much.

Jill Cooksey is an island. A beautiful Greek island.

My life was going to be so much simpler.

CHAPTER 5

"What do you mean he's dead?" I shrieked.

That got everyone's attention.

It was just after eight o'clock the following morning, and the production staff, cast, and crew had been asked to gather in The Pen for a special announcement. An ashen and shaken Marcus Sanderson had delivered the news that my date of the previous evening was now deceased. Everyone else reacted with stunned silence. I, on the other hand, had shrieked like a banshee.

"He was discovered on the set this morning by our floor director. He...had passed away. Paramedics and police have been called. They should be here shortly. We're asking everyone to stay off the set until further notice."

My legs were moving towards the set before conscious thought could register my actions. Vaguely, I heard people calling after me, but I kept moving until I was running. I burst through the door to the set. Leaping over coils of cable, dodging Flavia's podium, I ran until I faced the interior of Gingerbread Cottage head-on and was brought up short by a scene out of a nightmare. Bryce Camplen lay sprawled like a sacrifice across Mr. Snicklefritz's rustic coffee table. His mouth was agape, his eyes open and bulging. Across his chest lay the odious puppet Jim-Bob. They had died together, skewered by some sort of sword that pierced their chests and pinned them to the rough-hewn wood of the table.

"Like a toothpick in an hors-d'oeuvre," I said before succumbing to hysterical laughter. From far away, I heard a door open and close, but I couldn't look away from the profane tableau in front of me, a place of innocence and laughter now defiled by death. Moments later, I felt hands on my shoulders and a gentle pressure turning me away from the grisly scene. A pair of arms held me close, forcing me to lay my head on a rock-solid shoulder. Soon my crazy laughter dissolved into tears for the man who lay dead in the place that had held all of his dreams.

What seemed like an eternity later, the crying stopped, replaced by intermittent hiccoughs.

"Can you walk now, Jill?" I knew that voice. I nodded my head and then looked up into a face I had hoped never to see again.

"Detective Donato?"

"Walk of shame" is an apt description of the next few minutes of my life as the police detective escorted me from the studio, down the corridor, and into the offices to face my grieving coworkers. They all watched, the speculation written clear across their faces, as Donato escorted me to Marcus's office. I couldn't blame them. I had been working on the show for four days. I barely knew any of them, yet I had made a scene worthy of a soap opera. They wanted to know why. So did Donato.

He, Marcus, and Carl now faced me as I told them the tale of the date from hell. With every new detail, Donato's expression became more perplexed while Marcus and Carl seemed unbothered. This was old territory for them. Carl even cracked a sad smile when I described Jim-Bob's temper tantrum.

"And so I left," I finished. Those four words tasted like guilt. Bryce's last hours hadn't been pleasant ones, and I had been part of that.

"That sounds like Bryce," admitted Carl. "A brilliant puppeteer, but he sometimes took it too far."

"He seemed very insecure," I added. "He really wanted me to like his puppet."

Donato shook his head, and I could tell he was struggling.

"Mr. Sanderson, Mr. Biersdorf, could you give us a moment?"

When they were gone, he settled in the chair behind Marcus's desk and let out a huge sigh.

Detective Anthony Donato had been the lead investigator on the murder of a famous actress that had coincided with my PR campaign for a new perfume. I had frustrated him with my attempts to solve the crime, but in the end, I had laid the killer at his feet, literally. I may have been a pain in the butt, but I had been a great help in the end, no pun intended. Still, I couldn't imagine that he was very glad to see me. He stared at me thoughtfully for a moment before resuming his questions.

"And after the restaurant, you went straight home?"

"Yes."

"Can anyone verify that?"

"Maybe my landlady. She keeps tabs on me."

"I remember her well." I was sure he did. When I'd been attacked during the Fall Fantasy perfume campaign, he'd had to get past Mrs. Maroulis to question me. "I'll check in with her of course, but I'm sure it's just a formality."

"So I'm not a suspect?"

Donato gave me a knowing look.

"Technically, everyone's a suspect. Let's just say an awkward date doesn't make a good motive for murder."

He had a point.

"I do have one more question, though." He leaned forward. "How did you come to be here?"

"That's easy. I'm on vacation."

Not so easy, in fact. I spent the next several minutes explaining the situation to his satisfaction.

"Unbelievable," he muttered as he led me from the office back to The Pen. On cue, my friend, PR Posse member, and fellow crime-fighter Kate Vogel was there to verify my story, thank heaven. Donato knew Kate too. His day was getting better and better.

EVERYONE WAS STARING AT ME. I sat at a corner table in the cafeteria picking at some sort of pasta dish. My appetite was nonexistent, but I had nowhere else to be. All set visits had been canceled, Donato was still in the process of interviewing the cast and crew, and forensics had commandeered the set for the foreseeable future. Everything was on pause, and I thoroughly expected the anniversary celebration, if not the rest of the season, to be canceled. Meanwhile, gossip had spread through the cast and crew like wildfire, gossip about me and Bryce. Marcus or Carl or both had said something to someone. Maybe they'd felt the need to explain my outburst that morning. Whatever the reason, it didn't matter. The news was out that Bryce and I had been on a date the night before he turned up dead, and folks who had lost a friend or who were frightened needed something on which to fixate. The woman who scorned Bryce Camplen fit the bill.

For my part, I felt guilty as sin. I kept replaying the evening in my mind, wondering if there was some way I could have turned the date around. Did I say something to set off Jim-Bob? Was my inflection off? Did my face betray my feelings towards the puppet and the whole crazy situation?

"I know what you're doing." Kate's voice broke into my reverie. She placed a tray of food on the table and sat down across from me. After carefully placing a napkin in her lap to protect the skirt of her forties-era vintage suit, she looked at me with concern in her green eyes.

"What am I doing?"

"You're analyzing. You're picking through every interaction you had with Bryce Camplen to figure out how it was all your fault. You did the same thing when Mike ghosted you. You needed something to take your mind off Loser McCall but not this."

"I'm totally over him, thank you very much."

"Uh-huh. Sure." Kate took a bite of pasta, chewed, and swallowed. "The point is, his disappearance and Bryce's death are not your fault. You couldn't make Mike's poor decisions for him, and you didn't skewer Bryce, did you?"

I gave Kate my best withering look. She wasn't fazed.

"All you did was go out on a date, one date, that didn't go well. So you weren't compatible. Big deal. Happens every day." Kate was talking very loudly now for some reason. "How could a bad date have anything to do with someone running Bryce and that freckle-faced puppet through with Sting?"

"I beg your pardon? Sting?"

"You know. Bilbo's sword from *The Hobbit?*"

I had thought that sword looked familiar.

"The most important thing, Jill," Kate paused and looked around the cafeteria significantly where, I now noticed, no one was looking at me anymore, "is that NOBODY blames you for what happened."

I wanted to hug my best friend, and I would have if there hadn't been a table and two dishes of pasta between us. A little bubble in my chest that I hadn't realized was there suddenly burst. I felt lighter. My lunch actually smelled pretty good.

A moment later, Flavia paused by our table.

"You doing okay, Jill?"

"I'm hanging in there, Flavia."

"Good." She smiled, patted me on the back, and moved on. Soon Devon stopped by, and then Chuck and the PAs. Absolution complete.

"Well, I guess that once Donato is finished questioning everyone, my job here will be done," I mused as I forked up a bite of cannoli cake.

"About that. It might be better if you stayed."

"To do what? The anniversary celebration is canceled, isn't it?"

Instead of answering, Kate dug into her own slice of cannoli cake and avoided my eyes.

"Kate?"

With a sigh, she put down her fork and leaned in conspiratorially.

"Between you and me," she whispered, "it's a very delicate time. The network is thinking of pulling the plug."

I was shocked, but should I have been? The *Mr. Snicklefritz Show* had been beloved for thirty years. There were movies and merchandise and an entire publishing wing. But, a little voice reminded me, children's programming and murder were incompatible. Could the show survive such a blot on its record?

"The network's been looking for an excuse for some time," Kate continued. "Carl has had a bit of a publicity problem." I nodded in agreement. "And these days it's far more cost-effective to make animated shows. *Snicklefritz* is one of the last puppet shows standing."

"But what can I do about it?"

"This show is my client, not the network. It's my job to

protect the show, even if that means tracking down a killer." She stared at me until the penny dropped. When it did, a wave of adrenaline crashed over me, and I had the urge to bolt from the cafeteria, the building, and maybe even the state.

"No way! No. Way. You were there in September. You remember how much fun that was. Do you remember that I was attacked? Do you remember the flames at the Waldorf Astoria Hotel? Do you?"

"Of course I do, Jill, because I was with you every step of the way."

Poop.

Poopety, poop, poop.

Kate was right. She'd had my back one hundred percent. Without her help, my campaign would have gone up in flames, and, more importantly, an innocent person would be in jail.

Reluctantly, I gave in.

"What would you like me to do?"

"Just watch and listen and let me know what you learn. If I'm going to save this show, I need to know who's working against it."

I thought about it. Watching and listening I could do. I had already heard so much without even trying—arguments between divas and producers, the hopes and dreams of ambitious puppeteers, even Carl's entire sexual history. It wasn't going to be a difficult assignment.

"No problem," I said and stuck out my hand. Kate shook it solemnly, and we dissolved into giggles, which we quickly squelched when someone at a nearby table cleared their throat loudly. Kate grimaced.

"Probably not appropriate."

"Probably not."

Kate and I parted ways after lunch, she to try to save *Mr. Snicklefritz*'s reputation and I to see a man about a sword. With the set closed, I had to go out to reception and through another door, down a hallway, and through the green room to get to the corridor that contained the puppeteers' dressing rooms. I moved quietly down the hall, but I soon discovered that the place was deserted. That suited me fine. When I got to Larry's dressing room, I knocked lightly on the door. No answer. I tried the doorknob, which turned easily. In a trice, I was standing in the temple to fantasy that was Larry's inner sanctum. A quick glance told me all I needed to know. Larry's replica of Sting was gone.

I turned to leave and collided with Detective Donato. His demeanor may have been hard as nails, but his midsection was surprisingly squishy.

"Why am I not surprised?" He shook his head at me.

"I was just coming to see you! I thought I recognized the sword, you know, on the set." Sadly, the image was crystal clear in my mind. "I think it belongs to Larry Stubbins. His replica of Sting is missing."

"Yeah, we figured that out about three hours ago, but thanks anyway." Sarcasm stabbing! Ouch!

"Well excuse me for trying to be helpful!" I expected the detective to berate me about interfering, given our history, but he just rolled his eyes and sighed. As he exhaled, he seemed to deflate like a balloon.

"Are you okay?" I asked.

"It's this place." He loosened his tie. "It doesn't make any sense. You wanna know who I just interviewed? A moose. I interviewed a moose. And before that, I interviewed a squirrel. And that squirrel! One of the toughest interviews I ever conducted! At one point I threatened to haul him downtown, and then I realized I was talking to a puppet!"

"Squirrelly-Joe is a sphincter."

"He IS!"

Tentatively, I reached out a hand to pat Donato on the arm.

He had clasped his hair in both fists and was on the verge of pulling it out. He needed soothing.

"Repeat after me," I said as I gently patted his bicep. "The puppets aren't real. The puppets aren't real."

"The puppets aren't real," he repeated. "But they seem real."

"They do."

He closed his eyes for a moment, and I continued patting. Considering he had let me cry on his shoulder that morning, it was the least I could do. After a time, he opened his eyes and focused them on me. I stopped patting.

"This is going to be a tough one," he said. "I can feel it."

It seemed strange that he would admit that to me, but I credited the puppet world. The first time I met Detective Donato, he'd done his best to intimidate me, and it had worked. Later, I had broken several rules and maybe some laws in my quest to save my PR campaign, which hadn't endeared me to him. But now, in the face of trash-talking, lederhosen-clad, woodland creatures, Donato was letting his guard down with me.

"I don't know this world…I guess what I'm trying to say is… I'm a little out of my depth."

Well, knock me over with a feather! Mr. NYPD wanted my help.

Part of me wanted to crow. Three months ago I had been as annoying as a kid sister to this man, and now he needed me. Sweet vindication! But another part of me, the part that felt she was finally learning how to handle men, knew to play it cool.

"How can I help?" was all I said.

"I need someone who knows this world to be my eyes and ears."

I didn't remind him that I myself had only been there four days.

"I need you to listen to the scuttlebutt and let me know what you hear. Can you do that?"

"Do you want my first report now?"

"Huh?" He blinked at me in surprise.

"Do you want my first report now?"

"No, I heard you. What do you mean 'first report'?"

"Well...." And I told him, all about the fights between Carl and Marcus, about Marcus wanting to leave his wife, and about Squirrelly-Joe being a lecher.

"No surprise there," muttered Donato.

I told him about Bryce being the heir to the Snicklefritz throne and Devon expecting to move up as well. I even told him which Princess Gretels hated Carl the most. When I finished, Donato scribbled notes for several more minutes. Then he tucked his notepad and pen into his inside pocket.

"Well, it's a start," he said and headed toward the door. "You and everybody else need to stay out of these dressing rooms. They're part of the crime scene." He paused at the doorway to see if I was following him. Like a good, annoying little sister, I was. "And thanks," he mumbled so low I could barely hear him.

"You're welcome," I replied loudly and grinned back at him.

"I know you're eating this up."

"Like biscuits and gravy."

Donato and I parted ways, and I made my way back through the lobby and to The Pen to find most of the cast and crew milling about. Kate sidled up to me.

"Marcus has called a meeting. You're just in time."

The man himself emerged from his office, and the crowd settled faster than when Flavia yelled "Quiet on the set!"

"Today has been a terrible day," he began. Most of the audience nodded in agreement. "We lost one of our own today, and we don't know why. We don't know who took our friend from us. We don't know how anyone could harm Bryce Camplen, a man who loved puppeteering as much as breathing. His entire purpose in life was to make people smile."

I heard a sniff and looked over to find Britney weeping

quietly on Carl's shoulder. Carl himself looked stricken. Gone was the alcoholic bravado and simmering anger. What was left? I wasn't sure, but it appeared to be shock and sadness.

"We've brought in some grief counselors. They will set up in the cafeteria, and anyone who needs to talk should go to them. If you've been released by the police and you would like to go home, feel free to go. If you'd like to stay, we'll have a small vigil tonight at six in the small studio. Tomorrow we'll figure out what happens next, but I don't want anyone worrying about the future. The show must go on, but for now, take care of yourselves. Take care of each other." Then Marcus moved about the room, shaking hands, patting backs and shoulders, and giving hugs where needed. He was a good leader when he wasn't insulting his puppeteers. No wonder he'd been so successful. In his wake traveled Patricia following up his hugs with her own. Mom and Dad to the Snicklefritz family. Did the kids know their marriage was on the rocks?

Kate gestured to me, and I followed her into the hallway. Her face was grim.

"I'm going into A & C for an emergency meeting." A & C was Anstruther and Cole, the entertainment PR firm where Kate worked.

I nodded.

"I'm going to stick around for the vigil tonight…and keep my ear to the ground."

After Marcus's announcement, The Pen quickly cleared out, leaving only the PAs and me. They were sitting in a circle on the floor, like college kids in a dorm room, and Chuck the loner was with them, which made a nice change. The three young women seemed very friendly, and I hoped Chuck would give them a chance. A fog of depression hung over the group, so I made a quick detour to craft services and returned with the entire bowl of peanut butter cups. I set it in the middle of their circle and joined them on the floor.

At first, no one moved or said anything. Then one of the PAs, a tall brunette named Madison, reached for a peanut butter cup. The others followed suit until we were all sucking on chocolaty peanut ambrosia. A little of the tension lifted.

"I can't believe he's dead," croaked Madison.

"He was so nice," offered Tameasha.

"So nice," whispered Julia, and a tear trickled down her pale, drawn face. Tameasha leaned over and hugged her, which only served to unleash Julia's quiet sobs until her shoulders shook. I gave Chuck a questioning look. He held up his hands, touching thumbs and forefingers together to form a heart. *Aah.* Someone had a crush on Bryce. I thought he would have liked that. Too bad he hadn't known. Or maybe he had.

I took another peanut butter cup.

"He was going to be the next Mr. Snicklefritz," said Chuck.

"No, Devon is," asserted Madison. "He told me."

"Well, Bryce told me different," replied Chuck.

"Devon deserves it," trumpeted Tameasha with so much fervor that her braids vibrated. "He's worked here longer, and he shares his knowledge with others. He gives puppeteering lessons."

"So did Bryce," countered Chuck. "He's been working with me for the last month."

"Yeah but Devon's been a right hand for twenty years. He deserves a shot."

I didn't offer up what I knew, which wasn't anything different. Both men wanted the leading role on the show, but who was in the better position to get it? If Bryce had been handpicked by Carl, it would have been hard for Devon to overcome it. Clearly, they both had their supporters in The Pen. It was hard for me to imagine Devon committing murder, but I barely knew him. Were his fans capable of such an act?

The PAs were quiet again, this time stilled by anger.

"He was a good guy," I offered, "a creative guy. Did y'all ever meet Jim-Bob?"

That had them smiling.

"Jim-Bob was a hoot," chuckled Madison.

"He was like a brother to Bryce," smiled Julia through her tears. Bryce had clearly been dating the wrong girl.

"He was a little freaky," admitted Tameasha with a giggle, "but he made me laugh so hard my stomach hurt."

The PAs started swapping Jim-Bob stories, and soon even Chuck was laughing. But I had no desire to share my story because the pain and guilt were too fresh. I mumbled something about needing the restroom and stood up to go. As I walked away, Tameasha and Chuck cackled at Madison's imitation of Jim-Bob, and even Julia managed a giggle. I patted myself on the back for a mission accomplished. Now if I could only cheer myself up.

My next stop was the cafeteria, where two grief counselors sat at tables looking at their phones because they'd had no takers. I moved on.

Peeking into the small studio where the Princess Gretel fiasco had transpired, I saw that most of the PG paraphernalia had been removed. The thrones remained and were still arranged in a circle. Members of the art department were erecting blown-up production photos of Bryce working with his fellow puppeteers on the set. A chill washed over me as I remembered a similar memorial service just a couple of months ago. That time had been the most stressful period of my life, and here I was again involved with a murder. What was wrong with me? Just like last time, I was trying to help a friend. Would all my friendships require me to put my life on the line?

I told myself to simmer down. I wasn't necessarily in danger. Bryce's killer could have been anyone and was probably some Joe Schmoe off the street. New York had more than its fair share of crazies who wandered around talking to themselves, shouted at random people who passed them on the street, or contemplated pushing people in front of subway trains. I was probably in the same amount of danger as I was every other day.

Moving on from the small studio, I wandered back through the production offices. The place was eerily quiet. There was now no sign of the PAs, and I assumed many people had gone home to grieve. As I passed a door, it opened, and Larry Stubbins emerged looking sweaty and shaken. From Larry's own arm, Squirrelly-Joe glared at him.

"Pull yourself together, Larry!" spat Joe. "Time to grow a pair!"

I gave the two a wide berth, but they trundled past without a glance in my direction. When they were out of earshot, I peeked into the office to find Donato in his makeshift interrogation room. I entered and quietly closed the door.

"Larry didn't look so good."

"Well his sword or dagger or whatever was found plunged through Bryce Camplen's heart, so he's a little worried."

Images from the morning flashed across my vision. Donato must have seen something on my face because he offered a sheepish "Sorry."

I waved it away and took a seat.

"So is Larry your prime suspect?"

"Wouldn't that be neat and easy? But no. Right now he doesn't seem to have a motive. Of course he might just be crazy. I'm going to let him sweat a bit before I question him again."

I felt for Donato. Murder investigations were tough enough without an overlay of surrealism.

To be helpful, I relayed what I knew about Bryce and Devon both gunning for the lead role and the PAs who fell into their respective camps. Donato confirmed that he knew about the rivalry.

"We're looking closely at Devon, and at Carl."

That surprised me.

"What motive would Carl have had? Bryce was his choice."

"Yeah, but Carl didn't want to retire. Marcus confirmed it."

I thought back to the arguments I'd heard between Carl and Marcus. Carl had changed his mind about retiring. That made sense given what I'd heard.

"It's possible Bryce was putting pressure on Carl to step down," continued Donato. "Marcus was too."

"And maybe Carl thought the only way to take the pressure off would be to eliminate his hand-picked successor?" It seemed a bit thin to me.

"It's just a theory." Donato sounded defensive. "We have a lot more work to do."

"Speaking of work, I'm going to the vigil tonight. I'll keep my eyes open."

Donato relaxed a hair. "I doubt anything will transpire, but you never know."

Taking my leave, I continued my desultory inspection, but the offices were either empty or closed. I found my way back to my cubicle, sat down, and wondered how I would pass the time until Bryce's vigil. I checked my email and my bank account. Then I logged on to *The New York Chronicle* website to read the news. Until recently, I had subscribed to *The Gazette,* but I canceled my subscription when World's Worst Reporter exited my life. I didn't care to stumble across his byline. In *The Chronicle,* the story of Bryce's murder had broken, but there was a lack of details, thank goodness. I was also grateful that we worked in a studio complex with high security. Pesky reporters wouldn't be much of a problem. With nothing else to do, I pulled my phone out and read an e-book until I dozed off. The next thing I knew, someone was shaking me. I opened my eyes to find the PAs, all of them, with eager expressions on their young faces.

"Are you coming to the vigil?" asked Julia tearfully.

"I wouldn't miss it."

I followed the gang to the small studio. As we entered, an assistant producer handed each of us a candle in a paper cup. The thirteen thrones were already filled with the cast and high-ranking production staff. The rest of us stood, filling in the gaps between the chairs. In the center of the circle, the production stills of Bryce had been arranged in a smaller circle facing outward. The photo facing me depicted Bryce controlling Martin the Marten while Devon controlled the right hand. The puppeteers were intent on the job and didn't seem to notice the camera. Their expressions showed focus and determination, while Martin's fuzzy little puppet face expressed joy and exuberance. I felt a lump in my throat and pressure behind my eyes. That little face would never be the same because the man behind the puppet was gone. Swiping a tear, I studied Bryce and Devon, heads together as they worked. The photo showed teamwork and concentration. It didn't show rivalry, but I cautioned myself that one photo could hardly tell the whole story.

I looked around the room. Sure enough, Devon was there. Actually, everyone was there. Even people who had gone home earlier must have returned. Perhaps they'd just gone around the corner to the local pub. The assistant producer who had handed out the candles now lit her own and turned to light the candle next to her. This chain continued around the circle until all the candles were lit. Then someone dimmed the lights. The room was silent. I couldn't have spoken if I wanted to because the effect had stolen my breath. Marcus, Patricia, Phil, Larry, Carl, Devon, Britney, Flavia, and others sitting in the thrones with lighted candles were a vision from some mystical cabal. The thrones themselves, silver and crusted with rhinestones, refracted and reflected the candlelight, and the effect was otherworldly, magical. Malevolent? I couldn't shake the thought that I was witnessing some cult ritual. I had the heebie-jeebies and then some.

Focus.

I shook my head to clear my fancies. Then I zeroed in on Devon to start. He was solemn, which was to be expected, and stared into the candle flame in front of him. Next to him, Phil was gazing around the studio with a look of wonder on his face. I think he was having the same reaction I had to the psychedelic lighting. Larry, next to him, was crying silently. Fat tears rolled down his cheeks. In the next throne, Carl seemed to be having an internal conversation with himself. Occasionally his lips would move and his head would shake. Beside him, Britney was sniffling, and her mascara had made black rivers down her cheeks. She tried to take Carl's hand, but he shook her off. Marcus, on the next throne, was composed and staring into the middle distance, lost in thought. In a strange parallel to Carl and Britney, Patricia, seated beside Marcus, tried to take his hand, but he shook her off too. Her compressed lips hinted at her displeasure. Flavia was the only one with eyes closed. Her lips moved slightly, and I think she might have been praying.

After a time, Marcus took charge and spoke about Bryce and what he had meant to the show. From the control room, an audio tech played back some of Martin the Marten's most beloved songs from the show's history. At first, Martin's voice brought more people to tears, but after a while, the songs became a trip down memory lane, making folks smile and lean over to their neighbors to share a reminiscence. That sweet little puppet voice soothed spirits and lightened hearts. When the songs ended, we all blew out our candles and filed out of the studio.

CHAPTER 6

That night I dreamed I was trapped in Gingerbread Cottage. It was the dead of winter, and snow lay deep on the ground outside the cottage's fake windows. I was alone, but I couldn't leave. Some unseen force was keeping me inside. I wandered around the house trying windows and doors, but they wouldn't open. Even the drawers, the cabinets, and the giant grandfather clock wouldn't budge. Again and again, I moved around the house trying to open something to no avail. A loud *bang* on the front door made me jump and frightened the breath out of me. The bang came again and again. Now I didn't want to get out. Somehow I knew that whatever was on the other side of that door needed to stay there. With the next bang came a splintering sound. I watched in horror as the front door began to give way more and more with each pounding. Then I saw the ax blade penetrate the wood. I opened my mouth in a silent scream. Two more whacks and a hideous, grinning, freckled face appeared in the gap.

"Here's Jim-Bob!"

I sat bolt upright in bed, gasping for breath. Sweat poured

off me. Maniacally, I began stripping off the bedclothes and my pajamas, but I couldn't cool off. Even though it was the beginning of December, my apartment felt like a steamy tropical jungle.

Then I noticed the hissing sound, and I dove for the light.

As I suspected, a steady stream of steam issued from the relief valve on the radiator just a few feet from my bed. The banging in my dream had been the infernal device, and I had somehow worked the sound into my nightmare. Yes, the dream was terrifying, but much of the sweat was down to faulty heating.

Radiators were a complete mystery to me, a country girl from down south. I was more than a little fuzzy on how they worked, and I couldn't seem to regulate the temperature no matter what I did. Once the radiators came on in late October, I was at their mercy.

Clad only in my underwear, I padded over to the ginormous vaporizer and began twisting knobs and playing with valves. Sometimes I got lucky and the radiator simmered down. Other times I ended up having to vacate the apartment until Mrs. Maroulis could come tame the beast. A glance at the clock told me it was only three a.m., so I was hoping to get lucky and go back to sleep. Sure enough, after about fifteen minutes of turning things this way and that, the steam started to ebb. A few minutes later, it quit completely. I put my jammies back on and cracked a window to vent some of the heat and moisture, and then I lay back down and turned off the light.

Except now I was wide awake. I shook my fist at radiators, nightmares, and how quickly my body had adjusted to being an early riser. After venting my angst, I got up and started my day.

My coffee wasn't set to brew for two more hours, so I hurried it along. While it was brewing, I took a long lukewarm shower, which sounds weird, but as my apartment was at that moment a tropical biosphere, it was quite refreshing. Afterward, I wrapped myself in my silky summer robe, poured a cup of java juice, added ice cubes, and settled down to catch some very early morning news. I nearly dropped my cup, however, when I saw Bryce Camplen's face grinning at me from my TV. It was *Hollywood Report,* a syndicated entertainment news show. Apparently, the previous night's episode ran again in the wee hours of the morning. The report about Bryce's murder gave some details about the crime scene that I thought Detective Donato wouldn't be pleased about, including the position of Bryce's body on the set, but Donato wasn't the only person destined to be dismayed.

"A source close to the production tells *Hollywood Report* that the last person to see Camplen alive was a coworker with whom he'd had a date the night before his death."

Now the cup did drop, and coffee spilled all over my futon.

The segment cut to the reporter in front of Uncle Nick's restaurant where two nights before I'd had one of the worst dates of my life, and he was interviewing our server!

"It didn't go so well," said our traitor of a waiter. "She left before we served the entrees, but I couldn't blame her."

Christmas fudge!

I wasn't supposed to be part of the story. I was a PR professional. I controlled the story, spun the story, made the story. I was never ever the subject of the story. Worse, the report clearly implied that there was something suspicious about our date. At least the source had been kind enough not to mention my name. I wondered who had ratted me out. It could have been anyone—even the killer. That thought had me pausing on my way to grab a towel to mop up the coffee. What if the killer had tipped off the media about our date to deflect suspicion? But if that were the case, wouldn't he (or she) have mentioned my name to do a thorough job of it? Only the cast and crew of *The Mr. Snicklefritz Show* knew about our date. Was this confirmation that the killer was one of them?

Back in motion, I snatched a towel from the bathroom and attempted to save my futon. The comforter, normally a sunny yellow, had soaked up most of the coffee, turning it to a muddy brown. I doubted I could get the stain out, but since I was the only person who saw the comforter, I would just live with it. A new bedspread was not in the budget. Luckily, the coffee hadn't seeped into the sheets or the futon itself. When I finished the mop-up, I bundled the comforter into a trash bag so I could haul it to the laundromat the following day. I turned my futon back into a sofa, poured another cup of joe, and settled in for a think.

While I had acquiesced to both Kate and Donato and agreed to spy on the happenings at *The Mr. Snicklefritz Show,* the problem was that I didn't know where to start. I had one viable suspect, Devon Cauthorne. Donato had suggested Carl could be another, but with the evidence on hand, his motive seemed flimsy. He didn't want to retire, so he killed his replacement? Who hates the idea of retirement that much? But who else had a reason to kill Bryce? That was a question I needed to answer.

Because the murder was committed on the set, I reasoned, it had to be related to the show. Getting past security was difficult, so someone from Bryce's personal life would most likely have tried to off him elsewhere. I made a mental note to check with the security guards to see when Bryce had returned to the studio and whether he was alone. I was sure Donato already had that information and would have mentioned another suspect if Bryce had returned with someone, but I didn't yet feel comfortable ringing him up for a chat to confirm. Most likely, the killer was someone related to the show, which meant I was going to be busy. I foresaw a lot of interrogation disguised as casual chitchat and office gossip.

When I finished my coffee, it was four thirty. My apartment

was cooling down, so it was safe to get dressed. By five I was ready for work and heading out the door.

My first stop was the doughnut shop near the subway station. They hadn't seen me in a while because I hadn't been taking the subway, so they were very pleased when I ordered an entire dozen instead of my usual one or two. Doughnut box in hand, I headed for the studio through the pitch-black morning.

Security was also surprised to see me there so early, but they were all smiles when I handed over the doughnuts. These were the night shift guys, whom I normally didn't see because I didn't come in this early.

"Yesterday must have been rough for you guys," I said sympathetically, by way of explanation.

"So many questions," said a guard named Amir, according to his badge. "We want to be helpful, but how many times can you tell the same story?" The Donato treatment. I knew it well.

"And what story was that?" I leaned in and kept my voice low to imply discretion.

"The log showed that Mr. Camplen came in a little before nine p.m. Our shift started at ten. We never saw him."

"Didn't you think it was odd that he never left?"

"We just thought it hadn't been logged," piped up the other guard named Jason around bites of a Boston cream doughnut.

"Happens more often than you think," confirmed Amir, "although management has read us the riot act. Everyone gets logged from now on."

I pointed to the small camera mounted above their heads. "What about the security footage?"

"That's what finally ended the questioning," said Jason as he chose a chocolate frosted. "We showed them the videos. Mr. Camplen came in alone, and he never left. No one came in after him."

"There must be other doors into the building," I mentioned. "Maybe a loading dock?"

The two guards confirmed that there were but they were kept locked at all times. Someone had to open the doors from the inside, or security had to use a key from the outside.

"So the killer had been lying in wait, or Bryce had let him in."

"Looks that way," said Amir as he eyed me speculatively. "You ask almost as many questions as the police."

I forced a bright laugh, maybe a little too bright for five a.m.

"Sorry guys. I'm just a big *Law and Order* fan. What can I say?"

"Hey, I was an extra on that show once!" cried Jason. Distraction complete, I urged him to tell me all about it.

Twenty minutes later, I took my leave of the security team and headed for the production offices. The hallways were dark except for some dim security lighting. At zero dark thirty, I expected to be alone.

That's what Bryce expected too.

With that thought, I froze like a possum in the face of oncoming traffic. The dim corridor was lined with doorways to dark offices. At any moment, one of those doors could open and a homicidal, sword-wielding maniac could burst forth intent on shedding my blood. I willed myself to turn around and move back toward security, but I was frozen with fear. There were offices behind me too, the threat of danger in all directions. I strained to hear any telltale sound that would alert me to the presence of another.

Was that a *click*?

A footstep?

A door opening?

Was someone moving towards me?

Should I move?

Could I move?

A loud *bang* as something somewhere fell to the floor made my decision for me. I took off running.

You're going the wrong way!

Ignoring my inner voice, I sprinted down the hallway into deeper darkness. Adrenaline flooded my system as a single instinct took over—to get away.

This is just like a horror movie!

One corridor dead-ended into another, and I made a left turn towards The Pen and the area with all the cubicles. So many places for a killer to hide. At any moment, I expected someone with a gun or a shuriken to pop up from a cubicle and take me out.

You idiot!

That thought had me putting on the gas, and I flew past The Pen. Now there was another corridor that would eventually lead to the studio itself, but it was a closed crime scene. A murder scene. I would have to go back the way I came. A fresh wave of adrenaline washed over me.

A sliver of light forced its way into my consciousness and brought me up so short that I fell to my knees. An office door was cracked and a small line of light pierced the darkness of the corridor. Vaguely, I heard voices. Someone was here. As I feared, I wasn't alone.

It could be the killer.

I ignored the rational voice in my head in favor of my primitive instincts. Light meant safety. Darkness meant danger. I hauled myself to my feet and moved toward the light, a wave of relief washing away the adrenaline.

The relief I felt quickly dissolved when I realized the voices were raised in argument.

"For pity's sake, the man isn't even in his grave yet!"

That was Carl's voice.

"Network is just looking for an excuse to cancel the show." And Marcus.

"Not after thirty years!"

"Yes, after thirty years! Would you stop living in the past? We're expensive. The network would happily replace us with a cheap little animated show, and they wouldn't think twice about it if it wasn't for our fan base. Only forward momentum will counteract the bad publicity. The show must go on, and to go on we need a Martin. It's as simple as that."

"But why Devon?"

"Why not? He's lost out on becoming Mr. Snicklefritz because you won't retire—"

"He was never going to be Snicklefritz!"

"Whatever! The point is, he can do the voice and he's due a shot at the big time."

"Okay, okay. Devon makes sense for the role, but it's too soon! It's disrespectful"

"I know you loved Bryce like a son."

"I wouldn't go that far, but he was a good kid. Loyal, dedicated, and one helluva puppeteer."

The air suddenly seemed to go out of the argument as Carl and Marcus reflected on their fallen colleague. I stayed as still as possible and hoped they couldn't hear the beating of my heart.

"If there were any other way, Carl..."

My brain registered that the argument might be coming to an end, and I didn't want to be found eavesdropping. Slowly, I retreated down the hall until it was safe to run, and as I headed back the way I came, I was thankful for carpeted floors and sneakers.

When I got to The Pen, there were lights on, and Chuck the PA was sitting in a chair reading a book.

Five minutes before, I had been fleeing a murderer down darkened corridors. Now I felt completely silly and was glad no one had seen my overactive imagination run amok. I prayed there weren't any security cameras in the hallway because Amir and Jason might be having a hearty laugh at my expense.

"You're here early."

Chuck jumped at the sound of my voice.

"So are you."

"Couldn't sleep. Thought I might as well come in."

"Yeah, me too."

Chuck bent his red head to his book, ending our sparkling conversation. No one would call him chatty.

I went to my cubicle, fired up my computer, and opened up my email. There were some replies to emails I had sent canceling set visits. Everyone understood, but no one asked to reschedule, which was ominous. The murder may have done permanent damage to *The Mr. Snicklefritz Show*. But the darkest cloud on the horizon was another email from my mother. It had been sent late last night, and the subject line read "*AGAIN*?" Girding my loins, I opened it.

Jillian Elizabeth Cooksey, were you planning to tell me that another murder had happened in your place of business? Why do I always have to hear about these things from other people or, even worse, the media? You know I don't trust them to tell the whole story. If you don't call me and keep me in the loop, you will force me to come up there to find out the truth for myself. Is that what you want? There is a train for New York leaving at eleven a.m. tomorrow. If you don't contact me by ten, I will head to the station. You know I'll do it. I've done it before. All this could have been avoided if you had taken my calls last night.

The email ended there, no closing. Mom was ticked. I pulled my phone from the bottom of my Behemoth Black Bag. At this hour, it was still on "Do Not Disturb," which was why I hadn't taken my mother's calls the night before. Upon reflection, I should have made her a trusted contact simply to prevent tirades and unexpected visits, although I feared being woken up at all hours for questions like "What was the name of your best friend in the third grade?" or "What kind of handgun do you want for Christmas?" Without Dad to rein her in, Mom was a force to be reckoned with. Miss you, Dad.

Sure enough, there were six calls from Mom along with two others from numbers I didn't recognize. It was coming up on six o'clock, and Mom was an early riser, so I called her.

"I was just starting to pack for my trip," she said icily.

"Put the suitcase away, Mama. Everything's fine."

"Has the killer been apprehended?"

"Not yet."

"Then everything is not fine. Don't pee down my back and tell me it's raining!"

I sighed. This was going to be more of a challenge than I thought.

I explained to Mom that the police were on the case and that I was helping as much as I could.

"So you're in danger!"

"Nobody wants to kill me, Mama. I've only been here four days."

"You can't undo a bad first impression."

What was that supposed to mean?

"I'm barely part of the team here. I'm just going to keep my eyes and ears open, do my job, and go home with a paycheck. Detective Donato is investigating—"

"That doesn't inspire confidence, Jilly. He hasn't got the sense God gave a mule. We had to solve the case for him last time, remember?"

I was Jilly again, which meant things were moving in the right direction.

"The point is, I only have one more week here. The investigation will probably take longer than that, so I'll be back at my real job having left murder far behind me."

"You would leave before solving the case?"

I couldn't win with my mother. Safe or in peril? Which would she prefer? I said as much.

"Fine. I've said it before, and I'll say it again. You have always found it hard to ask for help."

Jill Cooksey is an island.

I took a deep breath and tried another tack.

"Mama, I'm not that involved." That was a lie. I was going to pay for that later. "If I need help, I'll ask."

Silence.

"I promise." Boy, that cost me. The last thing I wanted was my mom showing up guns blazing like last time. Don't get me wrong. It's always nice to see her, but I'd prefer to meet her for a weekend at The Biltmore instead of for a murder investigation.

My promise did the trick. Mom relented.

"See that you do, Jilly. I love you." She hung up. Mom was not completely mollified, but she wasn't headed for Amtrak, either. I had bought myself some time.

I listened to the other two voice mails—another dodgy guy (no, I don't want to see *The Rocky Horror Picture Show* with you) and another hang-up. Eventually, I reasoned, I would run out of sketchy men to whom I had given my number, and these calls would end. Delete. Delete.

Finished with email and voice mail, I headed for the cafeteria and a little breakfast. I met Flavia on the way. She was coming from the direction of the studio and Marcus's office, and she had a smile on her face.

"You look happy."

Her smile vanished.

"I probably shouldn't be so happy. It's wildly inappropriate."

"How can being happy be inappropriate?" I asked as we entered the cafeteria. We both took trays and headed for the line. The cafeteria was empty owing to the early hour, but Flavia still glanced around as if to make sure we were alone.

"Because of Bryce."

Now she had me intrigued, but our conversation was interrupted by the chef, who asked if we wanted omelets. We did, so the pause continued while he threw eggs, cheese, peppers, and ham into little skillets, set them on the flame for a bit, and then flipped them. Soon we both had steaming omelets on our trays to which I added a biscuit, some fresh fruit, and another cup of coffee. I was definitely developing a coffee habit. I followed Flavia to a corner table, we sat, and I picked up the thread of the conversation.

"Why should Bryce prevent you from being happy? Unless of course you're happy about him being dead."

Flavia winced. "I'm not happy he's dead, but . . ."

"But?"

Flavia exhaled a huge sigh of resignation.

"Marcus told me today that I'll be directing the next episode."

"Wow! That's huge. Congratulations!"

Flavia smiled again, but her smile didn't meet her eyes.

"It's just that Bryce was supposed to direct the next episode."

I gave her a sympathetic look. "So you feel guilty."

"Sort of...no...I don't know." She looked around again to make sure we were alone. "It's just that it was my episode to start with. I was supposed to direct. Then Marcus took it away from me and gave it to Bryce for some reason."

Probably because Marcus had no intention of letting Bryce be the next Mr. Snicklefritz, I thought, but I kept it to myself.

"That must have stung," I said instead.

"No kidding. It has taken me years to convince them to give me a shot, and they just took it away without an explanation. Marcus said something vague about me directing next season, but I didn't believe him. Right before it happened, I had been on a couple of dates with Bryce, but I said no to a third. No chemistry. I wondered if Bryce, or Marcus on behalf of Bryce, was trying to punish me."

"Was your lack of chemistry with Bryce or Jim-Bob?" I spoke without thinking.

Flavia arched an eyebrow. "Is there a difference?"

Flavia and I shared a moment in which I felt we understood each other perfectly. I so wanted to tell her that I was pretty certain Marcus had allowed Bryce to direct as a consolation prize and not as a punishment for failed romance, but I couldn't let that cat out of the bag. I refocused.

"So now you're happy that you get to direct again, but you feel bad because Bryce's death made it happen."

Flavia's jaw and her eyes hardened. For a moment, I think she was gritting her teeth.

"That's just it. I don't feel bad because it was mine to begin with. Getting it back feels fair. I think I feel bad about not feeling bad. Does that make any sense?"

She was talking to the queen of self-doubt and second-guessing. She just didn't know it.

"That makes complete sense."

She sighed again and smiled sadly.

"I'm an awful person."

No, she wasn't. Bryce's death and Marcus screwing her over were two separate issues. She was allowed to feel bad about one and happy about the other, and I told her so.

"Thanks, Jill. Only another woman would understand."

Too right.

As we continued our breakfast, Flavia began to share her plans for the next episode. It had a big musical number, and she was hoping to bring in extra puppeteers to play a whole host of woodland creatures. As she described her plan, her enthusiasm blossomed and grew. I could feel it expanding to fill the room, and I could see the creative fire in her eye.

"I want to shoot from above for a Busby Berkeley effect, which is going to be difficult because when you see the set from above, you see the puppeteers, so we're going to have to find a workaround. But I want the big number to have a 'cast of thousands' feel. It's going to be big. It's going to put me on the map."

Yeah. Directing meant a heck of a lot to Flavia.

CHAPTER 7

After breakfast, we wandered back to The Pen to find the cast and crew gathered. Since the dressing rooms were considered part of the crime scene, the puppeteers had nowhere to call home. They looked a little lost wandering around.

I hadn't made it all the way to my cubicle before two grips turned up hauling a huge metal crate. Marcus and Devon followed. The grips deposited the crate in the middle of The Pen and stepped aside.

"May I have your attention please?" bellowed Marcus. "Everybody gather around."

The cast and crew circled the wagons. Because of the conversation I'd overheard earlier, I had an inkling of what was about to happen.

"I think we need some good news, and I'm glad that there's some to share today. Devon Cauthorne has been part of the Snicklefritz family for twenty years. He has been integral to our success, as a right hand and playing many supporting roles. But today, his role changes."

Bump.

Bump!

Bump! Bump!

I looked around for the source of the noise and saw a few crew members smiling. It almost sounded like the bumps came from the…it couldn't be.

Bump!

"Ood fumwump met rhee doooda wheer."

What the—? I looked around some more. Now the cast and crew members were grinning at each other. What did they know that I didn't? And where was that voice coming from? It sounded like it was coming from inside the crate!

Devon approached the big silver box and began undoing the fastenings.

"Today Devon takes center stage as the new voice of Martin the Marten!" announced Marcus.

While we watched, the lid flew open, and Martin's voice could be heard clear as day.

"Get me out of this thing! I'm suffocating!"

In a trice, the furry brown marten puppet was out of the box and on Devon's arm. He shook, like a dog after a bath, then smiled at the crowd.

"Finally! I thought I'd never get out of that sarfogafus… sargacafus…that coffin!"

Everyone laughed except for me and Julia and Carl, because, while I knew it was Devon controlling the puppet and speaking, it sounded exactly like Bryce. It was uncanny. Everything Bryce had told me about puppeteers waiting in the wings was completely true. Julia, whose torch for Bryce still burned, was appalled. I saw her turn away and wipe her eyes. Carl's mouth was set in a grim line. I could tell he was trying very hard not to react.

Meanwhile, Martin was making the rounds meeting the cast and crew, cracking jokes, and posing for selfies. I watched Devon as he manipulated the puppet. His mouth moved normally as he voiced the character, so he must have been throwing his voice when Martin was in the crate. At least I hoped he'd been throwing his voice. It is not inaccurate to say that I sometimes wondered who was controlling whom.

When Martin got to me, I shook his hand, and he gave me a little kiss on the cheek. I tried to look past the puppet to signal my congratulations to Devon, but Martin wasn't having it. I would just tell Devon over lunch, unless of course his change in status meant that he would be eating at the cool kids' table from now on. I was interested to see how the dynamic would change.

"There's more good news to come, everybody!" cried Marcus as he waved his hands to catch everyone's attention yet again. "Everybody follow me."

Marcus took off down the hallway toward the cafeteria, and the crowd followed. There was much shoulder shrugging as people wondered what was happening. When we got to the cafeteria, Marcus kept going. I'd never gone this way, never needed to. About fifty feet past the cafeteria entrance, on the other side of the hallway, we came to a set of studio doors. Marcus stopped in front of them and turned to face the crowd.

"Behold! I give you the future!"

The double doors swung open, and the crowd surged forward into a sea of green.

The studio space we entered was mostly empty. A smooth green backdrop hung from a frame near the ceiling all the way to the floor where it became a floor covering. With no wrinkles or joints, it created an illusion of infinite space.

"That's a cyc wall," said Chuck to the other PAs.

"We know what a cyc wall is," said Madison with a roll of her eyes.

I didn't know it was called a cyc wall, but I kept quiet.

In the foreground sat several large, green boxes. Just like in the Gingerbread Cottage studio, three cameras faced the green area. A row of lights on stands flanked the set as well. Was it a set? What was with all the green?

Marcus positioned himself on the green floor in front of the middle camera.

"Ladies and gentlemen, welcome to Snicklefritz 2.0."

Two grips appeared with a monitor on a stand and rolled it out to where we could all see it. On the screen was Marcus, except he wasn't standing on the green set anymore. The green had been replaced with the Gingerbread Cottage.

"CGI," said Chuck.

"Huh?" I decided to stop playing it cool.

"Computer-generated imagery," explained Chuck. "A virtual set."

I looked closer. Sure enough, the set wasn't real. It was animated but in a lifelike fashion.

Marcus gave a nod to the camera, and the background changed. Now he was standing in a dense forest. He nodded again, and soon he was floating in space.

"With our new virtual system, Mr. Snicklefritz and his pals can go anywhere. They're no longer constrained by the four walls of Gingerbread Cottage. Imagine the flexibility we'll have with storylines, all the new adventures."

"Not to mention the educational opportunities," chimed in Patricia. "With a CGI set, we can add more STEM material."

"What's STEM?" asked a member of the art department.

"Science, technology, engineering, and math," pronounced Patricia.

"Science in Gingerbread Cottage? It's a fairy tale show."

"That's just it," countered Marcus. "It doesn't have to be. We're going to take Mr. Snicklefritz into the twenty-first century."

The cast and crew were abuzz. Everyone had a question or a comment, and the cliques were alive with conversation. Some folks, like the writers, were excited. I think they were already spitballing new ideas. The puppeteers, minus Carl, had their heads together and were talking low. I couldn't tell their reaction. The PAs were in a disagreement, with Chuck for computer generation and Tameasha firmly against it. The loudest group was the art department, and they eventually brought all the other conversations to a halt.

"Excuse me!" shouted the art director (I think her name was Deja) as she thrust her hand into the air like a student with a pressing question. The group didn't fall silent, but the volume fell considerably. "I have a question."

"Shoot," said Marcus amiably. Despite the buzz, his smile hadn't faltered.

"Since there won't be a physical set to dress and modify, what exactly will the art department be doing in this brave new Snicklefritz of yours?" Her voice, her expression, and her body language radiated challenge.

Marcus's smile slipped a little.

"We'll still use physical props on the show, so the art department will still be tasked with their design and creation." He smiled reassuringly around the room.

"Okay," replied Deja, "but that's going to be a lot less work, so you're not going to need all of us, are you? And without sets to build, you won't need the carpenters and most of the grips, either. Am I wrong?"

A hush descended while the cast and crew waited for Marcus to answer the challenge. He bit his lip nervously before he answered.

"There will be some adjustments as we learn to navigate our new world, our new normal—"

"Screw this!"

"I'm calling my union rep."

Evidently, the crew could recognize corporate-speak, and they weren't having it. Kate had warned me about the "suits versus ponytails" mindset in TV production, and now I was witnessing it firsthand. Still, Marcus tried to save the moment.

"We just need to sit down and talk..." But it was too late. Already Deja was leading the art department out of the studio, and the carpenters and most of the grips followed suit.

Marcus was stunned, unable to speak. Open rebellion must not have occurred to him. Next to him, Patricia bit her lip nervously and wrung her hands. Her usual poise had abandoned her.

Clap!

Clap!

Clap!

Every head left in the room swiveled to see the source of the disrespectful slow clap. No surprise, it was Carl.

"Oh, well done, fearless leader!" His voice dripped with sarcasm. "It wasn't enough that we lost one of our own yesterday. Now you want to take our whole world away from us, in the name of what? Education?" He turned to Patricia. "So concerned about education, about the children. A bit late to that party, aren't you?" Patricia blanched.

"Shut up, Carl," she hissed. "Can't you see Marcus is trying to do what's right for the show, to keep it going? To keep it relevant?"

"If we don't stay relevant, no one here will have a job." Marcus had found his voice again. "Snicklefritz is an institution, and even institutions have to change with the times. Otherwise, they get left behind." Now Marcus had everyone's attention again. "Yes, we'll have to make some adjustments, and it won't be easy. But think of the adventure we're about to undertake. We're moving in a new direction; I can't wait to see—"

CRASH!

Every head swiveled again to find Carl clutching his chest, his eyes bulging out of his face. Britney stood next to him in a similar state, while a little farther away stood Larry and Chuck in better shape but clearly startled. Scattered at Carl's feet were shards of glass, like mini icebergs, interspersed with pieces of twisted metal. A metal light stand lay on its side just inches from his foot, and I could only think that the light must have brushed against him as it went over. As if he read my mind, Carl reached up to rub his right arm.

"No one moves!" shouted Flavia, taking charge. "We don't want anyone stepping on glass." There was so much of it. The lights on the stands at the front of the studio space were quite large, shaped like drums with glass lenses that could focus the light. Just how much glass was in those lights was now in evidence on the floor. Flavia looked at Tameasha

"You're not near the glass. Run and get the first aid kit. Julia, you get a broom and dustpan from the maintenance closet. Madison, hand me that mat." She pointed to one of the heavy, black rubber mats that was sometimes positioned on top of bundles of electrical cable to keep people from tripping. Madison lugged the mat over to Flavia, who then laid it across the sea of glass. "Get me another." When she was finished, Flavia had constructed a black rubber bridge over much of the glass, and Carl, Britney, Larry, and Chuck crossed it into a glass-free area. Now Marcus appeared at Flavia's side.

"What happened?" he barked.

"The light just fell over!" cried Britney. "I saw it hit Carl on the way down." Flavia moved to look at Carl's arm where he was holding it, but he shrugged her off.

"I'm fine! Just a bruise."

"You were lucky it didn't fall right on you, baby!" Britney was close to tears.

Marcus rounded on Larry and Chuck. "You two were standing closest to the light. What happened?"

Chuck, lowly PA that he was, looked like a deer in the headlights. His green eyes were wide with fear, and his mouth hung open, but no sound came out. Larry filled the silence.

"All I know is the light was upright and then it wasn't. The stand must have failed. You know how unsteady they can be. And it wasn't sandbagged."

I looked at the other lights on stands in the row, and sure enough, the rest of them had sandbags lying across their bases to keep them steady.

Marcus looked at Chuck expectantly. "Well?"

"I…I don't know what happened. Larry's right. It was upright and then it wasn't." He looked at Larry, who nodded at him encouragingly. Sometimes Larry could be so normal.

"Well, we need to be more careful," pronounced Marcus. "Whoever set that light up without a sandbag could have killed someone today. We've had enough tragedy on this show. We need to take care of each other."

Tameasha and Julia returned with the first aid kit and a broom, but Marcus held up a hand to stop them until he was finished.

"Let's break for an hour and then meet in the cafeteria for a table reading of the next episode. I'm pleased to announce that our beloved floor director, Flavia, will be directing. See you in an hour." With that, Marcus fled the studio with Patricia hard on his heels. The grips who hadn't walked out and the PAs began cleaning up the shattered light. Tameasha started to approach Carl with the first aid kit but thought better of it and handed it off to Flavia. She didn't seem enthusiastic herself, so I took the kit and approached him. After all, soothing clients and making nice was my bread and butter.

"It's just a bruise," growled Carl when he saw me heading his way.

"You're probably right," I admitted, padding my southern accent just a tad, "but better safe than sorry." I distinctly felt Britney giving me the side-eye. "May I?" I asked as I reached for the sleeve of Carl's shirt. He answered by rolling up the sleeve all the way to his shoulder. There was a red streak dotted with crimson pinpricks—an abrasion but not a cut. Underneath and surrounding the scratch, an ugly bruise was forming. I told Carl I would bring him an ice pack and asked where he would be hanging out until the table reading.

"Don't worry," snapped Carl as he yanked his sleeve down. "You'll know where to find me." He marched out of the studio, but Britney didn't follow.

"I already have a headache from the crash," she explained to me, although I hadn't asked. "I don't need to be around a shouting match. I'm gonna get out of here for a while." With a hand to her temple, she scurried out of the studio. I couldn't blame her, but while she didn't need to be present for the shouting match, I did. The crew was busy with the cleanup, so I edged toward the door.

The shouting was audible long before I got to Marcus's office. The rest of the office was deserted, just like that morning, and I thought it likely that everyone else had run away from the conflict. Who could blame them? What a fun work environment.

I didn't have to worry about eavesdropping because the door was open, so I paused several feet from the doorway.

"You keep pulling crap like this, and I will spill my guts!" yelled Carl.

"You wouldn't do that!" wailed Patricia.

"Oh please! Like you haven't been threatening him with it yourself. It's the only reason you two are still married."

"At least we *are* still married! You couldn't hold on to Dominique!"

"And who's fault was that?"

"Enough!" broke in Marcus. "Carl, we aren't the only ones who will take a hit. You'll go down too."

"Could it be any worse than what you're doing to my

show?"

"Then retire!"

"Sure! Walk away and let you turn *Mr. Snicklefritz* into who knows what? Over my dead body!" Carl punctuated his words by slamming the door.

Dang! Now everyone was muffled. I moved closer, careful to stay away from the floor-to-ceiling glass sidelight that flanked the door. Even though the blinds were closed, I couldn't risk casting a shadow.

I strained to hear what was being said, but I could only make out a few words. "Kids" came up several times, along with "fraud," or maybe it was "frog." And the word "lies," or maybe it was "flies," which would have made sense if they were talking about frogs. I edged closer to the window in the hope that I could hear better through the glass. It worked, sort of.

"I'm warming you!" said Carl. "If I don't like how rings are showing, you will bake angels on the spot. If I hunt the sun to fee flew, you'll bake it flew. Otherwise, there will be hell to pay." The last sentence was dead clear because Carl was passing the window on his way to the door. Not for the first time that day, I took off running.

Back in my cubicle, I quickly jotted down what Carl had said. "I'm warming you" was clearly "I'm warning you," but the next two sentences were a mystery. I spent the next fifteen minutes pondering the puzzle before me. I managed to figure out "If I don't like how things are going," but I couldn't make heads or tails of "bake angels."

When I finally looked up again, it was to find the cast and crew had returned from wherever and that it was time to head into the table reading. Truth be told, I didn't know what a table reading was, but I was going with the flow and acting like I belonged. That strategy had helped me a lot in life. I picked up my notepad and pen and followed the crowd moving to the cafeteria.

CHAPTER 8

In the dining hall, the tables had been rearranged to form a massive square conference table. Marcus, Patricia, Flavia, Carl, Devon, and Phil were on one side with two empty chairs that must have been saved for Larry and Britney. Everyone else spread out around the table in descending order of importance, although I noticed that only two members of the art department were present, and they didn't look any happier than when they stormed off the set. I sat next to the PAs. At every place around the table was a copy of the script for the next episode.

"So that's what a table reading is," I whispered to myself. Next to me, Madison chuckled. I smiled at her and held my finger to my lips. She pantomimed zipping her mouth shut, and we giggled.

Then Britney breezed in all smiles, headache forgotten, with Larry close behind. They quickly took their seats, and the reading began.

"We haven't had a table reading since the beginning of the season, but as we are moving to a new set and a new way of production, it seems right," said Marcus. "Flavia, how would you like to proceed?"

After a short discussion, the reading commenced. It basically consisted of reading a scene and then discussing the blocking of the puppets and the technical aspects. The video editor had a lot to say because he evidently was now in charge of the computer-generated set. Necessary props and costumes for each scene were listed and discussed with the art department reps. The fun part was when the puppeteers read the script in their character voices, but the technical discussion afterward had me yawning. I soon turned my attention back to my puzzle and was looking for words that rhyme with "angels" when a flurry of movement caught my eye. Carl, who was sitting opposite me, had written something on a sheet of paper. Then, with a flourish, he folded it several times, wrote something on it, and passed it to Flavia, who passed it to Patricia, who reluctantly passed it to Marcus. Was it my imagination, or did Marcus sigh as he opened the letter? After a moment, he interrupted the reading.

"Hold up for a sec. I think we're going to change the musical instrument prop from a violin to a flute."

"But that will change the whole nature of the scene. It's going to need a rewrite," spluttered one of the writers.

"I'm sure you can handle it," said Marcus with a tight smile. "Now where were we?"

The reading continued, but everyone was looking around the room having silent conversations with friends and colleagues. It was clear that Carl had written the note to request the change, but why had Marcus caved? That small change was going to have a domino effect.

I looked at my puzzle again, and everything came into focus.

"If I don't like how rings are showing, you will bake angels on the spot."

"If I don't like how things are going, you will make changes on the spot."

"If I hunt the sun to fee flew, you'll bake it flew."

"If I want the sun to be blue, you'll make it blue."

"Otherwise, there will be hell to pay." That part needed no translation.

Carl had been yelling about spilling his guts before he shut the door and ended my eavesdropping. Evidently, whatever he was holding over Marcus's head was big, and Carl was going to make the most of it. But what was it? And what did it have to do with Bryce's death? Correction. Did it have anything to do with Bryce's death? For all I knew, I had stumbled across a completely unrelated drama. After all, a show that had been on the air for thirty years most certainly had its fair share of skeletons in the closet.

Carl passed notes two more times during the reading, but the two changes were minor. He was simply reminding Marcus who was in control. He seemed to take great pleasure in flexing his muscles, and my dislike for Carl grew with each flex.

When the table reading ended, we broke for lunch with the directive to meet afterward in the new studio for rehearsal. Carl and Britney immediately left the cafeteria, while Marcus was instantly besieged by the writers, presumably with questions about the changes to the script. The rest of us got in line for food.

It was Mexican day, and I filled my tray with nachos, tacos, refried beans, and churros. After the stressful morning, a Mexifeast was just what the doctor ordered. I headed back to my place at the conference table, but instead of Chuck taking the seat next to me, Devon sat down.

"I didn't see the churros! Where were they?"

I offered him one of mine because I had taken two. Okay, three.

"Congratulations on the Martin role! Please accept this

congratulatory churro." I handed it to him on a napkin with great ceremony.

Devon smiled at me, but there was sadness in his eyes.

"It's not the way I wanted to move up," he said, "but I'm grateful for the opportunity, even if it's not the one I thought I'd be getting."

"Mr. Snicklefritz?" I asked. He nodded.

"Carl will never retire. I just need to accept that fact. And now I have a great role. Really, I'm grateful."

My happiness for Devon was tempered by my sadness over Bryce's death, a death everyone seemed to have forgotten rather quickly. I looked at Marcus, who was in deep discussion with the writers. He should have worked in PR because managing people's perception and directing their attention were skills he had perfected. I realized at that moment that Marcus had been bombarding people with changes all day, forcing them to think about things besides Bryce's murder. I couldn't decide if he was being kind or cold-bloodedly opportunistic. Granted, morale had rebounded in the sense that people weren't overcome by grief. Instead, some were excited about the future while others were spitting mad, but one could argue that both emotions were preferable to grief. More importantly, Bryce's murder and the closing of the set had given Marcus the perfect moment to make swift and lasting changes.

And Bryce was forgotten. That didn't sit well with me for two reasons. First, he had faithfully served the show for fifteen years and shouldn't have been tossed out like yesterday's news. And second, if no one was talking about the murder, how was I going to help Donato find the killer? I decided to stir the pot.

"So who do you think murdered Bryce?" I asked rather loudly just as Devon bit into the churro. Shocked by my question, he inhaled cinnamon sugar which set off a coughing fit. Everyone on my side of the table paused, forks and tacos halfway to their mouths, to watch Devon either recover or choke to death on a churro and to see how he would answer. Pot stirred.

After a long swig of water, he wiped his streaming eyes and then met mine.

"Sorry. I didn't mean to make you choke."

"It's okay. You just really took me by surprise."

No kidding. I leaned in closer and dropped my voice so that only he could hear me.

"Who could've had it in for Bryce? He was such a nice guy."

"Your guess is as good as mine," said Devon. "There's a lot of competition in the puppet world, but we're not that cutthroat. We make children's programming, for heaven's sake."

"Maybe it was a stranger, someone who wandered in off the street."

"That would make more sense than anything else," said Devon.

I nodded my head in agreement, even though I wasn't sure I agreed, and picked up my glass.

"I need some more iced tea. Back in a sec." I got up and meandered over to the drink dispensers. After filling my cup and making a circuit of the room, I ascertained that most of the cast and crew were talking about Bryce, as was only right. And when I got back to my seat, Devon had disappeared, which was interesting.

Picking up a taco, I tried to focus on the conversations around me. The PAs were on my left, including Chuck, who had pulled up another chair when Devon took his.

"They're going to need a new right hand," asserted Tameasha. "Maybe it will be one of us."

"Fat chance," said Madison. "There are a lot of puppeteers waiting in the wings. They're not going to consider a PA."

"Depends," said Chuck. "If Devon puts in a good word.

Tameasha, you've been working with him. Do you think he'll recommend you?"

"Maybe. If I ask him. But you were working with Bryce. You have a shot."

Chuck laughed bitterly. "Bryce isn't here to say anything."

"I'm telling you," insisted Madison, "it'll be a pro."

"Do you think we'd be switching sets and going CGI if Bryce hadn't died?" asked Julia in a small voice. The PA's chewed on the question for a moment while I chewed on my taco.

"I think so," answered Chuck. "The move has been a long time in the making even if it was kept secret. The studio space was set up and the digital backgrounds were generated. That all takes time."

"Yeah, but did you see Carl's face?" demanded Tameasha. "He was shocked. How can the lead on the show, who is also its creator, not know about the changes?"

"Is that really so surprising?" put in Madison. "Marcus and Carl may have been besties in the olden days, but all they do now is fight."

"Children's television isn't what I expected," murmured Julia.

Amen, sister.

After lunch, I ran back to my cubicle to check my email before rehearsal started. There was one from Kate asking if I would come to Anstruther and Cole for an emergency meeting the next day. I had expected something of the sort. Most likely Kate and her team had been working on emergency PR plans in the wake of the murder, and as I was the boots on the ground, I needed to be briefed. I replied in the affirmative and then shot an email off to my mom to let her know that all was well in Gingerbread Cottage, further forestalling a visit from my concerned parent. She immediately responded with a phone call.

"I've sent you a package," she said without even a hello.

"Okay, thanks. What is it?"

"That's not important." Not important? Before I could ask her what that meant, she plowed on. "What's important is that you pick it up tomorrow between nine a.m. and five p.m. I'll text you the address."

"If it's being sent to me, why do I have to pick it up?"

"Don't be impertinent. Do as I say. Pick up the package tomorrow."

"Mama, you're being cryptic, and it's freaking me out."

Mom sighed in a particularly exasperated fashion. "You always were a nervous child. Just do your mother a favor and pick up the package tomorrow. Can you do that? Is that too much to ask?"

"No, ma'am."

"That's better. Call me when the package is secure." She hung up.

Thoroughly put in my place, I stared at the phone. *When the package is secure?* Why was my mother talking like a spy or a drug dealer? Oh no! Was this the beginning of dementia? Was Mama beginning to lose it? She had always been the most capable person I knew, but maybe even the strongest people give out eventually. And what was in this package? I had a strong feeling it wasn't a care package full of blackberry jam, grits, chow-chow, and banana bread.

With a renewed sense of dread, I headed to the new studio and Snicklefritz 2.0. When I arrived, three PAs and a grip were attempting to get the very large Larry Stubbins into the green suit that he would have to wear to be invisible on the virtual set. He almost fell over twice while stepping into the jumpsuit, and then there was an epic battle with the zipper. It seemed no one had taken Larry's measurements.

"Dude, it's better if you don't wear anything under it," advised Phil as he stretched languorously. "The suit is actually quite liberating." To demonstrate, the wiry little puppeteer did a quick sun salutation and ended in tree pose.

"Well, it's too late now," muttered Larry. "I'm already in the suit. Jeez, it's hot in here!"

"Too many clothes, man."

Devon appeared on the set with a slim young woman, both attired in green.

"Hey everybody. This is Susan, our new right hand." I looked at the PAs. Madison wore a distinct "I told you so" face, while Tameasha and Chuck looked crestfallen. It was probably better that their hopes had been dashed before they got any higher.

Marcus, Patricia, and Flavia arrived next. They were powwowing with the puppeteers when Britney glided into the studio in her Princess Gretel gown followed by Carl in his Mr. Snicklefritz woodcutter costume.

"Great!" said Flavia. "Let's get started." She began giving everyone direction in her calm, authoritative way, and I realized that being the floor director had been great training for being the actual director. Moreover, this cast and crew were accustomed to following her directions, so rehearsal started off smoothly. I was enjoying the show when I felt a presence at my side. It was Patricia.

"Hi, Jill."

"Hi, Patricia."

"I was just wondering…"

"Yes?"

"There are no set visits today, right?"

"That's correct. No interruptions." I smiled brightly.

"So…how to put this…why are you here?"

I should have seen it coming. With the set closed and the anniversary special in limbo, I really didn't have a role except to spy on everyone for Kate and the police, but I couldn't very well mention that. Luckily, I speak spin.

"Well, Patricia, things are in flux right now, but Anstruther and Cole asked me to stay on to get the lay of the land. Understand the new order. Perhaps tours will resume and the anniversary special will proceed. Until we know for sure, it's best that I understand the new form of production. That way, if tours recommence, I will be well-positioned to explain procedures to our guests and give them the most infor—"

"I understand." Patricia cut me off. With a nod, she stalked off, and I mentally patted myself on the back for spin well done. Yet I wondered why Patricia would care that I was hanging around. Was her question legitimate, or was she trying to shoo me away? Had my pot-stirring at lunch alarmed her? Or Marcus?

"Hey, Marcus." A voice sounded over the intercom, making me jump.

"Let's cut for a second folks," said the producer. "What's up Bruce?"

"We're having some trouble keying Snicklefritz. That green trim on his costume is wreaking havoc. Is there any chance the trim color could be changed? Maybe to red?"

Marcus eyed Carl, and with good reason. While the trim on his costume remained green, his face was fast turning scarlet. Carl was going to blow!

"Bruce, let's talk about it later. Just do your best for now."

"Roger that."

Before Marcus could tell Flavia to continue, the volcano known as Carl erupted.

"The color of this costume changes," bellowed Carl, spewing spittle like venom with every word, "when hell freezes over, pigs fly, and all the grips on the set have something to do at the same time! In other words, NEVER!"

Carl's roar froze everyone. I had never witnessed such fury up close, and it was terrifying. Not even Marcus could manage to speak. The master of soothing words was tongue-tied. Tense to the point of pain, we just watched to see what would come next. Amazingly, Carl was getting redder, his face and neck a shade of burgundy that nearly blended in with his rustic brown woodcutter shirt.

"And another thing," he began, and then he fell over in a heap.

CHAPTER 9

When I awoke the next morning, it was as if from a terrible dream, when waking brings sweet relief. It was a pleasure to find myself nestled in my own bed in familiar surroundings. The radiator was emitting gentle puffs of steam, cocooning me in warmth. I could smell the coffee in the pot across the room, and I lazily contemplated my breakfast options. An omelet? French toast? I had downloaded a new time travel romance on my e-reader. Maybe I would spend the day in bed reading.

Then I remembered the meeting. The emergency meeting. The emergency meeting in response to the collapse and hospitalization of the star of *The Mr. Snicklefritz Show*. The hospitalization that came on the heels of his co-star's murder.

Snicklefritz!

With a groan, I hauled myself out of bed. After coffee and a cheddar cheese omelet, I ran a bubble bath and let myself read my time travel romance for half an hour. Just as the heroine was coming to terms with the fact of time travel, I shut down my e-reader and toweled off. A glance out the window showed me a steel gray sky and snow flurries. The pigeons were fluffed up and trying to keep warm. It was a day for layers. It was a day for staying in.

With no choice in the matter if I wanted to get paid, I donned tights, jeans, thick socks, and a dark green cowl-necked sweater. I brushed my hair straight and pulled on a dark burgundy wool beret. I laced up my sneakers, slid into my navy blue parka, and wrapped a scarf that matched my beret around my neck. I grabbed my Behemoth Black Bag, checked for my key around my neck, and headed out the door.

The air on my face and hands was just as frosty as I'd imagined, and I rummaged in my coat pockets for the mittens that matched my hat and scarf. Before the emergency meeting, I was headed to pick up my mother's mystery package. The address she texted had turned out to be only a ten-minute walk from my apartment, and as I walked, I pondered the events of the day before. It was better than worrying about what was in the package.

When Carl collapsed, paramedics had been called, and he had been rushed to the hospital. Rehearsal ground to a halt, and Marcus sent everyone home while he followed the ambulance. I called Kate to let her know the situation, and she and the team at A & C went into crisis mode yet again and moved our Saturday meeting up an hour. I checked my email one last time before I left work. On my way out, I ran into the PAs, including Chuck, who had finally bonded with his coworkers. They were headed to a local pub for drinks and dinner, and they invited me along.

The group was quiet as we walked around the corner to the pub. It wasn't until we were settled in a booth, drinks acquired and dinner ordered, that conversation began.

"Do you think Carl's going to die?" asked Julia. Her brown eyes were bright with unshed tears. The week had definitely taken a toll on her.

"We should be so lucky," muttered Chuck bitterly.

"You don't mean that!" gasped Madison. The rest of us stared at him in shock. Carl was a curmudgeon of the highest order, but wishing his death seemed a bit over-the-top.

"What if I do?" challenged Chuck, his green eyes flashing. "Carl's been dragging the show down for years. The women, the booze, the temper tantrums. You can't tell me the show wouldn't be better off if a new lead took over. Then Marcus could guide the show in a more modern direction without any interference. We all know what Carl was doing today with his little notes. I just don't know why Marcus kept caving."

"But to wish him dead...," murmured Tameasha.

Chuck looked away, crossed his arms, and settled in for a good sulk. I took a sip of my drink and chose my next words carefully.

"Even if Carl recovers, and hopefully he will, it still could be the end of his time on the show. Who do you think would replace him?"

"Devon," said Tameasha and Madison at the same time.

"But Devon just became Martin," said Julia. "Wouldn't that be strange?"

"Other people can do Martin's voice," said Chuck from his sulky little corner.

"I think Mr. Snicklefritz should be a woman," offered Julia. "Ms. Snicklefritz would complete the modernization of the show."

"What about Princess Gretel?" I asked. "Should she become Prince Gerhart?"

Everyone chuckled except Julia.

"Princess Gretel needs to go. She's anachronistic and antifeminist."

Ouch! Kindly woodcutter's ax straight to my heart.

Just then the food arrived, and we tucked in. I ordered another round of drinks for everyone, and they all cheered, including Chuck, who, with a rise in blood sugar, was slowly rejoining the group. I felt a little guilty because I had an ulterior motive. I wanted to get their opinions on Bryce's murder and what could be behind the feud between Carl and Marcus. The PAs were often invisible to the higher-ranking members of the crew, and they saw everything.

"So much going on today," I began. "It feels like Bryce has been forgotten."

"I know, right?" Julia jumped in quickly. "It's disrespectful!"

"The show must go on," offered Tameasha. I could tell by her expression that it sounded just as lame to her.

"I'm just surprised that there isn't more of a focus on finding Bryce's killer," I prompted.

"Well, the killer was someone who came in off the street. We're not going to find him or her in the studio," said Madison.

"Why do you assume that?" countered Chuck. "Why can't the killer be one of us?"

"Because it doesn't make sense. We make children's television. How could any of us be a murderer?" asked Tameasha.

"Are you saying you couldn't imagine Carl killing anyone? I certainly could," sneered Chuck.

"But Carl loved Bryce," countered Julia, wiping her eyes with the back of her hand. "He wanted Bryce to replace him."

"Have you ever noticed how much Carl and Bryce look alike?" asked Madison. "It's like Carl found a younger version of himself to be his replacement. Weird, huh?"

We all chewed on that and our dinners for a moment. I had noticed that both Carl and Bryce had green eyes and similar complexions, but I hadn't thought they looked particularly alike. I filed that observation away to be investigated at a later date.

"I guess the thing to consider is who had something to gain from Bryce's death." I stirred the PA pot yet again.

"Devon of course," said Tameasha matter-of-factly. "But murder...it's just not in him."

"He's been a right hand for an awfully long time," observed Madison.

"What about the other puppeteers?" I prompted.

Chuck snorted. "Phil wouldn't kill a wasp if it was about to sting him. He's very into karma. And Larry, if you haven't noticed, has trouble functioning. There's no way."

"Larry has an ugly side," said Julia with distaste. "Or, I should say, Squirrelly-Joe has an ugly side." The women at the table all nodded in agreement.

"But when he's not Squirrelly-Joe, he's meek as a lamb," replied Madison. "I just don't see it."

We went through the crew, one by one, but while I heard a lot about them from the PAs, I didn't hear a motive for murder.

"So Devon is still the most likely suspect," I said finally.

"Except that he's a nice guy," said Tameasha as she sliced into her steak.

I had a thought.

"Chuck, you said a lot of people can do Martin's voice. Could another puppeteer, someone outside the show but waiting in the wings, have taken Bryce out in hopes of getting his job?"

"That person would have to be desperate and a complete psycho," replied Chuck. "How could anyone know they would be next in line for a gig?"

"You mean except for Devon?" asked Julia.

We were quiet after that, chewing on our meals and our thoughts.

I chewed on those same thoughts as I neared the address supplied by my concerned parent. Devon had the best motive for murder, but it was hard to imagine the uber-likable right hand as a killer. Unless there was some secret I hadn't yet discovered, no one else had real cause to kill Bryce, which made a lunatic wandering in off the street seem more plausible.

Reaching my destination, all thoughts of Bryce's murder

were replaced with plans for my mother's when I saw the sign over the storefront—Gun Island City Firearms Emporium.

Christmas had come early.

An hour and a half later, I exited the store a bundle of nerves. Nervous child, Mama? How about nervous adult with a handgun in her purse? It felt like a target was painted on my back. I just knew that criminals throughout the city could smell the gunpowder and were crawling out of their holes so they could beat me up and steal my gun. Clutching my Behemoth Black Bag, now home to a baby blue Ruger .22-caliber, I reached the subway and descended into the station. At the turnstile, I had to fish my MetroCard out of my purse. When my hand grazed cold steel, I nearly jumped out of my skin, and the station attendant gave me a funny look.

Be cool, Jill. Be cool.

Luckily, a train was already in the station, so I hastily boarded and took a seat. Then I noticed that I had both arms wrapped around the Behemoth Black Bag on my lap as if it contained gold bullion. My own body language screamed, "There's something valuable in my purse! Please come rob me!" I needed to get a grip. With great effort, I tried to relax my body and my mind. I dug my e-reader out of my bag, careful to avoid my Christmas surprise, and forced myself to read my time travel romance. It did the trick. Soon I was cavorting with the modern heroine stuck, not unwillingly, in the eighteenth century. Thoughts of firearms were replaced with thoughts of swords—and kissing.

Considerably more relaxed, at 59th and Lexington, I changed trains and headed downtown. Anstruther and Cole was headquartered in a Madison Avenue building in the mid-forties. I got off at Grand Central Station and walked north. Icy wind roared through the canyon created by the skyscrapers, hurrying me right along. I got to the building in record time and was heading up the elevator by eleven.

A & C was PR to the stars. They weren't agents, but they worked closely with agents, studios, managers, promoters, and the celebrities they represented to increase visibility and shape images. Kate had worked with *everyone,* and I was more than a little envious. As I stepped off the elevator and into the offices, I kept my eyes open for famous people, but as it was Saturday, I didn't hold my breath.

Surprisingly, a receptionist was stationed at the desk in the lobby, and she waved me through the glass doors into the inner offices. I had been here many times to visit Kate and to help out from time to time as part of our PR Posse. The Posse had taken shape when overworked me met overworked Kate at a beauty trade show a few years back. We were both in the same predicament: too much work and not enough help. Budgets in PR are forever shifting with the economy, so you could have a fully staffed team one week and a skeleton crew the next. Kate's roommate, Surya, was in the same situation, and she knew Anupa, who knew Liz, and pretty soon we were the best of friends and colleagues. Even though we worked for rival agencies, because our busiest work times were staggered, we helped each other out on the sly. Thus we stayed sane and gainfully employed.

I popped my head into Kate's office, which never failed to impress me. Entertainment PR certainly had perks, which included larger budgets. Kate's office was five times the size of mine at Waverly Communications. Her desk was a huge glass affair the size of a library reading table, the kind that accommodated four people cramming for exams. The filing cabinets and shelving were all black lacquer, and her chair was a black leather command module that should have been used to pilot a spaceship. In front of her desk was a tufted black leather love seat for guests, and on the other side of the room, near the huge window with a glorious view of Midtown, sat a glass conference table with black leather chairs for four. Kate was only a senior account executive, yet her office was plush. What would a vice president's office look like? My money was on a hot tub.

"Hello, sunshine," I chirped.

"Perfect timing!" smiled Kate. I was glad to see her dressed down like me, although her version of dressed down didn't quite make it to jeans. Vintage bell-bottom sailor pants? Yes. Denim? No. "We're meeting in Bob's office. You can leave your things here." Bob was a VP and Kate's boss, so my dream of seeing that office was about to come true. I just wished I had brought my swimsuit.

I left my outerwear on the sofa, but I had serious misgivings about leaving the Behemoth Black Bag and its contents. Kate noticed my hesitation.

"What's wrong with you?"

"I need to show you something." I opened my purse and held it out for her to inspect. She did, and her eyes nearly popped out of her head.

"Holy crap! Where did that come from? Why is it here?"

"My mom! It's my Christmas present. I just picked it up from the dealer."

"Well, that actually makes sense. Your mom loves guns." She whispered the word *guns* and looked around to make sure no one had heard. Her door was shut, so it was unnecessary, but I understood the paranoia that accompanied the appearance of unexpected firearms. "Are you even allowed to have it? Wait! Don't tell me."

"I have a concealed carry permit, so it's technically fine." And it was. After my mom discharged a gun in New York City and barely got away with it, I had acquired the permit to make sure I never found myself in such a situation. It had taken a little finagling and a favor called in by the cop-turned-reporter that I used to be in love with (ick), but I had been determined, and the jerk had loved me, or so I'd thought. Truth be told, after solving that case and bringing a killer to justice, I had been feeling my oats a little. For a moment, I had imagined myself a bit of an old-school, film noir gumshoe, and a pistol had seemed like a necessary accessory. Once I had the permit, however, I quickly realized that I really didn't want to own a gun.

But now I did. *Sigh.*

"Well, let's lock it in my desk," suggested Kate. When my bag was secure, I breathed a sigh of relief and followed Kate down the hall to Bob's office.

Okay, so there was no hot tub. But there was a foosball table, a popcorn machine, and several full-size cardboard standees of famous athletes and actors, including one of Mr. Snicklefritz himself surrounded by his forest friends. Bob, all business, plunged in as soon as he saw us.

"I just got an update on Carl. It wasn't a heart attack or a stroke, thank goodness, but his blood pressure was through the roof. They've upped his medication, and they'll discharge him later today. He can work, but he has to avoid undue stress. The anniversary is still on. Here's the schedule of events for the week."

Kate and I took the proffered lists, sat on a black tufted sofa similar to the loveseat in her office, and faced Bob across his desk. Somewhere around forty, he was clad in jeans and an Islanders jersey, and he was fighting a losing battle with his hairline.

I perused the list to find a few changes. In addition to the already scheduled set visits during the week and the live TV special the next Saturday, the network was sending a news crew for an in-depth report on the murder investigation. There was also going to be a Bryce Camplen retrospective at the Museum of Television and Radio, and another TV crew was coming to interview the cast and crew for an extra segment on

Bryce to go in the anniversary special. And to top it off, the Princess Gretels were coming back for round two.

"Since the first Princess Gretel roundtable was an unqualified disaster, we have to do it again," explained Bob. "The only part that was remotely salvageable was when you stepped in, Jill, so we'd like you to take charge and direct it."

I felt my jaw hit my lap. Me direct? The Princess Gretels were feral. Henry Higgins himself couldn't transform that bunch of broads into elegant aristocrats if he had a year and an infinite supply of marbles. Bob misinterpreted my hesitation.

"Don't worry. Your name will be in the credits as a segment producer."

My jaw fell even further, landing on the floor. Kate's eyes twinkled.

"Just think, Jill, you'll be in the Internet Movie Database."

"Yeah, and you'll get paid extra for the gig," added Bob.

Dollar signs had me reeling in my jaw and plastering a smile on my face.

"But how will Carl be able to avoid stress with all the added activity at the show?" asked Kate, dragging me away from my daydream of swimming in piles of money à la Scrooge McDuck. "We need to avoid another episode. A live thirtieth anniversary special without Mr. Snicklefritz would be a disaster."

I thought about all the recent changes to the show, the murder investigation, the personal conflicts, and the thirtieth-anniversary circus. *The Mr. Snicklefritz Show* was awash in chaos, a terrible sort of environment for the physically fragile, like Carl, and the mentally fragile, like our killer. Unless something changed, we were looking at the complete physical breakdown of Mr. Snicklefritz at best and a killing spree at worst.

"We're going to need Marcus's help," I proposed. "He can set the schedule and keep it manageable, but as his changes to the show are one of the main causes of Carl's stress, it's going to be difficult to get Marcus on board."

We took turns throwing out questions and trying to answer them while Kate took notes. When Bob's stomach growled noisily, I glanced at my phone to see it was after noon. We paused to order Chinese and then worked through lunch to hammer out a plan for the following week. By three we were finishing up the final details.

"I'll type it up and send it over to Marcus and the network ASAP," said Kate as we stood to leave.

"Better yet, *I'll* send it to Marcus and the network," offered Bob. "He's not going to like everything in this plan, and I want him to come at me instead of you when he gets his panties in a twist."

"You've got a good boss," I whispered to Kate when we were out in the hallway.

"Sometimes," Kate whispered back.

Returning to her office, Kate sat down to create the document that would be sent to Marcus. We recommended limiting filming to before lunch only. Set visits could still take place during that time. We also recommended no new changes to the show's format until after the thirtieth anniversary was over, even going so far as to recommend moving back to the old set for the current episode once the police cleared it for use. I knew Marcus would say no to that one, but it would at least underscore the seriousness of the problem. We suggested that the news crew and the crew filming for the special be as discreet as possible, staying clear of the set and only interviewing after lunch. The news crew was scheduled to film on Wednesday, while the special crew was scheduled for Monday. The Princess Gretel roundtable take two was scheduled for Tuesday afternoon, and we insisted that Carl and the Gretels stay far away from each other. The Bryce Camplen retrospective opening was Thursday night at the Museum of Television and Radio, and we excused Carl from attending, although I was now required to go. I was pretty sure that when my paycation was over, I would be an exhausted wreck, but Bob had mentioned overtime, so I slapped on a smile.

We added more security too. The studio might not like it, but they had most likely allowed someone to wander in off the street and kill Bryce. They would just have to suck it up. Hopefully, feeling safer would bring the overall level of tension down. I had told Kate and Bob about the arguments between Marcus, Patricia, and Carl, and Bob suggested a moratorium on personal business in the workplace. Requiring people to save their personal squabbles for home, while it sounded like common sense professionalism, also sounded like a tall order, but a reminder couldn't hurt. It struck me how our plan sounded a bit like a list of rules for a kindergarten class. Well, there *were* temper tantrums. I just wished I had the power to stick some noses in some corners.

Meanwhile, I had plopped down on the sofa to wait for Kate to finish and to mull over the case. Carl Biersdorf was holding something over Marcus and Patricia's heads, but what was it? It was serious enough that Marcus was catering to Carl's whims but not serious enough to keep Marcus from making big changes to the show despite Carl's disapproval. Perhaps he didn't think Carl would make good on his threats, or perhaps he felt he had pushed Carl far enough. And if Carl was blackmailing them, so to speak, why wasn't he the murder victim instead of Bryce? That question assumed that Bryce's death was related to the feud between Carl and Marcus, but there was no evidence to suggest a connection. In fact, I decided, it was more likely that there were two mysteries to be solved at *The Mr. Snicklefritz Show*.

Kate soon finished the document and emailed it off to Bob to proof and send. We retrieved my bag, wrapped up in our outerwear, and headed down the elevator to the street, where it was snowing to beat the band. Kate and I were headed for Brooklyn and our friend Liz's apartment where our Posse was gathering for the evening. We hustled our frozen buns over to Grand Central and caught an F train for the long ride out to Park Slope.

We both chose to read and didn't say much on the ride to Brooklyn, most likely because we both knew that we'd just have to repeat it all to our Posse anyway. I made a serious dent in my time travel romance, and the heroine was seriously considering choosing the hunky aristocrat over indoor plumbing when we arrived at the Park Slope station. A five-minute walk later, we were climbing the steps to a beautiful brownstone and ringing the bell.

Liz Gordon lived on the second floor in the best apartment of any of us. Her front room was in the round turret part of a Romanesque revival brownstone that had once been a single-family home and was now divided into four apartments. High ceilings, crown molding, and a claw-foot bathtub made the rest of us jealous, but none of us was willing to commute that far out. Luckily for Liz, her PR firm was located in lower Manhattan, so the subway ride wasn't so bad for her. I personally was also not willing to pay the astronomical rent that Liz had to shell out for such a beautiful place.

She greeted us at the door, and in no time she had taken our coats, settled us on a sofa near the gas fireplace, and pressed cups of herbal tea into our hands.

"You must be frozen," she exclaimed as she offered around a plate of healthy-looking oatmeal raisin cookies. I smelled cinnamon, so healthy or not, I helped myself. "After hockey practice this morning, I was so cold I had to soak in a hot bath for an hour just to get warm. Hypothermia is no joke."

Liz was the Sporty Spice of our group. She played every sport you could imagine, from ice hockey to kickball depending on the season. She also treated her body like a temple while the rest of us treated our bodies more like a drive-in movie theater. Her attention to fitness and healthy eating paid off in a supermodel physique packaged in clear, even, brown skin, springy, shiny, tight black curls, and dark brown eyes flecked with gold. I routinely told myself that it was all due to excellent genes, probably so I wouldn't feel compelled to exercise regularly or eat kale. But Liz's beauty was more than skin deep. For a competitive athlete, she had a gentle soul and cared deeply for the people around her, especially her Posse. Thus the tea, cookies, and roaring fire. I was a little surprised she hadn't tucked us in with blankies.

The rest of the Posse was already there, ranged around the room. Surya Smythe, Kate's roommate and a product PR specialist, was curled up under an afghan (speaking of blankies) on a Victorian settee next to Anupa Aranha, our expert in PR for high finance.

"Is pizza okay for everyone?" asked Liz.

"Only if it's Margarita's," replied Surya sternly. "I'm not wasting calories on bad pizza." As if she had to worry. Surya was the Audrey Hepburn of the group, tall and lithe with a pixie cut framing her enviable cheekbones.

"Of course it's Margarita's," countered Liz, justifiably offended. Margarita's ovens were coal-fired. Enough said.

"*And* we should go for cauliflower crust," continued Surya. This led to Kruschevesque protests from everyone else except health-conscious Liz. I was in the process of removing my shoe when Surya held up the pink pastry box.

"Are you sure cauliflower crust is a bad idea?"

Silence and salivation.

No Posse gathering was complete without French pastry, and ever since our favorite bakery, Payard, closed its doors, Surya and Kate had been exploring other patisserie options. Consequently, there were no more complaints about vegetable-based pizza crusts.

With food ordered, we finished our tea, switched over to red wine or sparkling water, and the real business of the evening began. Anupa called us to order. She was petite but formidable, with the straightest and shiniest black hair I'd ever seen cut in a sharp, angled lob and piercing black eyes to match.

"So the news reports are more than a little alarming. What on earth is happening to our beloved Mr. Snicklefritz?" Three sets of concerned eyes turned on Kate and me. I looked at her and shrugged. Where to begin? Kate shrugged right back, so I decided to start at the beginning.

"It all started when a puppet crashed my date."

Forty-five minutes later, I finished my tale and the pizza arrived at the same moment. While Liz went to the door to retrieve the pizza and Kate went to the kitchen for plates and napkins, we paused our discussion. Once the pizza was distributed and glasses refilled, we continued without skipping a beat.

"So Donato actually asked for your help?" Liz shook her head incredulously.

"He really did," piped up Kate. "I was there."

"He must be desperate," said Anupa between bites. "No offense, Jill. He just seemed rather territorial the last time we met him."

The last time had been at the Waldorf Astoria, and the whole Posse had been instrumental in bringing a murderer to justice. Detective Donato had seemed less than pleased, which still irked me because, hello, we stopped a killer.

"Has he mentioned He Who Shall Not Be Named?" asked Surya.

Out of the corner of my eye, I caught Kate making a "cut it out" gesture. When I turned, her hand flew to her side, and she flashed a big fake smile. Grinding my teeth, I faced the group.

"No, he has not brought up...Mike."

"She said his name!" exclaimed Anupa. "Does this mean we can talk about him now?"

"Thank the Maker," sighed Surya in her best Threepio imitation. "I am so tired of tiptoeing."

"Tiptoeing?" I looked around at my friends and saw Surya and Anupa high five. The only person who looked at all abashed was Liz, who saw the consternation on my face.

"We've been trying to give you time to come to terms with, you know, Mike leaving," she tried to explain.

"Leaving?" Anupa practically shouted around a mouthful of pizza. "More like fleeing, shaking the dust off his sandals, entering the witness protection program. He didn't just leave. He vanished."

"Not helpful, Nupe." Liz was trying to glower at Anupa and smile at me at the same time which only served to make her look insane. Everyone looked at me expectantly. What did they think I was going to do? Cry? I had cried myself out two weeks before. Yell? At my best friends? What purpose would that serve? Curse Mike's name? I finished that with the crying. Whatever my friends were expecting, it wasn't my job to deliver it.

"Look, Mike and I had six great weeks, fairy tale weeks. I can say that. But they were a fairy tale. I don't know what happened, and I don't think I ever will. One minute I was getting roses, and the next he was gone."

"Maybe he died," put in Liz quietly.

Kate shook her head. "I checked the obituaries. The rat's still alive."

"The point is," I said over-loudly in my attempt to hold onto control of the conversation and myself, "I'm past it." Four pairs of eyes brimmed over with doubt. I carried on resolutely. "Mike is history. I'm moving on, and by that I mean I'm focusing on myself and my career. I'm making changes, becoming a better person, focusing on my dreams, and making them a reality. I don't need a man to do that. I don't need anyone."

"Ouch." Surya was the only one who spoke, but I could see from my friends' expressions that I had wounded all of them.

"I didn't mean you guys. You're my life." I felt the tears pooling, the catch in my throat. Crap! Crap! Crap! "I'm just saying I don't need a stupid, thoughtless (sob), lying (hiccup), using (sniffle) male of the species!" I gestured awkwardly at my torso. "This (hiccup) is (hiccup) a man (hiccup) free (hiccup) zone!" And then they were on me, hugging the life out of me, or rather, hugging the life into me.

When the sobfest was over—because at least two of my friends had joined me in my despair—I think we all felt a lot better. I had no idea I needed to cry some more, to cry with friends, but I did. We warmed up the pizza in the oven and devoured all of it. Sometime later, Anupa brought us back to the murder.

"So the best theory anyone has is a random person came in off the street, found a replica Elven blade, stabbed a puppeteer, then went about his or her business?"

"When you put it that way, it sounds ridiculous," said Kate eyeing me significantly.

"Face it," said Surya. "The killer is among you."

"Then it's a good thing Jill has a gun in her purse," smirked Kate, leading to an entirely different conversation.

CHAPTER 10

When the alarm went off at five on Sunday, I leaped from my bed ready to begin my new life. On the long subway ride home from Liz's the previous night, I had done a lot of thinking. If I was really going to focus on self-improvement and pursuing my goals, then I needed to do more than talk about it. I had made a good start by getting up earlier and keeping my apartment clean. Now that my actual house was in order, I needed to set my metaphorical house straight. Furthermore, if I was going to focus on my goals, then I needed to get some that went beyond slowly climbing the corporate ladder. Sure I could go to work and hang out with my friends, but I knew that I would wake up one day several years from now and wonder what I had been doing with my life. It was time for more.

While I sipped my coffee, I opened a journal that had been taking up space on my shelf for a couple of years. I opened it to the first page and wrote "My Goals."

"Inspired start," I chided myself, but at least it was a beginning. Then I sat and thought.

And thought.

And thought.

Twenty minutes later, my coffee was cold, and I hadn't written down a single goal. The problem was, Jill Cooksey the island kept running into Jill Cooksey the peninsula or, worse yet, the continent. Translation: I kept running into goals for which I needed a man.

Get married.

Have kids.

Buy a house. Okay, I didn't need a man to buy a house, but the image of the house in my head was always inhabited by me, my husband, and our two children. Technically, I didn't need a man to have children, either, but I shuddered at the thought of raising them on my own.

I needed to change my worldview. Desperate to get something down on paper, I turned my attention to my job.

1. Become a VP at a PR firm.

There! I had one goal down, even if it did fall into the "climbing the corporate ladder category." Oh well. It was my goal. After a crisis of confidence a couple of months ago, I had decided that PR was where I wanted to be and that I was good at my job. Goal number one was a keeper.

Next, I turned to things I wanted to learn. My high school Spanish was abysmal. Actually mastering the language could open up a lot of business, travel, and friendship opportunities. At the very least I would be able to understand my pal and favorite cab driver Jorge when he insulted me in his native tongue.

2. Learn Spanish.

Foreign language led to thoughts of travel, including *3. Spain, 4. Portugal, 5. Costa Rica, 6. Peru, 7. Israel, 8. Australia,* and of course *9. Bali.* But then thoughts of Bali led to thoughts of money. So I had to add perhaps the most important goal of all.

10. Get my financial house in order.

This goal would make most of the other goals possible,

including Spanish classes and world travel. It could also make that house possible, with or without a mate. On a roll, I dove into creating a financial plan for myself. Two hours and an entire pot of coffee later (my arteries and veins were humming), I came up for air. The plan in front of me was as complex as the most elaborate PR plan I had ever created. It would require discipline, sacrifice, accountability, and most likely depression and loneliness, but it would get me where I wanted to go. The island nation known as Jill Cooksey was declaring independence.

After a shower and some toast (to soak up the coffee), I got ready for church, which was a fifteen-minute walk from my apartment. I left my Behemoth Black Bag and the peacemaker therein in my closet under the laundry hamper, and I hid the ammo in a box of cornmeal in the kitchen cupboard. I was pretty certain I could make it to church and brunch and then home again without a crazed, sword-wielding puppet killer attacking me.

Astoria was a winter wonderland after the snow of the previous day and night. My boots made a satisfying crunch as I walked, and the cold dry air made me feel truly alive and alert. Because the snow was past my ankles in some places, it took me longer than fifteen minutes to get to First Mt. Zion Baptist Church Inner City Ministry, my spiritual home in New York. While it wasn't exactly like attending Mt. Olivet Baptist in Luthersburg, Virginia, it had its moments. Reverend Calhoun, a transplant from South Carolina, always made me feel right at home. The choir was already singing when I took a seat in the back of the sanctuary. It felt good to block out the world and to focus on the divine...until Reverend Calhoun took the pulpit. The day's sermon was based on Genesis chapter two.

"The Lord God said, 'It is not good for the man to be alone. I will make a helper suitable for him,'" intoned the good reverend.

Not good to be alone? I balked at the scripture. My new life plan was based on being alone. How could that be so bad? Throughout human history, when men and women got together, they got into all sorts of mischief. I knew for a fact that just a couple of chapters later Adam and Eve were going to get into the biggest mischief of all time for which we were still paying the price. Unconvinced by Reverend Calhoun's theology, I resolved to do some research of my own later.

Overall, however, church was just what I needed after a week of murder and mayhem. I made a prayer request for Bryce and his family, and it felt comforting and right to pray for them with the whole congregation. I was feeling better and more centered than I had all week as I walked out of the church and into the brilliant winter day. I had no inkling that my sense of calm would be swept away before the day was through.

I was blissfully ignorant as I rode the subway toward Manhattan and brunch with my Posse. Even though a major plank in my financial freedom plan was to cut eating out, I couldn't eschew brunch with the girls. Thai takeout on a random Tuesday because I was feeling too lazy to cook, yes. Sacred girl time, absolutely not.

Our brunch spot was the UN Diner, named for the nearby landmark. The UN Diner made much of its theme by assigning a different country to each table and boasting a menu of international flavors. It took me a while to find the Posse sitting at a completely new table—Denmark.

"I checked it off!" exclaimed Kate as I sat down. She was referring to the paper placemat which listed all the countries represented by tables in the restaurant. Whenever we sat at a new table, she checked it off.

I chuckled as I surveyed my Posse. Every one of them, myself included, was dressed for the snow. Boots, parkas, beanies, mittens, scarves. (Vintage for Kate of course.) We all looked like we were headed for the slopes after brunch.

"What's so funny?" asked Anupa.

"Look at us!"

It took a moment for everyone to get the joke, but soon we were all giggling.

"You know what that means," said Liz with a competitive gleam in her eye. "Snowball fight after brunch!"

"In the Ramble!" suggested Surya. "It will be awesome."

The Ramble was a section of Central Park designed to feel like a walk through a forest in the mountains. It was full of twists and turns and places to hide—the perfect location for an epic snowball fight.

"Then we can have s'mores at the Park Cafe," piped Kate. The day was going to be one to remember.

Excited by our plan, we all ordered hearty breakfasts. While we waited for our food, everyone shared what they had done after our party the previous evening had broken up. Kate, Surya, and I had headed straight for the subway and our long rides home. Liz had gone for a walk in the snow and had taken some beautiful pictures that she showed us. Anupa, as usual on a Saturday night, had gone dancing. I didn't know how she made it to brunch every Sunday, but she never missed.

When our food arrived, we tucked in with gusto. I had a large plate of French crepes dusted with powdered sugar and drizzled with maple syrup, and a side of bacon. I had just taken the first ambrosial bite of crepe, bacon, and syrup when Surya made her announcement.

"It's time to take your investigation to the next level."

"Pardon?"

"I've been thinking," she explained. "You're only keeping your eyes and ears open at *The Mr. Snicklefritz Show*. What's that going to net you? Any criminal worth his salt is going to keep his mouth shut and act normal. You're never going to figure out who did it that way."

"First of all," I countered, "I wouldn't necessarily call it an investigation, but even so, what do you suggest I do? Interrogate and torture everyone until someone confesses?"

"What do real private investigators do? They look for clues. You need to actively look for evidence. Rifle a few desks. Look in some personal planners. Peruse the files. You need to collect data."

I looked at Kate to measure her reaction to Surya's suggestion that I walk the line between legal and illegal, but she wasn't as affronted as I'd expected. In fact, she looked intrigued.

"Maybe I could run interference," she suggested, confirming my suspicions. "I could distract people while you snoop."

"You know who can snoop and get away with it? Detective Donato. He even has these things called search warrants that force people to cooperate." I glared at my friends. They glared back.

"Jilly Elizabeth Cooksey," pronounced Surya in an imitation of my mother that was so good it gave me goosebumps, "I do believe you're chicken."

I was still annoyed at Surya for calling me a coward when we headed for the Ramble after brunch, and I daydreamed about pelting her in the back with an icy snowball as we rode the subway uptown. Chicken? Me? Hadn't I proven myself a few times over? I wasn't chicken. I just had a healthy respect for the law and for my job. If I got caught ransacking an office, the least that would happen to me is that I would get fired. That was bad enough. I didn't want to imagine getting arrested. My mother would kill me and then die.

A full-on snowmageddon battle did much to release my frustrations. I got some good shots in, but Liz, curse her pitching arm, rang my bell with a wicked fast snowball that I now refer to as The Polar Express. I was lying face down in the snow off the path when the Posse arrived.

Liz, my assailant, was the first to reach me.

"Jill, I'm so sorry! I got caught up in the moment. Are you okay?"

With her help, I managed to get off my stomach and into a kneeling position. Liz's fastball had punched me squarely in the back, and I had fallen face first.

"Oh my gosh!" yelled Anupa. "It's like she did a reverse snow angel!" And then she cackled. Soon we were all laughing because I had indeed made a perfect Jill-print in the snow. You could even make out my facial features. And where I had struggled to push myself up looked just like snow angel wings. The downside was that my entire front was covered in snow, and my face was starting to burn with cold. I tried to dust myself off but only made it worse because my mittens were crusted with snow and ice. Kate saw the problem and stepped in like a mom to brush me off. On that note of epic snow violence, we decided to call it quits, declared Liz the winner, and headed toward the Park Cafe for coffee and s'mores. We hadn't gone ten feet when Surya held out her arms to stop us.

"He's got a lot of nerve!"

I followed her line of sight to its conclusion which, unfortunately, was my ex-boyfriend Mike walking arm and arm through the snow with another woman. We'll call her Jadis because my feelings toward her were on par with those I had for the White Witch of Narnia, and as she was dressed in a spotless white parka with white fur trim, the comparison was apt. He was wearing his leather coat, the one that smelled so great, with the collar turned up, and his brown hair, longer than he usually wore it, almost touched it. Jadis tousled his hair and whispered something in his ear, and he smiled. Curse him. She was probably offering him Turkish delight, and the traitor was taking it.

In silence, we all watched Mike and Jadis saunter down the path headed toward the Upper West Side where he lived. Perhaps they were headed for his apartment. Certain scenarios flashed unbidden through my brain.

"Jill, your nostrils are flaring." Kate broke the silence.

"Are they?"

Without conscious thought, I started to move.

And by move I mean run.

Full out.

Leaping over those little chain fences that line the paths in Central Park.

Going cross country so I could intercept the traitor and his evil queen.

When I got ahead of them, I planted myself firmly in their path, crossed my arms, and stared them down.

When Mike and Jadis reached me, they were holding hands. I didn't move. I didn't blink. I stared straight at Mike's face and projected all my fury. I expected him to blink, to blanche, to come to a screeching halt. I expected him to stammer and to grovel and to declare his undying love for me and to send that witch packing.

But he didn't stop, and neither did she.

When they reached me, they let go of hands and walked right around me on either side like I was a lamp post or a fire hydrant.

"Bread and butter!" laughed Jadis.

I whirled around in time to see their hands reconnecting. I opened my mouth to yell…something…anything…but I couldn't make a sound. Something was caught in my chest making it difficult to breathe much less speak. Where only moments ago I'd been charged up for a fight and raring to go, I was suddenly enervated, weak even. I could barely stand. The pull of gravity (or was that depression?) was coaxing me to lie down in the soft white snow and drift off to sleep.

Then a white blur zoomed past my head and hit Mike square in the middle of his back. It knocked the wind right out of him. (I heard the air leave his lungs!) Down he went taking Jadis with him. They crashed together on the sidewalk, and I heard their heads *clunk* together, the most satisfying sound ever. Suddenly, a painless death by hypothermia in a snowdrift didn't seem as appealing.

Then Liz was at my side.

"Sorry, Jill. I couldn't help myself."

Liz is the best.

We watched as Jadis recovered first.

"What just happened?" she cried as she gingerly rose to her feet and clutched her head. The asphalt footpath had left black marks all over her once-white jacket. That stain would never come out.

"I slipped on some ice," I heard Mike say. Clearly stunned, he took several moments to recover. Between the Polar Express and the Three Stooges routine, his bell had been thoroughly rung, I was glad to see.

I felt more than saw my Posse gather around me. In silence, we watched Mike struggle to his feet. He managed to rise without ever turning in my direction.

That's how I knew.

He was fully aware of me. Although I had stared straight at his face, he'd never focused on mine, and his expression had never faltered. I was a nonentity. But now his refusal to turn even a few degrees toward me made him awkward and stiff—and revealed his thoughts. I hoped he could read mine.

I'm still here. I'm not going anywhere.

S'MORES and coffee wasn't the laughter-laced, post-snowball fight fun-fest we were all hoping for even though the girls tried. I was lost to them, my mind perpetually replaying the scene in the park. As soon as my coffee cup was empty, I excused myself. The girls urged me to stay, and I could tell they were worried about me, but I desperately needed to be alone.

I don't remember the subway ride or the walk home. I just know that I found myself in my apartment. It was warm and clean. Divesting myself of my outerwear, I collapsed wearily onto the futon, pulled the blanket over me, and let the hiss of the radiator lull me to sleep.

Sadly, I dreamed.

"This is why you never leave the city," breathed Mike over the steering wheel. In front of the car, behind it, beside it, were cars to the horizon, and none of us were moving.

"Are we all going to the same place?" It was an early weekend in October, and I had suggested apple picking upstate. It took the promise of a homemade apple pie, but Mike had rented a car and picked me up at nine a.m. It should have been five a.m. because everyone else seemed to have the same idea.

"Probably," sighed Mike. "There won't be any apples left by the time we get there."

I looked above the traffic at the beautiful fall sky, Delft blue and cloudless. This was my favorite kind of day in New York. The lack of heat and humidity guaranteed me a good hair day, and the cool temperature allowed me to wear a deep orange sweater that made my blue eyes pop. But all of that was wasted on Mike, who was glaring at the traffic.

"If you want, we can just go home," I offered. Maybe it was the note of defeat in my voice, but Mike tore his eyes from the sea of vehicles and turned to me with a look of concern.

"No way. I want my apple pie. That was the deal. You aren't going to welch on a deal, are you?" He winked, and I relaxed. Then he turned on the radio, and we fought about the station.

We loved to argue, and I knew the day was going to be great after all.

I awoke from the dream instantly alert but feeling nothing. Normally my dreams were an odd mishmash of reality, fantasy, and movies, but this time my brain had presented a perfectly accurate recollection of one of our dates. So why didn't I seem to care? Why wasn't my heart hurting? Had I successfully turned off my feelings, and if so, how? Maybe I could write a best-selling book about it. I turned over, repositioned my pillow, and fell back to sleep.

To dream again.

We were in a small movie theater in SoHo seeing one of my all-time favorites, *Citizen Kane,* and I was waiting for my favorite moment from the film, when squawking Susan Kane walks out on her husband, Charles Foster Kane, and the film cuts to a screeching cockatoo that literally flies the coop, telling us symbolically everything we need to know about Susan and her situation. Every time I watched this film, I waited for this moment. Even though Mike had seen the film before, he didn't believe me about the cockatoo. He hadn't noticed it before, but after tonight, he would never forget it.

We were getting close. I gripped the popcorn tub in anticipation. Charles Foster Kane was about to tell Susan that she couldn't leave him.

Don't do it! I willed Charlie to say something else, anything else, so Susan wouldn't leave, so they could save their marriage. So he wouldn't have to die dreaming of his sled and his cold, unfeeling mother.

"You can't do this to me." Dang. He said it.

"Oh, yes I can," Susan said quietly but triumphantly and walked serenely out the door.

I always felt great for Susan at that moment, for freeing herself from a miserable situation and finally sticking up for herself, but I also felt really bad for Charlie. His life was such a train wreck, and he didn't know how to fix it. He wasn't equipped. As I pondered the film, a couple of scenes passed by, and soon we were almost at *the* moment. The butler was recounting his memories of watching Susan leave. And then—

Squawk!!!

Out of nowhere came that crazy cockatoo, which spread its wings and flew off, transitioning the viewer back to Susan's birdhouse of a bedroom, where Charlie was in emotional turmoil. It was the climax of the film, and he trashed that room like a rock star and a supermodel rolled into one. It was cathartic and raw and, sadly, signaled his undoing. I looked at Mike. His eyes were wide, and he was holding his breath.

I chuckled triumphantly, breaking the spell.

"How did I miss that?" Mike breathed again.

"Everybody does. Don't feel bad."

"This is a great film!"

And then he kissed me, a laughter-filled, joyful kiss that expressed how much he enjoyed just being with me. Despite the serious film before us, I felt light and filled with joy myself. Then he put his arm around me and pulled me close, and we watched the rest of the movie cheek to cheek.

It was a great film, but it always left me thinking about how Charles Foster Kane could have changed his life and held on to his marriage. To the viewer, it was so obvious, and I wondered if the changes that we each needed to make in our lives were obvious to the people around us while we groped in the dark.

I awoke again instantly alert. I still felt nothing even though I seemed to be living my own version of *A Christmas Carol*, except with dreams instead of ghosts. I wasn't even afraid of what the next dream would teach me, because I was getting the feeling that my mind was trying to tell me something important, to help me understand.

I rolled over again and was soon asleep.

We were having drinks in our favorite pub on the Upper West Side.

"It's going to be big." Mike kept his voice low, but it was suffused with excitement. "Career making." He ran his hands through his hair, the way he always did when he was frustrated. "I just wish I could tell you more."

"I understand." I smiled at him, happy for the chance to be supportive of him. He understood there were things I couldn't tell him about my job because he was a reporter, and I was only too glad to return the favor. "I can't wait to read it when it's all done."

"That will be months from now. This story will require all my focus. My editor has already approved it. She thinks it could win awards." Mike's eyes shone.

I raised my glass.

"To the Pulitzer and the Best Boyfriend of the Year!"

We clinked glasses and took a sip, but then his expression grew serious.

"With this story, Jill, I doubt I'm going to be Boyfriend of the Year. It's going to be a lot of work, a lot of irregular hours. I just want you to know the score. We may not see each other as much for a while, but it's just because of work."

I covered Mike's hand with mine.

"Hey, it's me. PR woman. I know what it's like to be consumed by work. I understand." I squeezed his hand.

And suddenly we were on the sidewalk by the subway station. Mike reached for me, pulling me against him, and I melted into his solid warmth. I snaked my arms around his neck and looked into his eyes. They were blue and deep and seemed to see into my soul. And then his mouth was on mine, laying a claim to me. I lost myself in his kiss, in the heat. When his fingers dug into my hips, my knees nearly buckled, and I sagged against him, breaking the connection.

"Cooksey," he breathed raggedly into my ear. For a time, we

just held each other. An eternity later, when I finally pulled away, his expression was tormented, as if he couldn't bear to let me go. I felt the same with an intensity that was new and thrilling to me, and even though our date was ending, I was already thinking about the next one, already feeling giddy anticipation. I was head over heels. Happier than I'd ever been in my life, I brushed my lips gently over his and whispered, "See you soon," before heading down to the train.

At the bottom of the stairs, I found myself not in the subway station but in my office standing behind my desk. Jeannie Jacobsen, our administrative assistant, came bustling into the room carrying an enormous vase full of two dozen red roses.

"How did you manage to score such a good guy in this city of losers," bemoaned Jeannie in her permanent smoker's rasp. She plunked down the vase on my desk and unashamedly waited for me to read the card. I plucked it from its little pitchfork holder and smiled when I saw "Cooksey" scrawled across the envelope. I liked how Mike referred to me by my last name. It made me feel like Rosalind Russell in *His Girl Friday*.

I opened the card to find more of Mike's adorably messy handwriting.

Dear Jill,

I have to cancel our plans this weekend. Something has come up with the story. I'll be in touch as soon as I can. Until then, I'll be thinking of you.

Love,
Mike

I had kept those roses alive for three straight weeks using flower food and 7Up, but when they finally dropped their petals and I hadn't heard from Mike again, I realized that he was gone for good.

The next time I awoke was when my five a.m. alarm went off. This time I wasn't instantly alert, but thankfully I was still numb. I couldn't figure out what the dreams were trying to teach me, if indeed that's what my subconscious was trying to do. Was I supposed to scrutinize everything I did and figure out how I, like Charles Foster Kane, had wrecked my relationship? I had already been down that road and had no desire to travel it again. Or was I supposed to see a parallel between Charlie Kane and Mike? Had Mike's ambition killed our relationship like Charlie's ambition killed all of his? Or maybe I was supposed to focus on the happy times and just be grateful for them. That must be it, I decided. I must have accepted Mike's betrayal and absence from my life because I could now look back on the good times without pain. I was numb because I actually didn't care anymore. I had moved on.

Keep telling yourself that, Cooksey.

CHAPTER 11

Kate and I arrived at the studio on Monday at the same time. We had a meeting with Marcus at seven a.m. to brief him on the PR plan for the rest of the anniversary celebration. I could see the concern on Kate's face.

"I'm fine," I whispered as I signed the log at the security desk. When she had done the same, we pushed through the big double doors and started down the hallway towards the production offices.

"I'm here if you want to talk about it."

"The only thing I want to talk about is where I'm going to start snooping first. I'm thinking Marcus's office."

Kate agreed. "I'm sure I can distract him with an imaginary PR crisis at some point. While we're meeting with him, let's make a mental list of the best places to search."

We headed straight for said office without a stop for coffee because it was already 6:55. Marcus was there, and after brief pleasantries, we got down to business. He had already seen the PR plan via email, so this meeting was really about push-back and compromise. Kate handed around printed copies of the plan, but before we could begin discussing the first bullet point, Marcus announced that it all looked good to him—except for moving back to the old set.

"We're only moving forward." He said it like a mantra. "I think going back to the old set, even briefly, would confuse the cast and crew."

I had expected as much, so it was easy to let that point go. Besides, the police hadn't cleared the set for use anyway. Marcus had already set up a meeting with the entire cast and crew to go over the plan before the day's filming began, so we adjourned and made our way to The Pen.

"My money's on the filing cabinet," whispered Kate in my ear.

"I say desk drawers," I whispered back. "But I hope you can give me time to search both." I really felt that if there was something important to Marcus that was incriminating, he would keep it close at hand. I had no idea when the search of Marcus's office would take place, but I knew my friend would make it happen.

When we got to The Pen, most of the cast and crew were already gathered. I also noticed a couple of guys I hadn't seen before hovering at the perimeter of the area. They were dressed in black pants and gray polos with the word Securtech embroidered on the pocket. They also wore black Securtech ball caps and had tasers on their belts.

"Extra security, courtesy of Bob," said Kate. "And mighty fine, I must say."

They certainly were. Chiseled chins, tree trunk arms, and gorgeous smiles down to a man, because they actually were smiling. Really, they were too cute to be security.

"I half expect someone to whip out a boom box," purred Kate. "Do you think those pants are Velcro down the sides?"

"Get out of my head, Kate!"

The hottie security team was adding to the festive air of today's meeting, but so was the coffee and pastry buffet that craft services had provided. Those high priests and priestesses to sugar had supplied everything from cronuts to baklava, and the cast and crew were eagerly chasing a sugar high.

Then Carl entered the room, and the result was surprising.

"Carl!" everyone yelled together and moved en masse to bestow a group hug.

What the what? I could swear I heard the *Cheers* theme playing in the background. One of the all-time great curmudgeons was being feted by the people he routinely tormented. Marcus must have seen the incredulity on my face.

"Lotta history," he said with a shrug by way of explanation.

Group hug completed, with Carl actually seeming to enjoy it, slaps on the back and the shaking of hands ensued.

"Glad you beat the reaper, man," said Phil as he high-fived Carl.

"Don't scare us like that again," offered Devon as he and Carl fist-bumped.

Just when I thought *The Mr. Snicklefritz Show* couldn't get any more surreal, every Who down in Whoville was love-feasting the Grinch.

"It's just like my sisters and my brother," grinned Kate. "He torments us regularly, but it doesn't matter in the end. We still love him."

With everyone assembled, Marcus called the meeting to order. One of the producers handed out packets to everyone detailing the schedule for the week. Marcus went over it point by point, emphasizing how he wanted to make sure Carl got plenty of rest and recuperation along the way. He then introduced the new security team, and they got a big round of applause, confirming for me that everyone was feeling less than secure in the wake of Bryce's murder.

Marcus was wrapping up the meeting when Detective Donato entered the space causing Marcus to trail off in mid-sentence.

"I'm sorry to interrupt," said Donato, "but I have some news that I wanted you all to hear first."

Marcus gestured to the center of the room as if to say "You have the floor."

"Thank you." Donato took a moment to look around the room and make eye contact with as many people as possible. That gesture gave me a solid sense of foreboding. Whatever he was about to tell us, it was going to be big.

"We now know how Bryce Camplen was killed."

Cast and crew looked at each other in puzzlement. Didn't we already know how Bryce was killed? I, for one, would never get the image of the sword piercing his chest out of my brain.

"There was a distinct lack of blood at the scene," continued Donato, "leading us to suspect the cause of death wasn't actually...stabbing."

I mentally slapped my forehead because I should have noticed it. I didn't have to dodge puddles of blood on the set when I encountered Bryce's body. I could have felt for his pulse without staining my clothes. Why hadn't that registered with me?

"The autopsy has shown conclusively that Bryce was poisoned, and his corpse was staged after the fact," pronounced the detective.

If you want to break up a party, just enumerate the details of a gruesome murder. Works every time. Instantly, the collective sugar high evaporated. Julia began to cry, and Chuck pulled her into his embrace so she could weep on his shoulder.

My mind switched into overdrive. Poisoned? When last I saw Bryce, he was sitting in a restaurant. Had he eaten something tainted at Uncle Nick's?

"The poison, strychnine, was delivered via an alcoholic beverage, specifically whisky, specifically O'Sullivan's."

Every head in the room turned to look at the man who

could have been O'Sullivan's spokesperson if he wasn't a children's television icon.

Carl gulped.

"An empty bottle of O'Sullivan's was found on the set," Donato continued. "Tests show that it contained the poison that Mr. Camplen ingested. Tests also revealed three sets of fingerprints on the bottle belonging to Camplen, Carl Biersdorf, and Britney Spears."

Hold up! Britney Spears?

"Wait, the pop icon?" asked one of the grips.

"No, idiot." Britney rolled her eyes. "My name is Britney Spiers—S-P-I-E-R-S. No relation. Do you ever read the credits or the call sheet?"

"S-so," stammered Carl, "you think I poisoned Bryce?"

"No, Mr. Biersdorf," replied Donato calmly. "We think you were the intended victim, that the poisoned whisky was left for you. We believe the killer saw Mr. Camplen ingest the poison and die and then staged the body using the sword to draw attention away from the real cause of death. Perhaps the killer meant to use that means again."

Carl's normally florid complexion turned white as a sheet.

"Someone get him a chair!"

A rolling chair was thrust against his legs, forcing him to sit down. While Carl took a much-needed moment, Donato powwowed with Marcus, Kate, and me.

"Because Carl and Britney's prints are on the bottle, we believe that Bryce took it from Carl's dressing room where there is a considerable stash. This wasn't a random killing. I see you have extra security. If you're not going to shut down production, someone needs to be with Mr. Biersdorf at all times."

While they worked out the details, I wandered over to Carl, who was being tended by Britney, Flavia, and Chuck. Britney was patting him and making soothing sounds while Flavia held his hand. Chuck offered him a bottle of water, but Carl knocked it out of his hands. Water went everywhere.

"I can't drink that! I can't drink anything! It could be poisoned." He looked beseechingly at Britney, and his eyes were full of unshed tears. Chuck just hunched his shoulders and slinked away.

"Baby, it's okay," soothed Britney. "No one here wants to hurt you."

"They should," sobbed Carl. "I'm not a good man."

A silent conversation passed between Britney and Flavia.

"Why don't we go someplace private?" suggested the floor director. "Can you lift your legs?" Flavia nodded at the PAs, and Tameasha rushed over. Together they wheeled Carl on the rolling chair down the hallway to Donato's makeshift interrogation room with Britney close behind.

"You're not taking me somewhere to kill me, are you?" I heard Carl say before the door shut.

"We're going to be taking a harder look at everyone's movements last Wednesday," Donato was saying when I rejoined the group. "If only the facility had CCTV."

"Celebrities and privacy," said Marcus with a shrug.

"Yeah, I get it. It's just very inconvenient."

What was also very inconvenient was emotion, specifically mine at that moment. I realized that, like Carl, I needed to get away and come to terms with this new information. Blindly, I left The Pen and headed down the hallway in the opposite direction from Carl. I was fighting tears and not really thinking about where I was going, but I wasn't surprised to find myself at the door to the old studio. Police tape couldn't hold me back. I ripped the yellow plastic and pushed through the heavy door.

Minimal lights burned overhead, but I could still make out the set even though much of it was bathed in shadow. Slowly, I picked my way through the darkness, found the cleverly hidden stairs, and mounted the set. Intending to thoroughly torture myself, I made my way into Mr. Snicklefritz's living room and sat on the sofa that faced his rustic coffee table, the makeshift altar on which Bryce had been sacrificed. Then I let the tears come.

Bryce had come to the studio looking for booze, of that I was sure. There was always whiskey to be found in Carl's dressing room, and he wouldn't miss it because his supply was endless. So Bryce knew where he could get rip-roaringly drunk, but more importantly, I knew why.

I had rejected him. He had taken a chance and shared who he was with me, his crazy, his uniqueness, and I had rejected him. I was surely not the first, but it broke my heart that I was the last. Had he turned to drink before to numb the pain? I couldn't know, and it didn't matter. This time, it was on me.

I don't know how long it was before Kate found me. Thankfully, she didn't say anything. I wouldn't have responded to any pleas not to feel responsible. That die was cast. She just wrapped her arms around me and held me in a hug.

"Kate, I'm going to find Bryce's killer if it's the last thing I do."

CHAPTER 12

It was a long time before Carl emerged from the office. He was moving under his own steam, and his color was better, but one look at his face told me he was a changed man. Knowing someone hates you enough to kill you can have that effect.

Flanked by two bodyguards and with Britney trailing behind, he headed for his dressing room. I had returned with Kate to discover that the old set and dressing rooms were now cleared for use. The forensics team had taken all the photos and fingerprints they could.

"Well, at least we didn't contaminate the crime scene," chirped Kate in an attempt to cheer me up. I didn't care. Forensic science wasn't going to find the killer. I was.

The scheduling producer had managed to move things around so Carl wouldn't have to participate in filming that morning. The start was delayed by the aftermath of Donato's announcement, but eventually the offices and studio began to take on an air of normalcy. I even had a set visit to conduct.

Thank heaven the children and their parents were well-behaved because I wasn't yet at my best, but the visit was going great until one little boy inevitably asked, "Where's Mr. Snicklefritz?"

I was struggling to come up with an excuse when a cheerful voice bellowed, "I'm right here!"

There was Carl in all his Snicklefritz glory beaming a gentle smile at all the children who ran to him and started hugging his legs. Behind Carl stood two of the hottest woodcutters I had ever seen. Their gorgeous smiles were replaced with uncomfortable frowns, but I couldn't blame them. They appeared to be wearing brown woodcutter shirts with leather laces over their Securtech polos, and perched on their heads were Robin Hood-style hats adorned with huge scarlet plumes. They were ridiculous—hot, but ridiculous—and the irony startled a laugh out of me and everyone else.

"Who are they?" asked one father.

"I don't know. I would have remembered those guys," replied his wife, who used to be a producer on the show.

"These are my assistants," announced Carl. "I'm teaching them all about wood."

"Did he just say what I think he said?" asked Squirrelly-Joe.

"Joe, your mind's in the gutter!" sneered Moose, who, oddly, had a British accent between takes.

Joe smiled wryly. "Ain't it the truth?"

"Rainbow morning!" Flavia reminded everyone, although she barely got the words out because she was laughing so hard. Everyone was laughing, even the kids, who didn't get the joke, thank goodness. I saw the moment Carl realized what he'd done because he turned bright red, which made me laugh even harder.

"I mean, I'm teaching them all about woodcutting! Being safe in the forest!"

Everyone laughed even harder, and now Carl was having trouble holding it together.

"And making furniture...and stuff." Now he was crying from laughter.

Production ceased until the catharsis was over. Never had a group of people been more in need of a laugh. I know I felt a lot better, and the cheerful atmosphere made the rest of the set visit fantastic. Carl was a dream with the kids, and the puppeteers didn't make anyone cry when they unzipped their green suits to say hi.

The lighter mood, however, didn't temper my resolve to bring Bryce's killer to justice. I was just biding my time.

~

MY MOMENT CAME after lunch when the network news crew descended to cover the investigation. Normally it would be my job to liaise, but Kate was there to handle the press, and she promised to keep everyone occupied while I snooped. She was also my early warning system. We had devised an emoji code that would allow her to quickly text me if anyone was heading towards Marcus's office.

As nonchalantly as possible, I made my way towards the office and slipped inside. The lights were usually left on all day, and the door was normally closed when Marcus wasn't in there, which worked in my favor. I was also happy to discover the door could be locked from the inside. I pressed the little button and felt a smidge more secure.

Marcus's office was nondescript: a metal desk, a rolling chair, two guest chairs opposite the desk, a sofa against the far wall, and two tall metal filing cabinets to the side of the desk on the wall facing the door. Posters and photos of the show in high-quality frames graced the walls, but beyond that, there was very little to personalize the space.

I placed a file folder on the desk. It was my excuse for being there and contained some hastily printed articles about the murder, a sort of *ad hoc* clippings report. Then I took a deep breath and got to work. I tossed my ink pen under Marcus's desk, my excuse should anyone find me under it, and began my search.

I started with his desk drawers but found few surprises: a prescription for muscle relaxers, some bottled protein drinks, a paperback copy of Agatha Christie's *The Mysterious Affair at Styles*. I had read that book and knew it featured a poisoning. Coincidence? I felt around in the desk's cavities, hoping he had hidden away some important document or a bottle of rat poison, but my hand encountered nothing except cobwebs, which gave me the creeps.

Before turning to the filing cabinets, I checked my phone. No emojis. I was safe for now. I walked over to the cabinets wondering how I could explain why I was digging in the files. I would just have to trust Kate to warn me in time. Hardening my resolve, I opened the first drawer.

Budgets took up a lot of space in the drawer, and since the show had been on the air longer than I'd been alive, that made sense. Contracts were next, and they took up even more space. Anyone who had worked on the show and had a contract had a file, so all of the performers and many of the crew and production staff. I was so tempted to peek and see how much money everyone made, but I decided that would be unethical unless the investigation called for it. If a need for that information arose, I could always come back since Kate and I had such a great system going. Boy, was I getting brave. I glanced at my phone again for an emoji warning, but the coast was still clear.

Contracts took up the rest of the cabinet, so I moved on to cabinet number two. The first file tab was labeled "Complaints." I was surprised, more because of the violation of alphabetical order than because there were complaints about the show—Squirrelly-Joe alone probably generated several sexual harassment complaints each season. I hastily scanned the folders until I found one with Larry's name on it. It was surprisingly thin. I looked further and found a much thicker file labeled "Squirrel." If the executive producer of the show couldn't differentiate between the people and the puppets, what chance did the rest of us have?

Going back to the beginning so I could make a methodical search, I pulled the first file which had Carl's name on it and was pretty thick. Opening it, I found letter after letter from parents who were offended by Carl's behavior in public, echoing my findings online: drunkenness, swearing, womanizing. Were these complaints enough to push Marcus to murder? He badly wanted Carl to retire. Had Carl's refusal pushed him over the edge?

I flipped through the rest of the contents. There were also some complaints from various Princess Gretels, and I wondered, not for the first time, how the show had avoided lawsuits from that corner.

A complaint written on *Mr. Snicklefritz* letterhead caught my attention. It was from last season, and it was signed by Phil Rainey and Larry Stubbins. My eyes flew across the page. The complaint from his fellow performers echoed the parent complaints with one addition: they were upset about his behavior during set visits as well.

"Carl's behavior has alienated the parents of our fan base. Ratings have dropped steadily over the past decade indicating that parents are making different television choices for their kids. Uncool! We are afraid that further damage by Carl will lead to the cancellation of the show and the loss of our jobs. We think it would be righteous of management to replace him with a more responsible performer. If Carl wants to self-destruct, that's certainly his right. Live and let live. But we don't want him to take the show and us with him." I could hear Phil's voice in every sentence. For someone so laid back to take a stand like this, he must have been feeling desperate.

So the pressure to oust Carl had been coming at Marcus from all sides: the network, the fans, the cast. That sounded like a motive to me.

Ping!

The notification made me jump. I grabbed my phone and saw an emoji of a woman with glasses and a tight bun. She was supposed to represent a teacher. In our code, it meant that Patricia Miller-Sanderson was on the move.

Heart pounding, I replaced the file and closed the cabinet drawer. All of my movements felt too slow. I expected Patricia to rattle the door handle at any moment. I ran for the door and turned the knob, unlocking it.

I was just about to make good my escape when I remembered the pen I had thrown under Marcus's desk. It was supposed to give me an excuse for being under his desk, but now it was going to be my undoing because it was an erasable purple ink Hello Kitty pen. If I left it behind and Marcus found it, he would know someone had been in his office.

Panicked, I dove under the desk and patted around frantically for the pen. After what felt like six hours but was more like six seconds, I found it. I also found an envelope. It was a standard pink greeting card envelope, but written across the front in cursive swirls were the words "My Darling."

On autopilot, I stuffed the envelope and the pen down my sweater and ran from the office, which was a stupid thing to do because Patricia or anybody else could have been in the hallway to witness my asinine behavior, and there would have been questions. My luck was holding, however, and it wasn't until I turned the corner on my way to the ladies' room (best place to hide ever) that I literally ran into Patricia. The pen, which had lodged in my bra, practically cut open my heart when we collided, but I tried not to show my excruciating pain.

"Sorry! On my way to the ladies! Gotta go!" I babbled.

"Okay." Patricia nodded slowly at me. "You do that."

"Bye!" And I ran.

Why had I felt the need to hide the pen? I could have held it in my hand. It wasn't incriminating. What did it tell the world other than that I had awesome taste in pens?

I mentally berated myself until I was safely locked in a bathroom stall. Then I extricated the pen and checked for blood. Three crimson beads welled from a sizable scratch. Hello Kitty had cut me, the little wildcat. I nearly deposited the pen in the receptacle for feminine hygiene products, but as it was erasable, it got a reprieve.

After blotting the blood with some toilet paper, I carefully retrieved the card from under my sweater. The blood hadn't touched it, and it was only a little bent, thank goodness. The card I pulled from the envelope was a standard greeting card covered in hearts and flowers in shades of blue. When I opened it, the text I read was pretty much what I expected:

Marcus,

I know we've been going through some tough times, but our love is strong. It can endure anything. Never doubt how much I love you.

Always,
Patty

I felt for the woman. Her husband was trying to ghost her, and I knew what that felt like. At that moment, I wanted to take her out for coffee and a smorgasbord of pastry and explain to her that when they stop loving you, there's nothing you can do. I wanted to be her friend because everyone needed a friend when men became dogs.

Then I noticed something else in the envelope, a folded-up piece of paper. It looked to be a standard sheet of copy paper folded into fourths so it would fit in the envelope.

Was it a love poem? A photo of happier times?

Hardly.

August 16, 1995

Dear Dr. Miller:

It is with deep regret that I write to inform you that the university must sever ties with you and The Mr. Snicklefritz Show. Our independent research does not corroborate your claims about the educational content and efficacy of that television program. In fact, our studies indicate that children are learning very little if anything. I have included a detailed report of our findings, which I hope will be illuminating and helpful as you move forward in your career without the support of this university.

Educational research is open to interpretation, and it is for this reason that the enclosed report will remain in-house. The courses you were scheduled to teach have been assigned to other professors. On a personal note, until now, you have been a credit to this department, and it is my hope that you will do whatever it takes to restore your academic standards and credentials.

Howard Morton, EdD
Chair, Department of Education
Columbia University

Next to Morton's signature, in cursive swirls underlined several times, Patricia had written, "Never forget!"

Okay. So emotional blackmail. Some, but not all, of my friendly feelings for Patricia dried up. I didn't know exactly what Patricia had done back in the early nineties when *Mr. Snicklefritz* was new, but the letter suggested she had helped out the show in some way. Had she falsified data? Endorsed the show as educational when it wasn't? And did that even matter? As far as I was concerned, *The Mr. Snicklefritz Show* was children's entertainment, and boy had it entertained me.

No matter what had transpired, Patricia was trying to remind Marcus of something she had done, a sacrifice she had made. She was trying to hold on to him at all costs.

What had Carl said during the argument after he threatened to spill his guts? Something about why they were still married? Was that related?

I snapped photos of the card and the letter with my phone and then put them all back together as I'd found them. I would have to find a way to return the card, but now that my nerves had calmed, I could imagine a few very creative ways to accomplish it. Maybe I was getting better at the private investigator stuff. Then I laughed. Why would I need to get better at it? I couldn't imagine needing these skills again in the future.

CHAPTER 13

The next morning found me standing in front of my open closet in deep thought. I was tasked with directing the Princess Gretel debacle, I mean roundtable, take two, and I was afraid. Those women were sharks to whom fear was blood in the water. If I wanted to project confidence, if I wanted their respect, I had to dress for it. Forgoing those lovely jeans, I opted for a power pantsuit in black with a green silk blouse and black high-heeled boots. There was a chance I would slip and fall to my death on the icy sidewalks while wearing those boots, so I also opted to ride to work instead of walk.

With a full face of expertly applied makeup (thank you, beauty PR), my power suit, and my sexy boots, I felt ready to take on the streak of tigresses known as the Princess Gretels. I dialed 718-MEXICAR, and five minutes later I was climbing into the burgundy town car owned and operated by my friend Jorge.

"Hola, señora Jill."

"Morning, Jorge. So how long did it take you to deliver the

princesses to their respective homes last week? That couldn't have been fun."

He laughed.

"It took a few hours because some live out in Jersey. But I need to apologize. It wasn't until we were out of the city that I was told we had left someone behind."

That was news to me.

"Who?"

"I don't know which one exactly. I mean, how do you keep track? But one of the ladies was upset that someone had been left behind, but then the one in charge said it was no big loss because she was a total snob."

"Let me guess. Number Nine?"

"That's the one. What a woman! I tried to get her number, but no joy." He waggled his eyebrows at me. "I may have to go to Coney Island this weekend."

"Well, she's coming to Queens today. They all are. I have to work with them again."

"Better you than me!"

I sat back on the burgundy velour seat and wondered which princess had been left behind. I thought they had all boarded the bus, but the ordeal was a bit of a blur. If I had to guess, it was probably Dominique who had found her own way home. After all, she hadn't arrived with the others. Why would I assume she had left with them? I tried to remember the events after Carl had shown his face and the ladies had let him have it, but I couldn't remember if Dominique had left the studio with us. Had she stayed behind to talk to Carl? I highly doubted it. A Mississippi River of bad blood ran between them. Could she have stayed behind for a darker purpose? I made a mental note to mention Dominique to Detective Donato when I briefed him. I had already apprised Kate of my findings in Marcus's office, but I still needed to tell Donato what I had discovered. As my actions were not quite legal, I also needed to figure out a way to tell him that wouldn't make him hit the roof.

Two minutes later, we arrived at the studio. I bid Jorge goodbye and headed for the lobby, forgetting that I was wearing my sexy boots of death. Two steps out of the car, I hit an icy patch. I went down hard.

Jorge was out of the car and at my side in a flash.

"Jill, are you okay?"

I sat on the sidewalk, my butt freezing to the ice beneath it while pain washed over my lower leg and foot.

"My ankle," I managed through gritted teeth.

Stan from security arrived.

"I saw you go down. *Bam!*"

Together the two men helped me to stand and supported me while I hobbled into the building. They deposited me in a chair, and Jorge immediately set about removing my boot. The ankle didn't look swollen...yet. Jorge felt the joint and all the bones in my foot. Then he moved my foot around. No sharp pain.

"I don't think it's broken. You should try to put some weight on it."

With their help, I stood and gingerly put my weight on the injured leg. It wasn't bad. The pain had lessened greatly, and I found I could walk with a little limp.

"It's just twisted, I think. Nothing serious."

"You should try to stay off it," advised Stan.

"Si! Prop it up whenever you can."

"Duly noted," I replied. Just then we were joined by the PAs, who were arriving for work.

"What happened?" demanded Tameasha. While Stan filled her in, I reached for my boot to put it back on only to find the heel completely broken off.

"Shitake mushrooms! Now what am I going to do? It's too cold to wander around in bare feet. I'll catch my death."

"I know!" announced Madison. "Give me two minutes." The PA took off towards the production offices. She was back in sixty seconds holding something furry.

"Close your eyes!" she ordered. I'm a good sport, so I did. I felt my other boot being removed from my foot, and then both feet were surrounded in softness and warmth.

"Open your eyes."

I did, and then I closed them again. *Not today. Of all days.*

"I remembered that we had some slippers in the goody bag closet," Madison chirped happily. "You're going to be so comfortable all day long."

I opened my eyes again and forced a smile.

"Thanks, Madison." She really was trying to help. I looked at my feet and sighed.

Nothing takes the power out of a power suit like fuzzy Moose the Moose slippers, complete with oversized plush antlers. The Princess Gretels were going to eat me alive.

The kids, on the other hand, thought my slippers were awesome. I spent the first half of the morning conducting set visits. My slippers were a hit, and so was Mr. Snicklefritz. Carl was charming, effervescent, and downright loving with the kids. Gone were the temper tantrums, the insults, the bottles of O'Sullivan's.

"Who are you, and what have you done with Carl?" I heard Flavia remark.

"It's like the old days," Phil sighed happily. "There's nothing like attempted murder to align your chakras and open your third eye."

Phil made me laugh, but he wasn't joking. And that made me think. He and Larry were concerned enough about Carl's behavior to lodge a formal complaint. Were they concerned enough to try to scare Carl straight? Had Bryce died because of a prank gone horribly wrong? Putting rat poison in Carl's whiskey was a huge risk to take if they hadn't actually wanted him to die. Were Phil and Larry capable of taking such a risk with a human life? This was something else to mention to Donato when I saw him next. Maybe I would run into him at reception when I escorted the visitors out.

Well, I didn't run into Donato, but I did run smack into my entire PR Posse.

"What are you doing here?" I was glad to see them but very surprised.

"We need something to do," announced Surya.

"We want to help," clarified Liz.

"With your investigation," added Anupa unnecessarily. I pressed my finger to my lips to indicate that discretion was needed.

"Come with me," I whispered. Anupa and Surya smiled at each other and executed an elaborate fist bump while Kate and Liz shared an eye roll like two long-suffering parents.

I signed the gals in and led them through the single door towards the small studio where the Princess Gretel debacle had taken place. The ring of thirteen thrones had been reduced to only five because I had received approval to hold several smaller roundtables instead of a giant, uncontrollable Thunder Dome. The Posse happily claimed the thrones because who doesn't want to sit on a throne?

"Now this is a council of war!" proclaimed Anupa.

"One day, when we have our own PR firm, this is what our boardroom is going to look like," sighed Liz contentedly.

"Oh, yeah!" exclaimed Surya, her eyes dancing beneath the spiky bangs of her pixie cut.

"Well, I'm calling this meeting to order," announced Kate. "What are you all doing here? Honestly, Jill, they ambushed me at reception."

"We want to help. Duh!" Surya rolled her eyes.

"You know this is the dead time in PR. From Thanksgiving

to New Years' Eve, there's nothing to do. Put us to work," explained Liz.

"Y'all, this is so nice, but shouldn't you be getting your nails done or doing your Christmas shopping? You must have better things to do," I protested.

"Better than catching a murderer? I don't think so. As I recall, I had a lot of fun last time," Anupa slid her glasses down her nose to give me a schoolmarm stare.

"Your job ends in three days, Jill," Liz put in pragmatically. "How are you going to solve the case without a little help?"

"Wait a minute! I forgot. Jill is an island. She doesn't need help." Surya stabbed me with her sarcasm. "Well, too bad, Jill. Cooksey Island has allies. Deal with it."

"Isn't Cooksey Island a real nation?" Liz side-barred to Anupa.

"No, hon. That's the Cook Islands."

"Oh."

I looked to Kate, who just shrugged her shoulders. When the Posse wanted to help, there was no way to stop them. I gave in with good grace.

"Y'all are the best. The absolute best." My Posse-mates relaxed. I wondered what plan B would have been if I had said no. Probably a hostage situation but with the best of intentions.

I quickly brought everyone up to speed, running through the growing and changing list of suspects and conflicts in the Snicklefritz family. It took some time. Now that Carl had been revealed as the intended victim, everything had shifted.

"Flavia's out as a suspect because her beef was with Bryce, and even though Britney's prints were on the whiskey bottle, I think she's out too. She's always drinking whiskey with Carl, and she wouldn't be Princess Gretel if it wasn't for him. Devon's still in the picture because it was Carl who didn't want him to be the next Mr. Snicklefritz. We need to add Marcus and Patricia to the list, too, because Carl is holding something over their heads."

"Don't forget the Princess Gretels," added Kate. "That entire gang hates, loathes, and despises Carl, and they were in the studio on the day of the murder."

"Let me dig into Devon Cauthorne," offered Anupa. "Ambition alone is a thin motive for a nice guy. I'll see if there's a money component."

"I'll do some research on the rules governing children's television. I have some contacts at the FCC," said Liz. In healthcare PR, she had a lot of experience with government agencies and watchdogs, making her the perfect person for this research.

"I want to know more about these princesses. That Number Nine is a firecracker. Sounds like she has an ax to grind," mused Surya.

"I'll email you the whole list. By the way, Number Six never showed for the segment."

"Intriguing." Surya stroked an imaginary goatee.

"That just leaves me," smiled Kate.

"You have to be my eyes and ears while I'm stuck with the Princess Gretels this afternoon," I replied.

"No problem," she said. "And while I'm at it, I might investigate a few affairs of the heart."

CHAPTER 14

After we dispatched our Posse with a promise to meet them for dinner that evening, Kate and I headed to the production offices. We were passing the office that Detective Donato had been using for interviews when we heard a "Pssst!" from within. Sure enough, our favorite NYPD detective was seated at the desk.

"Close the door."

"What's up?" I asked.

"Nice shoes." Was that a hint of a smile? "Do you have time to brief me?"

I looked at my watch. The first round of Gretels was due to arrive in twenty minutes. Drat! I had time. So I told Donato about the letter of complaint that Phil and Larry had given to Marcus. Donato cocked an eyebrow at me.

"And how did you come across this letter?"

"Um, well, I can't tell you."

"Oh boy, this is just what I was afraid of."

"She found something else too," Kate chimed in. "Show him the card. This is even better."

I hadn't yet returned the card to Marcus's office, and it was currently in my jacket pocket. However, I thought that producing it outright might make Donato's head explode. Instead, I showed him the pictures on my phone.

"So you left this card and the complaint in place, correct?" Donato skewered me with his laser gaze.

"Uh-huh." I was careful not to look at Kate, and I applied a little pressure to her foot using my Moose slipper in an attempt to communicate that she should keep her mouth shut. Thankfully, it worked.

"Well, the complaint certainly shines a new light on the working relationship between the performers. I'm not really sure what this card means."

"In the conversation I overheard between Carl, Marcus, and Patricia, Carl implied he would reveal something if they didn't do what he wanted," I thought aloud. "When Patricia objected, Carl then implied that blackmail was how she had managed to stay married for twenty-five years. The two things must be related."

"Not necessarily," objected Kate. "They could be two completely different secrets."

"But what if they aren't?" I proposed. "If Carl exposed the thing Patricia is holding over Marcus's head—"

"Then Patricia wouldn't have any leverage anymore. Marcus could walk away," finished Donato. "It bears looking into."

I glanced at my watch.

"I've got to go. The Princess Gretels will be here any moment."

"About them," began Donato. "When they're done with the roundtable, be sure to have a PA bring them here. I need to ask a few questions."

"With pleasure! If they misbehave, will you cuff them? Pretty please?"

In the end, the princesses were good as gold, but then

again I tend to learn from my mistakes. I only interviewed five at a time, only bottled water was allowed on the set, and no Princess Gretel had to be in a roundtable with the woman who replaced her. I also carefully vetted the questions, and the difference between the roundtables was like night and day. The ladies even liked my slippers! I hoped Detective Donato was having as much success in his interrogation room

I was finished by five-thirty, and I headed back to my cubicle to put the day to bed. As I was passing the old studio, Chuck came barreling out of the double doors. I jumped out of the way before he could run me over, which was a good thing because he didn't see me. His head was down, and his shoulders were hunched up to his ears, which wasn't out of the ordinary. What was strange, in addition to the fact that he was running as if bloodhounds were chasing him, was that his face was beet red, and I was pretty sure he was crying.

"Chuck!" He didn't respond, and I don't think he could hear me. I was on the verge of following him when Dominique burst through the doors carrying a small binder. She had been in the first group of PGs, so she should have been long gone. She stopped when she saw me, and a moment later, Carl poked his head out the door as well.

"Anybody want to tell me what's the matter with Chuck?" I didn't try to be polite. I was pretty sure these two had upset the PA, and I didn't like it. I was beginning to feel very protective of the PAs.

"It's a private matter," mumbled Carl, whose face was also beet red, before he disappeared back the way he came.

"When you see Charles again," said Dominique, "give him this." She thrust the binder at me. "It explains...a lot." She gave me a meaningful look and then turned to follow Carl.

I started to open the binder and realized it was actually a photo album, but other than the first photo, I didn't get a chance to peruse it because Britney came bouncing down the hallway.

"Have you seen Carl?" Her smile seemed forced, and her eyes were red. Had she been crying too?

I didn't know how to explain what I had just witnessed, so I said, "I just saw him. He headed into the old studio."

"Was Dominique with him?" Britney's attempts to smile through her pain were making her look homicidal.

"Uh, yes."

"Okay!" More smiling. "That's cool! No worries. I'll just join them. Bye!"

And she was gone. I thought hard about following her because a huge argument was in the offing, and who knew what I could learn? The reappearance of Carl's ex-wife on the scene seemed to be stirring up trouble between Carl and Britney. But I was more concerned about Chuck and the contents of the photo album, so I headed for The Pen.

"He left a few minutes ago," said Tameasha when I caught up with the PAs. "He was really upset about something. I thought maybe he'd been fired for some reason, but I asked a producer, and she said no."

"Madison went after him," added Julia. "She's supposed to text us later."

"Would you mind texting me when you hear from her?" I asked.

"No problem," replied Julia. I put my number into her phone and bid the girls goodbye.

Moving farther down the corridor, I found Kate in Donato's makeshift office, but he wasn't there.

"You just missed him," she said. "But he didn't have too much to report. All the Gretels went home last Wednesday on the party bus except for Dominique, who stayed after to talk to Carl."

"Yeah, I just ran into her. I think I know what she needed to talk to Carl about. I'll tell you when we meet the girls. You ready to go?"

We bundled up and headed around the corner to meet the Posse at the pub that was fast becoming a hangout for me. I wondered if Chuck and Madison would be there, but when I scanned the room, I didn't see them.

The Posse had already commandeered a large round corner booth. Kate and I squeezed in at opposite ends, and the waiter came to take our drink order.

"You can get little individual pots of tea here," enthused Liz.

"You can also get Irish Car Bombs," added Surya with a wink.

I ordered a pot of tea with lots of sugar on the side while Kate went for a glass of Pinot Grigio.

"We have things to report," announced Liz.

"That was fast!" exclaimed Kate.

"Well, not all of us," cautioned Anupa. "I'm still waiting on Devon's financials."

"Let me start! Let me start!" Surya was bouncing up and down like a small child. "Princess Gretel Number Nine is writing a tell-all book! Actually, she's written it. It's in the final stages of editorial right now, set to launch in February. That's a great time of year for tell-alls because people are bored post-holidays and stuck inside because it's the dead of winter. People are going to gobble it up. I wish I had the account."

"How did you find this out?" Surya was a little scary sometimes.

"Well, I started with her YouTube Channel. It's called *Coney Island Confidential*, and it's a hoot."

I could imagine. Number Nine was feisty and funny. YouTube was the perfect venue for her personality.

"In one video she referred to her time on *Snicklefritz* and then hinted that we'd all get to read the whole story very soon. That's all she said, but it sounded like a tell-all to me, so I made some calls to my contacts at the big five publishers. Found her at number three." Surya looked so proud.

"Good work, roomie," praised Kate. "Now how do we parlay a tell-all book into a motive for murder?"

"Well, if Carl died scandalously, lots of people would want to read about his life," reasoned Liz pragmatically. "Coming on the heels of his death, her book would certainly become a bestseller."

"But when did she put the poison in the whiskey?" I wondered. "She may have motive, but did she have opportunity?"

"Listen to you sounding all *Law and Order*," Anupa poked me gently in the ribs. "I'm sure there had to be a time when you didn't have eyes on her, and she knows the studio, right?"

"When she went to the bathroom!" Kate snapped her fingers. "Didn't you tell me they all had to go after the champagne?"

"It's certainly possible," I admitted. I had sent PAs to the bathroom with the PGs, but once they left the green room, anything could have happened. "We'll have to let Donato know about this. Surya, did you find out anything else?"

"Oh yeah." Surya took a quick sip of her car bomb. "Number Six is deceased. That's why she didn't come to the roundtable. She died last year of an undisclosed illness leaving behind one child, a son named Charles, age nineteen. He's probably twenty now. I found her obituary today."

No one said anything, which was fine because my brain was whirring. I reached under the table for my Behemoth Black Bag and extricated Dominique's photo album. I placed it in the middle of the table where everyone could see it. Then I flipped it open.

The pictures were old, or rather copies of old pictures. I could tell right away they weren't the originals. Some were even copies of scanned Polaroids. Every one of them featured a young man with a shock of red hair, green eyes, and a florid complexion.

"Hey, that's that PA," said Kate. "What's his name?...Chuck!"

"Which is short for Charles," I replied. "Only that's not Chuck."

"Hey isn't that Dominique? How old are these photos?" Kate looked perplexed.

"Very old. That's Dominique...with Carl Biersdorf."

"But he looks just like Chuck!"

Indeed.

The waiter chose that moment to take our food order. I was eyeing the salmon Caesar salad but opted for the chicken Caesar due to budgetary concerns. Plus, I was jonesing for the strawberry rhubarb crumble for dessert.

"So this Chuck kid is actually the son of Mr. Snicklefritz and Princess Gretel Number Six?" asked Anupa after the waiter left.

"I think so. I saw him running away from Dominique and Carl this afternoon, and then Dominique asked me to give this to Chuck. She said it would explain a lot."

"Do you think he didn't know Carl is his father?" asked Liz. "It would be quite a coincidence for Chuck to end up working on his long-lost father's show."

"Agreed," affirmed Anupa. "He totally knew. Maybe he got the job so he could get to know his father."

"Or for a more sinister purpose." Surya was stroking her imaginary goatee again. "Raised by a single mom who dies before her time—this kid has anger issues, I guarantee it."

"Don't forget how badly Carl treated all his girlfriends," added Kate. "Do you think she got fired because she got pregnant, or do you think she found out after she was fired?"

"Motive much?" Surya cocked an eyebrow.

The case had suddenly shifted direction, and I didn't like it one bit.

"Y'all, Chuck may have started out a loner, but he's bonded with the PAs. I even think he's dating one of them. He seems like a nice, normal kid, *and* he wanted to learn puppetry. He was taking lessons from Bryce before he died. I don't want him to be the killer."

The girls all looked at me sympathetically.

"And none of us wanted Shelby to die in *Steel Magnolias*," Liz soothed, "but it happened, and we had to deal with it."

"Liz, are you speaking southern to help me come to terms?"

"I am."

"Well, bless your heart!"

Anupa cackled, and then we were all laughing.

Our food arrived, and we all tucked in. After a few mouthfuls, Liz spoke up.

"I finished my research on the laws governing educational television. Basically, starting around 1990, children's television programs had to prove their educational worth to the FCC. I emailed you some documents."

"That's right before Mr. Snicklefritz went national," I mused. "That has to be important. Thanks, Liz."

"Well, I guess that just leaves little old me." Kate's imitation southern accent was appalling.

"Stick to 'Yo, Adrian,' Philly girl, and tell us what you found."

A wicked gleam appeared in Kate's eye, and her grin gave me goosebumps.

"Well, I did a little bit of B and E myself today."

"B and E?" asked Anupa.

"Breaking and entering." Surya rubbed her hands together gleefully. "Excellent!"

"Not excellent!" I cried. "What did you do, Kate?"

"I just let myself into Marcus's office while he was in a meeting with the editor."

"You could have been caught!" I protested. "You didn't have

anyone to be lookout or to signal you with emojis. What were you thinking?"

"I was thinking that I could always claim I needed someplace to work since I don't have my own office there and Donato has commandeered the spare. Marcus might have been annoyed, but he wouldn't have been suspicious."

It made sense, and I had to admire her gumption.

"You beast!" laughed Anupa.

"Don't you want to know what I found?" Kate batted her eyelashes suggestively, then slid her cell phone across the table where we all could see a photo of a document of some kind.

"What is it?" I asked as I reached to enlarge the photo.

"A formal separation agreement. It's unsigned, but Marcus definitely wants out of the marriage."

"I wonder if Patricia knows," I breathed.

If she did, and if she was losing her leverage over Marcus because of Carl, that would make her a prime suspect, along with Devon, Chuck, PG Number Nine, Phil, and Larry. I had more suspects than I could shake a stick at.

CHAPTER 15

I slept poorly that night, my racing thoughts allowing me only snatches of slumber. Eventually I gave up trying to sleep and opted for a very early rise and a little sleuthing. I was out of the apartment by four thirty and headed toward the studio. The sky was clear, the air was frigid and dry —a static electricity sort of day. I had a feeling my ponytail would be standing straight up when I pulled my beanie off. Luckily I kept a dryer sheet in my coat pocket for just such static emergencies.

The streets of Long Island City were nearly empty. Only delivery people were out at this time of morning—delivery people and criminals. I kept my head on a swivel as I made my way to the studio and arrived without incident.

As I pushed through the double doors and headed down the dark corridor toward the production offices, I vowed not to be afraid. Security was tighter now. We all were safer. I made it to my cubicle where I took off my mittens, scarf, and coat.

Snap! Crackle! Pop! Out of the corner of my eye, I saw flashes of lightning as I removed the wool beanie, and, as expected, my hair was now standing straight out from my head in all directions. Straight and fine, it was the perfect conduit for electricity and could have charged a cellular device. Annoyed, I groped for the dryer sheet in my pocket and rubbed it all over my head.

Smelling like a laundromat, I moved toward the old studio. Now that Donato had cleared the space for use, I wanted a closer look at the dressing rooms. If the cast had any more secrets, their personal spaces would be the place to find them.

The old studio was dark except for a couple of security lights. I had no idea how to turn on the lights in that space, so I used the flashlight on my phone to find my way. I only tripped over coils of cable twice as I crossed the studio to the other corridor that led to the dressing rooms.

The first room was Carl's. I half expected the door to be locked, but it wasn't. After I shut the door behind me and turned on the lights, I did a double take. Was I in the right dressing room? The place was clean, so clean I could still smell Pine-Sol. There wasn't an ashtray anywhere nor any bottles of booze. The room had been scrubbed. Even the shelves of awards had been dusted and the cracked glass replaced. The space was immaculate.

First a complete personality change during set visits. Then a complete clean-out and, unless I found evidence to the contrary, a shedding of addictions. What would be next in Carl Biersdorf's transformation? Had the attempted murder really brought all this about? Aligned chakras indeed.

I tried to put aside my astonishment so I could focus on the search. I opened every drawer, every cabinet, even the fridge, but I found nothing of interest. At one point I thought I'd found a locked drawer in his dressing table, but it turned out to be just a bit sticky. Inside I found some photos of young Carl during the early days of the show. Had Carl been taking a walk down memory lane. With Dominique perhaps? Or Chuck?

Making sure everything was just as I'd found it, I moved on

to the next room. This was Phil's dressing room. When I flipped on the light, it appeared just as I remembered it from the previous week. I started with the drawers of his dressing table. Phil had a taste for voluptuous redheads if his choice of reading material was any indication. To his credit, however, I must also admit that he possessed copies of *Jonathan Livingston Seagull* and *The Celestine Prophecy*. Okay, maybe not so much to his credit, but at least his reading was diverse.

I also stumbled across Phil's stash of, let's just say, supplements. Indeed, from the quantities, herbs and fungi seemed to be a very important part of his diet. None of this was terribly shocking, but I did wonder if the police had found it as well. I couldn't imagine they'd missed it, unless of course Phil had recently replenished his stock. Phil's stash brought up an important question. If Phil and Larry had wanted to scare Carl, they could have just put some magic mushrooms in his whiskey. Why use a potentially deadly poison?

Other than Phil's vices, I didn't turn up anything interesting in the drawers, so I turned my attention to the rest of the room. Scanning the space, I realized that Phil had created a lot of hiding places simply because of his penchant for draping surfaces with fabric. Fabric covered walls and tables, pooling on the floor. Methodically, I made my way around the room, lifting the material wherever it hung or pooled to see if anything was concealed. I hit pay dirt under a small, draped table next to his papasan chair. A stack of magazines and worksheets was topped with a pencil and a calculator. I pulled out the stack and took a seat on the floor. Surprisingly, the magazines were all about horse racing, and the worksheets were racing forms. I wondered if I aligned my chakras and opened my third eye, would I be able to predict a trifecta at Aqueduct? I pulled out my phone and texted Anupa. We were going to need Phil's financials as well as Devon's.

The next dressing room was Larry's, and I dreaded it.

Maybe it was all the weapons or knowing that one of them had been used to skewer someone *and* his puppet, but the room just felt dangerous to me. Still, it had to be done. For Bryce.

Larry's dressing room looked just the same too. Or did it? Something was different. I scanned the room several times until I figured it out. Where the replica of Bilbo's Sting, now sitting in an evidence locker, had been displayed on a shelf next to the Morgul blade, another sword had taken its place. This one was even longer, although it too had an Elvish air about it. Before I even read the brass plaque on the mount, I knew I was looking at the sword reforged, Anduril, belonging to Aragorn in *The Lord of the Rings*. I had to smile. Larry was nothing if not consistent, and the fact that I knew the name of that obscure sword meant he and I were not so very different. Except for that whole sexual harassment thing of course.

With a slightly lighter heart, I continued my search, but I came up with nothing more exciting than some stomach-turning DVDs about young women making poor choices during spring break. After Phil and Larry's dressing rooms, I was congratulating myself on being a man-free island nation. Some men could be icky, but honestly, some women let them. True story.

Leaving Larry's dressing room, I headed across the hallway. The room across from Carl's was much smaller and belonged to Britney, probably because Princess Gretel was only supposed to work one day a week. Britney, however, had been at the studio every day since I had started at the show. Opening the door, I could tell immediately why she spent more time in Carl's dressing room than her own. Other than the fact that she purportedly loved him, her dressing room was tiny, about eight-by-eight, and much of it was taken up by the Princess Gretel gown. Still, she had tried to make the space her own. Everything that could be purple and glittery was—the dressing table and chair, the picture frames on the walls, and the rug.

Prince would have felt quite at home, and I didn't hate it myself. I perused the photos on the walls. Every last one was a picture of Britney and Carl—in costume on the set, seated at a restaurant, in a crowded bar, on a beach somewhere. I turned to the dressing table. The surface was covered in neatly arranged makeup and brushes. I checked the drawers and found nothing out of the ordinary. The bottom drawer was larger and empty, and I imagined that she stored her purse there, the same way I stored mine in my desk.

That little detail gave me pause. Britney was the only female performer in a cast dominated by men. What was it like for her? Did she ever feel alone? Was that why she seemed to stick to Carl like a shadow? Maybe she liked being the only woman in Gingerbread Cottage. She didn't have to be at the studio every day, and yet she was. Her constant presence and the photos on the wall actually indicated a deep affection for Carl the curmudgeon, wonder of wonders. I chuckled to myself and continued to search the tiny room for hiding places, but the space was so small that there wasn't much point. Britney's dressing room was all business.

Next door to Britney was another tiny dressing room—Devon's. His space was tidy, but with only sixty-four square feet, he didn't really have a choice. His dressing room was a bit more spacious than hers simply because it lacked an enormous ball gown. Without it, he had room for an arm chair and an ottoman tucked into one corner. It was well-worn and looked really comfortable. I was tempted to pull a Goldilocks, but if I were found sleeping in Devon's comfy chair, there would certainly be questions. Instead, I scanned the extensive collection of framed photos on his walls and found family pictures almost exclusively—Devon, his wife, and their daughter, I assumed, sometimes with extended family. A couple of photos of the puppeteers together and a single photo of Devon with a puppet I didn't recognize rounded out the collection.

So many family photos implied that Devon was a real family man, but was there a darker message? Twenty years as a right hand, relegated to a tiny dressing room, never feeling quite like part of the team. Were the family photos intended to be reminders of why Devon persevered? Had he surrounded himself with reminders of his responsibilities to keep himself from saying "Take this job and shove it"?

One could argue that his perseverance had paid off, albeit with a little help from homicide. It was also interesting that despite his recent promotion, Devon hadn't asked to move into Bryce's much larger space. Was that out of respect or to deflect suspicion? An ambitious, grasping person might not care that Bryce's body was barely cold, but a soulless, calculating killer might bide his time to appear respectful.

Before I moved on, I searched the dressing table. I wasn't expecting to find anything, so the hatbox in the large bottom drawer took me by surprise. How many men in this day and age owned a hatbox? I removed the lid and found myself looking at a green felt Tyrolean hat with a colorful band and a spray of oak leaves and acorns—an exact copy of the hat worn by Mr. Snicklefritz. A card lay next to it but only for a second before I snatched it up and read it: *Your day will come.—Marcus.*

Another reminder to persevere? Certainly. Evidence that Marcus was committed to giving Devon the Mr. Snicklefritz role? Absolutely. Proof that Devon wanted the role enough to kill for it? Possibly.

Devon Cauthorne was a friendly guy, without a doubt, but beneath that affable exterior, I suspected, were resentments and ambitions. And who could blame him? If they led him to murder, I could.

I moved on to the final dressing room, Bryce's, with mounting dread. I wasn't worried about finding anything shocking. Bryce was a victim, not a suspect, and an unintended victim at that. So what was I looking for? What could be of use to the investigation? I really didn't know, but I knew that I couldn't leave this stone unturned. I had to be thorough.

My hand shook a little as I reached for the doorknob, but I got a grip on myself and opened the door. Taking my first good look at the dressing room, I could see that Bryce's was a monument to the art of puppetry. When I visited the room on my first day on the job, I hadn't wanted to seem too inquisitive and had resisted the impulse to gawk at the performers' personal spaces, but I had registered that Bryce's was cluttered. Now I discovered that the "clutter" was actually the contents of an entire museum to puppetry crammed into a ten by twelve-foot room. Marionettes hung from the ceiling, and hand puppets were arranged on stands, their mouths gaping without a puppeteer's support. Propped in the corners of the room were giant, life-size puppets, and mounted on the walls were a hundred different puppets of sorts I had never seen before and that I would have no idea how to operate. From the look of them, they had come from all over the world, their expressions and clothing suggesting faraway lands and fascinating cultures. I moved about the room and studied the puppets, many of which were so complicated that it must have taken a team of puppeteers to operate them. No wonder puppeteers hated being called dolly wagglers. I marveled at the practice and skill required to bring these creations to life, but while the puppets filled me with wonder, they also filled me with sadness. Bryce had been dedicated to his art, maybe more so than any of the other performers on the show, but this master of the puppetry arts was gone long before his time. The world had lost someone very special. I could feel the tears coming, and I didn't resist them.

Sometime later, I managed to pull myself together. I conducted a search of the room but found nothing that seemed pertinent to the investigation. I had just turned off the light and was closing the door when the sound of voices turned my blood to ice in my veins. Those weren't just any voices. They were the Snicklefritz puppets, and they were nearby. Had the puppeteers noticed the lights on in the dressing room? I had closed the door while I searched, but surely the light had shown underneath it. Maybe it hadn't. If anyone had noticed someone in Bryce's dressing room, wouldn't they have investigated?

Following the voices, I tiptoed down the hall and stopped outside the puppet room. This was the room dedicated to storing and maintaining the puppets. I had only visited once on my first day. I glanced at my phone. It was only five forty-five. Was there an early morning rehearsal?

Suddenly, the puppets broke out in that modern-day classic "The Booger Song." What the heck was going on? If they thought they'd be performing that crime against humanity on the anniversary special, they were sorely mistaken. I marched into the puppet room to put a stop to the shenanigans and nearly collapsed in shock.

No, the puppets weren't performing without puppeteers controlling them. This isn't a Stephen King novel. They were, however, being performed by my favorite PAs, and the kids were slaying. Chuck was performing Martin, Tameasha Moose, and Madison Joe. And in the illustrious role of disembodied, booger-filled nose was Julia. The voices were spot-on! I couldn't believe what I was hearing. These kids were amazing.

It took about thirty seconds before they realized I was there and the singing stopped abruptly. The puppets came down, and the PAs' faces became masks of fear.

"Don't stop! That was incredible. Where did you learn to do that?"

"You're not going to tell anybody, are you?" asked Tameasha. With my compliments, the kids' looks of abject terror had been replaced with slightly milder expressions of dread and worry. I hastened to relieve their fears completely.

"Of course not! Unless you want me to. I mean, people should know what you can do."

"That's a really bad idea," moaned Julia,

"Yeah," said Chuck. "There's a hierarchy, and if you want to work in this business, you don't mess with it."

"But if someone was sick, you could fill in." It made sense to me.

"Yeah, there are about a hundred other people ahead of us on the list," laughed Madison a little bitterly. "We have to wait our turn."

I understood what they were saying, but it still rankled. I really liked these kids. They had become my Puppet Posse, and I just wanted good things for them.

"So do you practice here a lot?"

They traded some guilty looks.

"Sometimes," mumbled Julia. I had a feeling sometimes meant all the time.

"Look, Jill," began Chuck. He looked me squarely in the eye. "These puppets cost tens of thousands of dollars each. If anyone found out we had been practicing with them…"

"You'd never work in this town again?"

"Exactly."

"My lips are sealed…but I do have to remind you that you're taking a huge risk with your careers."

"We would never hurt the puppets!" exclaimed Madison.

"Yeah, we love them," said Julia as she caressed her disembodied, booger-filled nose.

I wasn't really worried about the puppets getting hurt. I was more worried about my PAs.

CHAPTER 16

I spent the morning on set visits, lots of set visits. Thursday and Friday were set aside for rehearsals for the live anniversary special on Saturday night, so Wednesday was the last day of shooting for the week and the last day for anniversary set visits. Despite Bryce's death, or perhaps because of it, everybody and their mother's uncle wanted to visit Gingerbread Cottage.

Carl 2.0 continued, and I was beginning to believe that his Damascene conversion would stick. He was a new man, and the only time I saw the shade of his former self was when Chuck passed by. I got the distinct impression that Chuck was freezing him out, hardly surprising, and Carl's happy-go-lucky expression would slip.

The rest of the cast seemed happy to follow Carl's lead, including Squirrelly-Joe. He was on his best behavior, but really, with so many children coming through the set, he never had the chance to act up. All this good behavior led to incredible productivity, and Flavia was simply thriving as director. I'm pretty sure she was also in the first flush of romance with one of the security woodcutters. All was right in the Snicklefritz world.

Until it wasn't.

I had just returned from escorting the last tour group to the lobby.

"Finally! The rug rats are gone, and you and I can be alone at last." Squirrelly-Joe leered at me from atop a large green box used to simulate set pieces. He patted the space next to him. "Why don't you come up here and get to know me a little better? I'll let you stroke my tail."

"Stuff it, Joe!"

"No, doll. That's my job. Am I right, boys?" Joe grinned at the grips around the set, and they all chuckled, the villains.

"You know what we do with squirrels in Virginia, Joe? Ever heard of Brunswick stew?"

The vermin didn't have time for a retort because Britney burst into the studio.

"It's Carl. He's hurt!"

We all took off after her, and I had to fight my way past some grips to get to Carl. He was sitting at his dressing table, cradling his right arm, which was slashed open and bleeding. A katana sword lay on the table in front of him.

"What happened?" I asked while I looked around for something to stanch the blood. His costume was the only thing handy, so I grabbed it and wrapped it around his arm.

"The sword just fell on me," mumbled Carl. He seemed dazed and might have been in shock, although the small amount of blood on the table indicated his shock was more emotional than physical.

"We're gonna need the first aid kit!" I shouted to no one in particular.

"I've called 911." That was Flavia's voice.

I turned back to Carl.

"So you're saying the katana just fell on you? From where?"

I looked up. There was no place directly overhead from which the katana could have fallen.

"I think it came from up there." With his good arm, Carl pointed to the row of lights over his mirror. It was certainly possible the Katana could have been balanced on the row of bulbs.

"What were you doing when it fell?"

"I was closing this drawer. It sticks, so you have to push it hard."

I almost said "I know," but caught myself at the last second.

"So the vibrations from forcing the drawer caused the sword to fall."

Carl grabbed at my hands with both of his, not caring about his wound. His eyes were wide with fright and filling rapidly.

"Someone's still trying to kill me! It doesn't matter what I do or how I change. Someone wants me dead." The tears spilled over, so I switched into publicist mode.

"Okay, everyone, show's over. Time to give Carl some space. He's been through a traumatic event. Everyone out. And keep those cell phones in your pockets!"

I herded everyone out of the room except Tameasha, who had the first aid kit.

"Go to the production offices. See if Detective Donato is there, and my friend Kate. Tell them what happened. And send two of the security dudes back in here."

Tameasha nodded and was gone. She was replaced by Marcus, who burst in.

"Carl! I was back in my office when it happened. I didn't know. How are you?"

In response, Carl backed his chair as far away from Marcus as he could.

"You! You're trying to kill me because of what I know. You want me gone! You won't stop until I'm dead!"

"Jeez! Carl! No! I would never! Has it come to this?"

Marcus's expression was tortured, but I had seen him give some good performances for the cast and crew over the last two weeks. I wasn't necessarily buying it. I stepped between the two former friends and deployed my southern accent.

"I don't think now is the time. I need to tend to Carl's wound, and he's been through a terrible shock. Best to give him some space. He'll be okay." I laid my hand gently on Marcus's arm and gave him a reassuring squeeze. Then I guided him to the door. The sight of two burly security woodsmen returning hastened his departure, and with a sigh of relief, I turned to Carl and the first aid kit.

The knot on my perfectly applied bandage (thank you, Girl Scouts) was just tied when Donato, Kate, and the paramedics arrived.

"I'm going to have to remove that bandage. Sorry," the handsome Indian EMT apologized. I recognized him from last September when I had been attacked.

"I know you!" I smiled at him.

"Mild concussion!" He snapped his fingers. "Good to see you alive and in good form. I'm Vignesh."

"Jill," I replied and shook his hand.

"Okay, okay," muttered Donato. "You two can flirt after you've seen to Mr. Biersdorf."

"I was just being friendly," I protested. I looked to the EMT for support, but he winked at me. I got out of the way and joined Kate and Donato in the hallway for a pow-wow.

"Nice work," quipped Kate with a knowing smile.

"Oh, not you too!" I rolled my eyes at her.

"So what happened?" demanded Donato.

I relayed what Carl had told me about the katana falling from the lights.

"The thing is, that's Larry's katana. I'm sure of it. But I don't think it was in his dressing room this morning. I was looking at the collection, and I'm pretty certain the katana wasn't there.

It could have already been in Carl's dressing room when I was searching it. I didn't look up at the lights."

"And why were you in the dressing rooms?" Donato cocked an eyebrow pointedly.

"Looking for clues for you! And would it kill you to say thank you? If that katana was over his dressing table this morning, then I could have been killed. I wrestled with that sticky drawer. Oh, and I found some *very interesting* clues too. Or do you not want to know what they are because I was snooping—because YOU asked me to!"

Donato and I glared at each other.

"Okay, everyone," soothed Kate. "Let's just take a step back."

I closed my eyes, took a deep breath, and counted to ten. The falling sword had me rattled. It might have been intended for Carl, but anyone visiting his dressing room—a cast member, a crew member, a child—could have been hurt. Whoever had it in for Carl must have been feeling desperate.

"Sorry," I said as I opened my eyes.

"No, I'm sorry," said Donato. Wow! A man who could actually apologize. The end of the world was nigh. "I asked you to be my eyes and ears, and it put you at risk. I shouldn't have done that."

"No!" Kate and I cried simultaneously. Then we looked at each other and laughed.

"I must admit, I wasn't too keen on the idea when you asked," I explained. "But I really am glad to help. I want to find Bryce's killer."

I want to atone, I thought but didn't say it.

"Well fill me in then," said Donato resignedly.

I told him all about the racing paraphernalia I had found in Phil's dressing room. Donato was skeptical.

"What does playing the ponies have to do with murder?"

"Well, people who gamble a lot can rack up a lot of debt. We already know Phil was worried about Carl costing him his job. Maybe he's so worried because he's broke."

"Or worse, maybe he owes money to some bad people," added Kate. "People who would break a puppeteer's hand if he didn't pay up."

Donato thought about it for a moment.

"Okay, it's worth looking into." He moved to go.

"Wait!" Kate and I cried simultaneously again which amused us to no end but made Donato clench his teeth.

"There's more," said Kate. "A lot more."

I filled them both in on Devon's Mr. Snicklefritz hat, but Donato already knew about it.

"We found it when we conducted our *legal* search. The hat is...concerning."

We also filled him in on Carl's long-lost son, PG Number Nine's book deal, and Marcus and Patricia's impending separation.

"It's important," I explained, "because to get the network to green-light the show, Marcus and Carl had to prove it was educational. I read up on it last night. A whole bunch of new rules had come down from the Federal Communications Commission in 1990. We think Ph.D. Patricia fudged the report because she was in love with Marcus. They married a couple of years later."

"Now Patricia's holding it over Marcus's head to keep the marriage together," added Kate. "But if Carl exposes the truth, she'll have no leverage."

Donato was writing furiously. After a moment, he paused, took a long look at what he had written, and sighed big.

"So we went from having one suspect with an alibi to...one, two, three...six suspects. Jeez Louise! This is just the beginning. I'm gonna need more cops. This is unbelievable."

Was it weird that I felt proud of myself while feeling bad for Detective Donato? Kate and I were seriously helping, but you wouldn't know it from the set of his jaw or the perspiration on his brow.

Just then my phone vibrated. It was Anupa.

"I got the financials, and you're not going to like it."

"Morning, Nupe. I'm going to put you on speaker. I'm with Kate and Detective Donato."

"Okay. So Devon first. He has two mortgages on his house. He may have said that being a right hand put his kid through college, but I call bull. He and his wife are barely hanging on, and he has almost no retirement savings."

"That jives with what we found," said Donato. "Although I don't want to know how you're getting your information, Ms. Aranha."

"And I don't want to tell you," laughed Anupa.

"But Devon has an alibi, right?" asked Kate.

"Just his wife, so it's thin. I've got people trying to break it, but so far no luck. We'll need to work harder."

"Yeah," said Kate, "because a doubled salary when you're broke is a pretty good motive."

"How do you know that?" demanded Donato.

Evidently, Kate hadn't resisted the temptation to look through the contracts when she rifled Marcus's office. I wonder what else she knew.

"I'm in charge of PR for this program, which makes me privy to certain information," she replied primly. Donato rolled his eyes.

"So Phil Rainey," piped up Anupa from my phone. "He's also in big financial trouble, not quite as bad as Devon, but for a children's television star of thirty years, he doesn't have much to show for it. His stock portfolio has been shrinking over the last decade, and I can't find any other assets except his cottage up in Tarrytown. He's bleeding money."

"Thanks, Nupe."

"Anytime, Jill. Gotta go." She rang off.

"So both Devon and Phil need *Mr. Snicklefritz* to continue, and Devon really needed a promotion," I thought aloud.

"It's time for me to sweat some people," announced Donato. "I need the weight of a police interrogation room behind me."

"Who will you start with?" I asked.

"I'm not sure."

Just then Vignesh emerged from the dressing room.

"Mr. Biersdorf is going to be fine. The wound is superficial. It doesn't even require stitches. If he had been positioned differently when the sword fell, it could have been a different story."

"Thanks for your help." Kate offered him her hand, and he shook it

"Anytime," he replied. I offered him my hand, and he took it in both of his. "See you around," he said with a smile, and then he was gone.

"I bet you will," grinned Kate, and I rolled my eyes. Vignesh wouldn't be visiting Cooksey Island any time soon.

We reentered the dressing room to find Carl perking up, so Donato got down to business.

"Mr. Biersdorf, we need to clear the room. This is a crime scene again."

Carl ran a hand over his face and sighed.

"When will this nightmare end?"

"I'm here for you, baby," cooed Britney as she walked through the door. Dominique was hard on her heels.

"Carl, thank heavens you're okay." She brushed past Britney and knelt by Carl's side.

"We need to clear this room," reiterated Donato impatiently.

"Let's find you some place where you can be comfortable," offered Dominique.

"Don't you think that's my job?" asked Britney. "I'm his girlfriend."

Britney held out a hand to Carl and looked pointedly at him. The message was clear. *Make a choice.*

Carl cleared his throat. "Dominique, we'll speak later." He took Britney's hand and rose. Then she led him from the room. Dominique watched them go, her expression inscrutable. I was dying to know what she was thinking or even why she was there, but I didn't get a chance to ask.

"Okay, everybody out!" Donato's patience had evaporated. Dominique went left, heading toward the small studio and ultimately the lobby, while Kate and I went right, heading towards the production offices.

Kate commandeered Donato's makeshift interrogation room so she could call Bob and apprise him of the situation. I wandered back to my desk, thinking I would get a little work done, but as soon as I sat down, three heads appeared above my cubicle wall: Tameasha, Madison, and Julia.

"Is it true that Larry's katana fell on Carl?" asked Tameasha without preamble.

"Looks that way," I affirmed.

"Do you think Larry is trying to kill Carl?" asked Madison. "First Sting and now the katana. All the weapons lead back to Larry."

"Larry wouldn't be that stupid," Julia argued. "It's just that his stash of weapons is convenient. Isn't that right, Jill?"

"Ladies, I really don't know." I shrugged my shoulders because I really didn't. Larry would be awfully stupid to use his own weapons to try to eliminate Carl, but maybe it was a blind. Maybe he was trying to deflect suspicion by doing something that would point straight at himself. Larry was odd but not dumb.

"Guys, the first weapon wasn't actually Larry's. It was poison," Tameasha pointed out. "The killer probably staged Bryce's body using Larry's sword hoping no one would think poison was involved because he—"

"Or she," Julia interjected.

"Or she," continued Tameasha, "was still hoping Carl would drink some poisoned whisky." Nothing got past Tameasha, or any of the PAs for that matter, but I had my own questions.

"Hey, where's Chuck?" I asked.

"Who knows?" said Tameasha.

"He's avoiding us," said Julia. "Unless we're working, he keeps his distance."

Madison said nothing, just looked at the floor.

"Did he ever tell you what was wrong?" I nudged.

"No," Madison whispered. Her feelings were definitely involved. Part of me wanted to invite her to be an ally island nation and save herself the hurt, but I also knew she had to learn these things for herself. At her age, I wouldn't have believed me either.

"Let's get some lunch," I suggested as I gave her shoulder a little pat.

We made our way to the cafeteria and discovered it was southern soul food day. Hallelujah! A little taste of home was always welcome. I loaded up my tray with fried chicken, mashed potatoes, collard greens, and macaroni and cheese. I was bemoaning the lack of fried okra when I spotted the hummingbird cake and had to do a happy dance. The PAs were highly amused.

We took our usual corner table so we could watch the show. As the crew came in, the usual cliques formed, not surprisingly. Then Devon, Phil, Larry, the new right hand Susan, and Flavia came in and sat together. Carl and Britney followed a few minutes later flanked by security. There wasn't room at the puppeteer table for all of them, so they sat one table over. I was relieved because I didn't want anyone slipping something into Carl's food. I saw potential killers everywhere.

Marcus came in next with Patricia hard on his heels. He started to walk over to Carl's table, thought better of it, and took the last seat at the puppeteer table, leaving Patricia without a place. An awkward moment ensued in which Patricia looked beseechingly at Marcus while he completely ignored her. I could tell the puppeteers were getting uncomfortable by the way they shifted in their seats and shot each other meaningful looks. Eventually, Patricia walked away and sat alone at a table for two on the other side of the room. I don't think she touched her food.

Chuck arrived next, and Madison pulled out the chair next to her in the hope that he would sit with us, but he just walked on by and opted for another table for two near Patricia.

"Jerk," I heard Tameasha mutter under her breath. Julia gave Madison's hand a squeeze as tears rapidly filled her eyes.

Island life, ladies. That's where it's at.

Before I could offer unsolicited advice that neither of them would take, Dominique entered the cafeteria. She walked directly over to Chuck, and I heard her ask "Is this seat taken?" He didn't answer, so she sat and began eating her lunch. A moment later, he got up and, taking his tray with him, headed for the exit. Unfazed, Dominique kept eating.

As Chuck left the cafeteria, he passed Detective Donato, who stopped him and said something that had Chuck doing a double take before scrunching up his shoulders in his Chuck way and stalking off like Heathcliff on the moors. Donato then headed for the puppeteer table where he had a quiet word with Devon and Phil. I saw Devon's jaw set in frustration, and he pulled out his cell phone as he rose from the table. Phil took a different tack.

"I smell bacon!" he proclaimed loudly. "Does anyone else smell bacon?" Then he made a show of sniffing Donato. "That's bacon alright!"

To his credit, Donato didn't react. Phil continued his protests and Devon his phone call, probably to his lawyer, as they followed the detective from the cafeteria, leaving the other performers in shock.

"What's going on?" I heard Larry say. "Marcus, do something!"

The producer stood and rushed toward the exit only to be brought up short by the appearance of Kate. Her expression told me trouble was brewing.

"Marcus," she said and stopped his forward progress with a hand on his arm. Then she scanned the room until she saw me. "Jill, I need you," she called out.

She waited until we were out of earshot of the cafeteria before she told us, "The network is pulling the plug."

"How can they do this now? Right before the anniversary special?" Marcus roared as we hustled back to the production offices. Kate didn't answer until we were in his office with the door shut.

"Because the publicity has been awful. The NYPD is taking a lot of heat because a beloved children's TV star was killed and they haven't had any real leads until now."

"Is that why they've taken Devon and Phil? There's no way they could have done it!" exclaimed Marcus.

"There was some speculation on the part of the public that someone else in the cast had killed Bryce, but when word got out that Mr. Snicklefritz himself was the target, speculation went through the roof. There's a Twitter war over who wants Carl dead, and the flames are being stoked by YouTubers with conspiracy videos. Not to mention the war between Carl haters and supporters. It has been the lead story on *Hollywood Report* for a week, but that's nothing compared to what's happening on the internet."

I was shocked, but I shouldn't have been. Focused on finding a killer, I hadn't paid much attention to the outside world. Kate echoed my thoughts.

"Working on the show, you're in a bubble. I get it. Everyone's focused on getting the job done, but Gingerbread Cottage is on fire as far as the outside world is concerned, and while that might make for good publicity if you were producing a soap opera, it's too sordid for children's television. The network wants to distance itself."

Marcus uttered an oath and buried his head in his hands.

"Isn't there anything we can do?" I asked Kate.

"Not where the network is concerned. They're burning the boats. The anniversary special is off. They're yanking the show immediately."

"What!" Marcus's head came up. "So we don't even get to finish the season?"

"Not with the network, but...," Kate hesitated, biting her lip as if she were making a big decision.

"What?" Marcus was desperate. "Tell me!"

"Bob and I saw this coming, so we began working on a contingency plan. We got NetPix interested."

Marcus perked up. "Really?"

"It's not a done deal, so hold your horses. They might be persuaded to pick up the rest of your season if, and it's a big if, the case is resolved quickly. As a streaming service, they're not as tied to public opinion as the network is, and I think they'd love to lay claim to an iconic show with worldwide appeal. There's still a chance, albeit small."

"Okay," breathed Marcus. It was a lot to take in, and he suddenly looked all of his sixty-something years. "I need to speak to that detective."

CHAPTER 17

We didn't see Detective Donato, Devon, or Phil for a couple of hours. Devon returned first with a face like a storm cloud. He walked straight into Marcus's office and closed the door. Unfortunately, the production office was full of people, so I couldn't eavesdrop.

While Marcus and Devon were talking, it was business as usual for everyone else. Marcus had decided not to tell everyone about the cancellation until the next day. He even made sure that people got to record their memories of Bryce for the anniversary special as if it were still happening. We were living on borrowed time, however, because it wouldn't be too long before someone's agent got word of the cancellation and called their client.

Phil finally returned looking about ten years older, and he joined Devon in Marcus's office. Donato reappeared soon after, and he found Kate and me in his makeshift office. He closed the door.

"Well?" I asked.

"Devon sticks to his story. I made him repeat it twenty-five times, and it never altered."

"Oh yeah, I remember." Donato had questioned me once, and by the end, I felt like I was living in the movie *Groundhog Day*. "What about Phil?"

"The night Bryce was killed, he had a meeting with a group of neopagans to plan a winter solstice celebration. Afterwards, he said he was, and I quote, 'unwinding with my lady.' I've already got someone checking his story."

"So who's next?" asked Kate. "We've got to keep this investigation moving because finding Bryce's killer is the only chance we have of saving this show." Kate filled Donato in on the happenings at the network.

"I want to talk to that PA, Chuck," Donato decided.

"I'll get him," I volunteered. "He and I are friends, of a sort."

I went to The Pen and found Chuck reading a book and waiting for his next errand or assignment.

"Hey, Chuck. Can you come with me?"

"Uh, sure."

On the way back to Donato, we stopped at my cubicle, and I picked up Dominique's album.

I ushered Chuck into Donato's office and gestured to a seat. Kate made a hasty exit, but I entered the office and shut the door behind me. Donato looked confused.

"What are you doing?"

"I'm staying."

"What's going on?" asked the bewildered PA.

"Jill was just leaving," said Donato between clenched teeth. I ignored him and took a seat next to Chuck.

"How long have you known that Carl is your father?" I asked. Then I flipped open the album and laid it across his lap. Surprised, he answered immediately.

"Since my mother was dying. She told me. She wanted me to know I wasn't alone in the world."

I waited for Donato to throw me out for overstepping, but

it didn't happen, maybe because I was getting results. I continued the questioning.

"Did you come to work here so you could get to know your father?"

"No! Why would I want to know that womanizing lowlife? After what he did to my mother?"

"What did he do to your mother?"

"He dropped her for the next blonde bimbo, only when Carl Biersdorf drops you, you don't just lose your relationship. You lose your job!"

"So you came here to get revenge," Donato spoke softly, mirroring my own tone.

"No! I mean, not originally. I wanted to work in this industry. I'm a good puppeteer. The job came open, and I applied. It wasn't until I got here that I thought about…about hurting him in some way." I felt Donato tense. Was an arrest imminent? "I thought about taking video of him acting out and putting it on Twitter, exposing him for the fraud he is. He's supposed to be a role model for kids, but he's the worst person I know."

"You never thought about hurting him in a more physical way, a more permanent way," I prompted. "After your mother sacrificed everything to raise you, after you nursed her through a slow, painful death? You didn't want him dead?"

"No! I could never…My mother thought he walked on water. She raised me on this show and never said a bad word about it or him. I wanted to destroy his reputation, but in the end, I couldn't hurt the thing my mother loved almost as much as she loved me. I couldn't hurt Carl, even though he's a pig, even though he wasn't there for us—"

"I never knew about you!" cried Carl from the doorway. Intent on the interrogation, none of us had heard the door open.

Here it comes, I thought. The "You're not my father"

moment. It wasn't difficult to imagine Carl, the great misanthrope, in a black suit, cape, and helmet, although I must admit it was more *Spaceballs* than *Star Wars* in my imagination. Then Squirrelly-Joe popped up as Salacious Crumb squeaking, "May the Schwartz be with you." I wondered if there was a long-lost sister who had also inherited great puppetry skills. I was brought back to Endor, I mean Earth, when Carl Vader lurched around my chair to get to Chuck and collapsed on his knees beside the boy. "If I had known, it all would have been so different."

Chuck squeezed his eyes shut and turned his head away as if it would block out what was happening. Out of the corner of my eye, I saw Dominique in the doorway with Britney right behind her. I stood and offered Dominique my chair, which she took. I didn't need to be in the middle of family drama.

Carl's hands were floating about in the air looking for a place to land, as if he wanted to touch his son or take his hand, but he knew he couldn't, not yet.

"I'm a selfish bastard. I wish I could've been there for you, and maybe if I'd cared enough about your mother, I would've checked on her and found out about you. But I didn't, to my eternal regret."

"She loved you," whispered Chuck. "To the day she died."

Tears were sliding down their cheeks, and their pain-racked faces looked so similar. Chuck and Chuck in fifty years.

"I thought very highly of your mother, but I would be lying if I said I was in love with her. I wasn't interested in love, hadn't been for a long time." He glanced at Dominique, and I felt Britney stiffen next to me. "But I want that to change. It *has* changed. I want to know you. Will you let me?"

"I don't know." Chuck's eyes were open now, but he still wouldn't look at Carl.

Dominique reached over and laid a hand on Chuck's arm. He tensed but didn't shrug her off.

"Some part of you wanted to come to this show so you could know your father," she whispered. "In all the good ways, you and he are a lot alike. You can show him who he used to be."

There is still good in him. Get out of my head, George Lucas!

Carl's eyes closed as a fresh wave of tears spilled down his cheeks. For a long moment, no one spoke. Then Chuck whispered, "I need to think about it."

"You take all the time you need," Carl whispered back. "I'm not going anywhere."

And then I found that I was crying. My face was completely wet. I looked at Britney and saw her in the same state. I gave her a wobbly smile that she answered with a wry smile of her own.

Then Donato ruined the moment as only he could.

"This is very touching, but it does nothing to change the fact that you're a suspect in the murder of Bryce Camplen and the attempted murder of Carl Biersdorf."

"What?" I shrieked. "Have you been in this room for the last ten minutes, or did you step out for a cup of coffee?"

Donato ignored me completely, which was just as infuriating as calling Chuck a murder suspect.

"Just because you say you were unable to harm Carl's reputation or person doesn't mean you didn't. You had a clear motive and plenty of opportunity, and that makes you a suspect in this case."

Okay, he had a point. Murderers generally denied the accusation. True enough. Even though I couldn't believe Chuck capable of murder, I had to admit that Donato wouldn't be doing his job if he eliminated Chuck from suspicion simply because of a moment of family melodrama.

"I refuse to believe it!" asserted Carl.

"With all due respect," said Donato, "you hardly know this kid."

"A situation I intend to remedy," snapped Carl.

At that, finally, Chuck looked at his father.

~

THE CHARADE of business-as-usual continued the rest of the day. Donato, Kate, and I met with Marcus late in the afternoon once the dust had settled from the Biersdorf family nuclear meltdown.

"Tomorrow is supposed to be rehearsal for the anniversary special," said Marcus once we were seated. "I'll announce the cancellation at tomorrow morning's meeting. I just want everyone to be happy and carefree for one more night."

"Understood," said Donato. "Now I need to inform you that we're looking very carefully at three of your staff regarding the murder. Devon Cauthorne, Phil Rainey, and Charles "Chuck" Cameron. You may want to put them on a leave of absence until the investigation is concluded."

"There's no way," said Marcus. "Devon and Phil, it's just not possible. You don't know them like I know them."

"Then at least send Chuck home," pleaded Donato.

"And have Carl revert to raging diva? Oh no. If I send his son away, he'll be worse than ever. And we have to finish the season."

"Not to mention Chuck is completely innocent," added Kate, winning her a frown from Donato.

"Wait a sec." I was confused. "The show was canceled. What season is there to finish?"

"We still have the budget to finish production," Marcus explained. "And if NetPix wants to pick us up, we must have shows to deliver."

That made sense, but I wondered how hard it would be to motivate a cast and crew to finish a season that might never be aired. It was going to be very depressing around the Gingerbread Cottage for the next few months, but I wouldn't be there to experience it. That thought made me a little sad.

"Now, Kate and Jill, if you'll be so good as to step out of the room, I need to speak to Mr. Sanderson privately." Donato's face was devoid of expression, but he didn't fool me.

This was my punishment for muscling in on Chuck's interrogation. Shut out. Donato was pulling rank because, well, he was the only person who actually had any. Kate looked as ticked off as I was, but a silent conversation passed between us with the disheartening conclusion that there was nothing we could do. Grudgingly, we got up to leave.

"Hey, what's that?" Kate suddenly bent down and peered under Marcus's desk. When she stood up, a pink envelope was in her hand. I had forgotten about Patricia's card, but Kate hadn't. She'd been biding her time.

"This was on the floor," she said as she handed it to Marcus.

"Uh, thanks," he replied as he crumpled it and tossed it in the waste paper basket.

With a pointed look at Donato that screamed, "Don't forget who's been feeding you information," she turned to go, and I followed.

"Well played," I whispered when we reached the hallway.

We left soon after. I was sorely tempted to go back to the pub for some comfort food, but I reminded myself not to let the problems of *The Mr. Snicklefritz Show* derail my plan to be a new and improved Jill. Cooksey Island needed to be fiscally prudent. So I walked home slowly and considered the suspects and what to do next. Chuck was innocent—I knew it in my bones—but I didn't want anyone else at *The Mr. Snicklefritz Show* to be guilty either. They were a frenetic and flawed family but a family nonetheless, and they had been my childhood companions. If they went away, would they take my childhood with them?

Yes, I was in that kind of place.

When I got home, I made myself some tomato soup and a grilled cheese sandwich and flipped channels for a long while before I settled on a movie—*The Island of Dr. Moreau.* With talking animals, strained parent-child relationships, a plethora of prima donnas, and murder, it bore a striking resemblance to *The Mr. Snicklefritz Show.* The film was a steadily intensifying fever dream, much like my experience over the last two weeks. Luckily, it was also boring, and I fell asleep.

I had the Gingerbread Cottage dream again, only this time it was worse. I was rushing frantically about the cottage trying to find a way out, but every time I managed to open a door or window, I was blocked by a half-puppet/half-puppeteer hybrid. Larry Stubbins with a squirrel's nose, ears, and tail leered at me when I opened the front door. The kitchen window led me to Phil Rainey with moose antlers, brown fur, and hooves instead of hands. He menaced me with his antlers, and I slammed the window shut. The living room window opened onto Devon Cauthorne's head atop a sleek, ferret-like marten body. And the back door opened up to the biggest horror of all—Bryce Camplen wearing Jim-Bob's cowboy clothes. He tried to throw a giant black duffel bag over me, but I dodged it and slammed the door.

Running back into the living room, I was stopped in my tracks by the presence of all the puppeteers and puppets, now separate entities, but now the puppets were wandering about of their own free will. The whole gang descended on me, surrounded me, repeating the same question over and over.

"What are we gonna do, Jill?"

"Jill, what are we gonna do?"

Plush paws and human hands poked and patted me as I fought to free myself from the mass of people and puppets. I began lashing out, punching, hitting, scratching, and kicking, but it didn't faze them. Then, just as I thought I would collapse and let them do their worst, they all disappeared, except for Bryce and Jim-Bob.

"What are we gonna do, Jill?" asked Bryce.

And then I woke up, and I knew what we were going to do.

CHAPTER 18

At eight the following morning, the cast and crew gathered in The Pen for what they thought was the beginning of a special day. Nervous excitement tinged the air. Everyone was stoked about the live anniversary special. Bless their hearts. Only a handful of us knew the real story, and we were the only ones not smiling, not bouncing around full of nervous energy.

"I wonder who's directing," said Flavia. "I hope it's someone famous. You know, an anniversary special qualifies us for another Emmy category. Live TV is so cool and so rare these days. This is going to be amazing." My heart sank even further. So many people were about to be so disappointed.

Around the room, the departmental cliques were gathered, the little families within the bigger Snicklefritz clan. Kate and I were a little clique of our own, the outsiders who were trying to save the show. But we had allies, the PAs, and they knew the score. I had told them early that morning when I enlisted their help to catch a killer. Now they were doing an impressive job of acting excited like everyone else. Only Chuck seemed subdued, but that was his normal demeanor, so no one would notice.

The only people missing were Marcus and Carl. As the creators of the show, they were going to make the announcement together. Upon arriving at the studio that morning, my first stop had been Marcus's office. I'd hoped he would reveal something about his conversation with Detective Donato, but I was disappointed. He only had cancellation on his mind.

"I told Carl last night," he said once I'd shut the door. "It was awful. He cried. No, he sobbed, and in front of that security guard."

"He brought private security into your meeting?"

"He doesn't trust me." Marcus held up his hands in defeat.

"Why would Carl think you were trying to kill him?" I feigned ignorance, hoping he would reveal something.

"It's not important. The important thing is, he apologized over and over for his misdeeds. He really believes he brought us to this place, and he's not wrong. I think if we can keep NetPix interested, Carl will be on his best behavior from now on."

"Maybe he can even be convinced to retire."

Marcus sighed. "From your mouth to God's ear."

Now, as we waited for the two men to appear, I watched the performers. The puppeteers were joking around, and Britney was laughing at their hijinks. The private security guards were dotted around the room interacting with the various cliques. Since everyone was in high spirits, Carl and the security guard must have kept the news to themselves. Best behavior indeed.

"I feel like I'm aboard the Titanic," whispered Kate.

"Have we hit the iceberg yet?"

"It's right ahead. Ooh, here it comes!"

Marcus and Carl entered the room, and a host of smiling faces turned towards them like sunflowers following the sun. I didn't envy them one bit.

"Good morning," began Marcus. "I know you were all expecting to rehearse the anniversary special today. But plans have changed."

Smiles faltered, and a low buzz of concern welled up.

"The anniversary special has been canceled," Marcus announced. "But that's not the worst of it. Owing to the bad publicity that has surrounded this show for the last few years, culminating in a PR crisis due to the death of Bryce Camplen and the attempts on Carl's life, the network has canceled *The Mr. Snicklefritz Show*."

The first reaction was stunned silence. It lasted several seconds before chaos erupted, a hundred voices raised in questions and exclamations of dismay. Marcus let them have their moment, and while I waited for it to pass, I wondered about his strategy of ripping off the Band-Aid. I had seen him coddle, flatter, and soothe tempers, but now Marcus chose a different way. Why?

When the mob started to settle, he continued. "There's a very small chance that our show could be picked up by a streaming service, but the odds are against us. We will finish filming this season, but I suggest you start lining up your next jobs right away." He gestured to Carl. "Now our own Mr. Snicklefritz has some things he would like to say to you all."

"Thanks, Marcus." Carl took center stage as Marcus moved off to the side and out of the spotlight. "Some of you may be thinking the situation in which we find ourselves today is my fault. In many ways, you would be right. I've had my fair share of run-ins with the press over the years. But there is someone else who is even more at fault and who is standing in this room right now. Everyone look to your left and to your right. Look at the person standing in front of you and the person standing behind you."

We all followed his directions even though it felt silly. I

looked at Kate on one side and Chuck on the other. But the silly feeling evaporated with Carl's next words.

"Any of those people could be Bryce's murderer. You could be standing next to a cold-blooded killer."

A couple of people giggled nervously as everyone looked around, sizing up their neighbors. I for one got goosebumps because Carl was right. There was a killer among us.

"It's a truth we've tried to ignore. The show has gone on while we ignored the murderous elephant in the room. One of our own killed one of our own while trying to get to me, and he or she is still trying to get to me. Well, to the murderer of Bryce Camplen, I have one thing to say. You may have managed to kill this show, but you will never kill me." And then he flipped the entire room the bird before stalking off to his dressing room followed by his bodyguards. Class act, Carl. Class act.

There were no nervous giggles now. Instead, if I had to guess, I'd say most people were one part ticked off and two parts freaked out. Many were still eyeing their neighbors nervously when Marcus spoke again.

"I know this is a lot to take in, and you probably have a lot of questions. My door will be open. I'm happy to meet with anyone who wants to talk. In the meantime, we'll take an hour break and then resume shooting the current episode. You all have jobs until the end of the season, so we'll do our jobs and show the network and everybody else what professionalism looks like. See you in an hour." With a nod, Marcus headed back to his office. It may have been my imagination, but those steps seemed difficult for him, as if he were trudging through quicksand.

When he was gone, the room came back to life, but an atmosphere of tension and fear permeated The Pen. Hard looks, whispers, and quiet finger-pointing replaced jokes, laughter, and hijinks as the cast and crew began to turn on one another.

"How long before Abigail accuses Goody Proctor?" murmured Kate in my ear.

"I'm just surprised it took this long."

Then, right on cue, Tameasha entered The Pen pushing a dolly full of crates marked with the O'Sullivan logo. Ignoring the curious looks of the cast and crew, she moved through The Pen and down the hall towards the old studio.

"Was that for Carl?" I heard Flavia ask.

"I thought he had quit," remarked a grip.

"I heard he is going to spend the night on the old set to say goodbye to the show. A sort of last fling," whispered Madison.

Excellent, I thought. Phase one of the plan was complete.

THE PLAN, also known as *Operation Puppet-master,* had been hatched in my apartment at three o'clock that morning. After waking from my nightmare, I made coffee and started working my phone. I started with Tameasha, whom I considered the de facto leader of the PAs. It didn't take too much convincing to get her on board.

"Chuck is on the hook for Bryce's murder, but he didn't do it. How would you like to help me prove it and catch the real killer at the same time?"

"I'm in."

"Excellent. Call Madison, Julia, and Chuck. Text me your addresses. I'm sending a car to pick you up." And thus was born the PA Posse.

Next, I called Kate and Surya.

"Jill?" said a sleepy Kate. "What's wrong?"

"There's a killer on the loose. That's what's wrong. But

we're going to stop him. Council of war at my apartment. Dress for the day. You won't be home until tonight."

"Uh, okay. Jill, are you all right?"

"I've had a lot of coffee."

"Okay."

"I'm sending Guadala-Car-a for you."

"I'm up. I'm up. Grabbing clothes. Surya, get your butt out of bed!"

I called Anupa next.

"I'm out and about," she told me. "No need to send a car. I can be at your place in thirty."

"Anupa, what are you doing out and about at three o'clock on a Thursday morning?"

"Recording studios are cheapest to rent in the wee hours of the morning."

Recording studios? I swear my friend had a secret life.

"Anupa, we really need to catch up."

Liz was the hardest to get in touch with. I had to dial her phone several times before she would answer.

"Sorry," she yawned. "I took some valerian to help me sleep. Works like a charm."

"Think you can wake up enough to help us bring a murderer to justice?"

"Some yerba mate should do the trick." Liz had a remedy for everything.

I hung up and dialed 718-MEXICAR. Sixty seconds later, vintage eighties town cars in shades of maroon were speeding across the city doing my bidding. I sat back on my futon and petted my imaginary hairless cat while I fleshed out the remaining details of my plan.

Kate and Surya arrived first. When I opened the door, they were both sporting dark sunglasses and fedoras.

"We're on a mission from God," they said in unison.

"Truer words have never been spoken."

I poured coffee and offered refrigerator cinnamon rolls that I had baked while waiting for them to arrive. Anupa showed up next followed soon after by Liz.

"So what's the plan?" asked Surya as she licked icing off her fingers.

"Patience, Padawan. All in good time. And save some cinnamon rolls for the others."

"The others?" Anupa wrinkled her nose.

The doorbell rang, and I buzzed the others in. I opened the door, and Tameasha, Madison, Julia, and Chuck came face to face with Kate, Surya, Anupa, and Liz.

"PR Posse, meet PA Posse."

"You've been dying to say that, haven't you?" Kate smirked.

"Oh yeah."

After a round of introductions, the pouring of coffee, and the passing of cinnamon rolls, everyone settled on the floor or the futon for the council of war.

"First we all need to get on the same page." I looked at Kate for permission, and she nodded. Then I looked at Chuck. Eventually, he nodded too.

"*The Mr. Snicklefritz Show* has been canceled." I closed my eyes and waited for the uproar. When there wasn't one, I popped open one eye.

"We already know," Tameasha shrugged.

"How could you possibly?"

"There's one AC vent in The Pen where, if you stand on a chair directly under it, you can hear everything being said in Marcus's office," explained Julia.

"We dust that vent a lot," giggled Madison.

Would it have killed them to share their vent with me?

"You don't seem torn up about it," commented Surya.

"We were," said Tameasha. "We went to the pub and drowned our sorrows."

"We've moved on to acceptance," offered Julia solemnly

The resilience of youth.

"Okay," I sighed. "Moving on. The next thing you need to know is Chuck is Carl's son."

"We know that too," said Tameasha matter-of-factly. "Is there more coffee?"

"I'll get it," offered Liz.

"Hold up," said Chuck. "You know?"

The girls had the good grace to look sheepish.

"There's another vent in The Pen, and if you stand under it, you can hear what's being said in the office that police detective has been using," explained Madison. "Sorry. We figured you would tell us when you were ready."

"Okay, okay." I dragged my fingers through my hair, forgetting they were covered in icing I had yet to lick off. Gross. "What else do you know?"

"Let's see," began Tameasha. "Marcus and Patricia are headed for divorce court. Phil has a gambling problem." She ticked off the items on her fingers.

"Devon and Phil were seriously ticked off to be hauled to the police station for questioning," inserted Julia. "They're thinking of suing."

"Flavia's dating one of the new security guys," offered Madison.

"Don't forget Britney," put in Julia. "She's jealous now that Dominique is hanging around more."

"The art department is planning a walkout over the new digital set," added Chuck. "Although that might not happen now that the show has been canceled."

"Anything else?" I asked.

"I don't think so," said Tameasha.

"Yeah, I think that's it," agreed Madison.

I blew out a sigh.

"Okay, now that we're all on the same page..." I waited for someone to contradict me. When no one did, I continued.

"We need to clear Chuck's name. He had motive and opportunity. The only thing Detective Donato doesn't have is evidence. If he finds a fingerprint, anything, I think he'll arrest Chuck."

"How come you're so sure I didn't do it?" he asked.

I thought about the question. Why was I so sure? I couldn't say.

"Because my gut tells me you didn't do it."

"So does mine," piped up Madison loyally.

"Mine too," said Julia.

"Me too," Tameasha nodded sharply.

"Well, my gut tells me nothing because I don't know you," Surya cut in. "But I trust Jill. She's going out on a limb for you, we all are, so don't screw it up."

Chuck nodded. I think he was a little afraid of Surya. Probably a good thing.

"Let's talk about the actual suspects," I said, moving us forward. "Devon Cauthorne needed a promotion badly. He's in debt and barely holding onto his house. Phil and Larry were afraid Carl's behavior would cost them the show and their jobs. Phil has been bleeding money due to his gambling problem. Carl is holding something over Marcus's head to hold onto his job and maintain a modicum of control over the production. Patricia, we believe, has been holding the same information over Marcus's head to hold onto her marriage and is afraid Carl will take away her leverage."

"Don't forget Princess Gretel Number Nine," added Surya.

"Oh yeah, PG Number Nine has a tell-all book coming out soon. It's less likely but still possible that she tried to kill Carl to boost book sales."

"That seems a bit extreme," protested Liz.

"You haven't met Number Nine," countered Chuck. "She's a head case."

"The killer could be any of these people," I affirmed. "We

need to lure the killer out, separate him or her from the herd, and I think I know how we can do it."

"We're going to set a trap!" exclaimed Anupa as she clapped her hands giddily.

"Yes, with Carl as the bait. We'll make everyone think that Carl is alone on the old set, providing the perfect opportunity for attack."

"What about the security guards?" asked Madison. "Won't they discourage the killer from making a move?"

I looked at Kate. "Not if Kate sends them home. Her company hired them. She can fire them, or at least make people think she has."

Kate nodded in understanding.

"But with the show's cancellation, some of these motives disappear," Anupa challenged. "The puppeteers are all out of a job. Carl's blackmail won't hold up. How can we be sure the killer will take the bait?"

"Because we're going to tell all of them exactly what they want to hear."

FOLLOWING Tameasha's performance with the crates of O'Sullivan's and Madison starting the rumor about Carl spending the night on the set, the team spread out to wreak even more havoc.

Julia was overheard outside the dressing rooms telling Chuck that there was a possible deal with NetPix, but it was contingent upon Carl stepping down, and he had refused. I then fed that fire by relating to Flavia how Carl had been rude to some fans who had stopped him on the street the previous evening and how I was trying to do damage control.

Surya called her friend at PG Number Nine's publisher to let her know the word on the street was that Carl Biersdorf had his own tell-all book in the works, set for a spring release. Kate was overheard talking on her cell phone in the hallway outside Marcus and Patricia's offices about the very same book deal and how her firm was going to handle the publicity.

Kate then gathered all the extra security guards in the middle of The Pen where everyone could see, thanked them, and told them that due to budgetary constraints they would be finished on *The Mr. Snicklefritz Show* at the end of the day.

All of this was accomplished within the hour after Marcus delivered the bad news of the cancellation. Soon rehearsal and filming began, and all we could do was wait.

We didn't have to wait long. It started with Larry complaining about his green suit.

"I swear this thing must have shrunk! Who washed it? I want that person fired. How am I supposed to work in uncomfortable, skin-tight clothing? Stupid green set."

"Calm down!" yelled Phil uncharacteristically. "You won't have to wear it much longer. Remember, we've been canceled." I had never seen a worked-up Phil. He was really starting to lose it.

"Guys, we gotta keep hoping," countered Devon. "There's still a chance we'll be picked up."

"Get your head out of your—" Phil was cut off by Carl's entrance.

"Let's make the best episodes of *The Mr. Snicklefritz Show* the world has ever seen!" he pronounced grandly in a booming voice. "Let's show the haters they can't take us down."

"Whatever," snarked Moose the Moose, now on Phil's arm.

"I'd rather make porn," smirked Squirrelly-Joe. "Where's Princess Gretel?" He looked around and saw Tameasha standing nearby. "I guess you'll have to do."

"You deserve to be canceled!" spat Tameasha, and she stalked off the set.

"Okay, okay. Cool it, everyone! It's time to get to work."

Flavia soon had everyone in hand, but I could still feel the tension on the set throughout the rest of the morning.

Lunchtime was a gloomy affair with lots of muttering and complaining within the cliques. We were sitting with the PAs and trying to look nonchalant. When Carl entered, the whole room went silent, and I was afraid that perhaps we had overdone it and the entire cast and crew were going to assassinate Mr. Snicklefritz Julius Caesar-style. Luckily, he was still flanked by bodyguards whom Kate had instructed on the sly to keep him safe at all costs. I hoped it would be enough.

"I hope Carl survives the day," bleated Kate, echoing my thoughts.

"Should we call it off? Have we gone too far?" There was a note of hysteria in my voice.

"Psst! Pull yourselves together," whispered Julia furiously. "This is for Bryce and for Chuck. Now get a grip!"

"Sorry," Kate whispered.

"My bad," I said and shoved a chocolate chip cookie in my mouth hoping that bravery was a byproduct of serotonin.

Then the unexpected happened, and I nearly choked on the cookie. PG Number Nine strolled into the cafeteria.

"Well, would you look at that?" breathed Chuck.

"She actually took the bait!" Madison sounded giddy. "I really want to fist-bump someone right now."

"I can't believe how well this is going," mused Tameasha. "No offense of course."

"None taken," I replied, and I meant it because I couldn't believe how well the plan was going either.

Number Nine took a seat across from Carl. He looked very surprised to see her. They engaged in conversation that we couldn't hear. Then Carl got a confused look on his face and said something while shaking his head no.

"I don't believe you," said Number Nine loud enough for

everyone to hear. "You always were a selfish scumbag." She stood to leave.

"No, really Carla!" Carl pleaded. Her name was Carla? Carl and Carla? I chuckled low in my throat because I just couldn't help it.

"Save it, Carl. May the best writer win!" Carla flounced out of the cafeteria, leaving Carl looking very perplexed and leaving everyone at our table feeling very pleased with themselves.

"Play it cool. Play it cool," murmured Kate, who was desperately trying not to smile.

"In my head, I am fist-bumping the heck out of all of you right now," said Madison as she made a big show of salting and peppering her meatloaf.

"We're hugging in my head," said Chuck from behind his paperback book.

"It's a full-on rave complete with glow sticks and foam in my head right now," whispered Julia as she furiously scrolled through her Instagram feed.

Me, I shoved a celebratory cookie in my mouth to keep from crowing. Then I choked on some cookie crumbs and Tameasha had to give me the Heimlich, which effectively dampened our spirits.

In the afternoon, Detective Donato showed up, which I should have planned for but hadn't. It was, hopefully, the one hole in the operation. Luckily, Donato and I were on the outs over Chuck's interrogation, so although we said hello, he wasn't asking me for info and I wasn't offering. Still, it was a good thing that the rest of the PR Posse wasn't supposed to arrive until the end of the workday. If Donato saw all of them, he would undoubtedly become suspicious and start asking questions. No, thank you.

Dominique also arrived in the afternoon. Instead of heading for Carl, however, she made a beeline for Chuck, whom she pulled aside for a quiet word. Because I couldn't hear what was being said, I watched them carefully. Chuck was polite. Dominique was friendly. Chuck seemed to listen carefully to what she was saying, and when she was done, he said something in reply and nodded in the affirmative. Dominique smiled and patted him on the arm. Then she walked over to where Britney was watching the rehearsal and greeted her. Britney gave her a tight smile. Then Dominique said something that took Britney by surprise, but I think in a good way. Britney also nodded in the affirmative. Dominique gave her arm a little pat and walked out of the studio. Britney's gaze followed her all the way to the door, her brow wrinkled as if she didn't understand what had just happened. I hastened over to Chuck

"What was that all about?"

"Dominique invited me to have dinner at her house this weekend."

"Just you and Dominique?"

"No. Carl and Britney too. She said her house could be neutral ground where Carl and I could get to know each other."

Dominique was really invested in reuniting Carl with his son. I wondered why.

"What did you say?"

Chuck blushed a little and looked at his shoes.

"I said yes."

Well done, Dominique.

"That's great," I said, and Chuck finally looked at me.

"Really?"

"Really."

CHAPTER 19

When filming wrapped for the day at six o'clock, Donato took his leave. Then the security woodcutters made a show of leaving the studio, although they had instructions to go around to the loading dock where Kate would later meet them with Carl so they could escort him home.

We didn't want Carl to know about Operation Puppetmaster because we thought he might object to Chuck putting himself at risk. Moreover, after his speech to the cast and crew, punctuated by his middle finger, we thought he might insist on being part of the operation. If he got hurt, it would totally defeat the purpose. Plus, there was no room on this Ocean's Nine team for a diva. Also, if I'm honest, if we were wrong about Chuck, and I was certain we weren't, then we didn't want to put Carl in harm's way. Mr. Snicklefritz needed to go home.

I knocked on Carl's dressing room door.

"Enter!"

Kate and I did. I scanned the room and was glad to find him

alone. Kate locked the door behind us, which made Carl a little nervous.

"What's going on?" he demanded.

"We have intel that there's a credible threat on your life. It may go down tonight," said Kate.

Carl blanched. "But Detective Donato didn't say anything about it."

"The tip just came in," I responded smoothly. "After he left. He called to let us know so we could make sure you were safe."

"But my security is gone!"

"We've rehired them," Kate assured him. "In a little while, we'll escort you to the loading dock where the team will be waiting to escort you home. We don't want anyone to know when you leave. It will be safer that way."

"In the meantime," I added, "you need to stay in this dressing room with the door locked. Let no one in. Not even Britney. If anyone knocks, tell them you want to be alone."

"I'll stay with you until it's time to leave," said Kate.

"Okay. Whatever you say." Carl nodded enthusiastically. "You wouldn't by any chance have a drink on you?"

I gave him a stern look, the one my landlady and my mother often employed on me.

"Just kidding!" Carl faked a laugh. I took my leave, and I heard Kate lock the door behind me.

I walked down the corridor past the other dressing rooms. Phil and Larry's doors were closed. Devon's was open, and he was packing up his backpack to leave.

"Goodnight, Devon," I called as I walked past.

"Goodnight!" I heard him reply.

When I reached the puppet room, I ducked inside, flipped off the lights, and closed the door, leaving only a crack through which I could see the dressing rooms. I sat on the floor in the dark and waited. Two minutes later, Devon came out of his dressing room. He turned off the lights and shut the door before walking past my position toward the little studio and ultimately the lobby. I wondered how long it would take the other puppeteers to leave.

What if they don't leave?

And that's when I fell into the second hole in my plan. If the puppeteers didn't leave—say, if they were waiting around to kill Carl—then how were we supposed to get Carl safely out of the studio while maintaining the illusion that he was still there getting sloshed on the set? Why had I assumed the murderer would go away and then come back?

Because the murderer would want to cover his or her tracks, that's why. I needed to believe the killer would at least act like he or she was leaving and then return or hide somewhere in the building. The arrival of Britney at Carl's door hit the pause button on my worries. She tried the knob and frowned when she found it locked.

"Hey baby, it's me!"

"Go away. I want to be alone."

"Wouldn't it be more fun to be alone together?"

"I'm not in the mood, Brit."

"Since when, baby? My Carl is always in the mood," she purred through the door.

"Not tonight!"

Britney's lips pursed in a pout. Then she opened her mouth to say something else, but Dominique appeared behind her.

"What's going on with Carl?" asked Dominique.

Britney looked annoyed. "He says he wants to be alone." She crossed her arms defensively.

"Carl," called Dominique. "It's Dom. I thought you might want some company. You okay?"

"I just want to be alone," he responded, sticking to the script.

"You sure?"

"I'm sure."

"Okay, just promise me you won't make any bad choices tonight." Dominique sounded like Carl's mother, and Britney rolled her eyes behind the other woman's back.

"I promise."

"Okay then. Goodnight." Dominique turned to Britney.

"I guess he wants to be alone."

"Yep." Britney's tone was clipped, and her smile didn't reach her eyes.

"Want to get some dinner?" asked Dominique out of the blue. Britney was clearly taken by surprise.

"Um…"

"It's just, I have some insight regarding Carl," explained the older woman. "It might be helpful."

Aca-awkward! I was cringing at the scene between Carl's first love and his current amour. Was Dominique seriously offering relationship advice to Britney Spiers? Was she really trying to help? Evidently Britney thought so because she said, "Okay," and the women left together. I was still trying to make sense of what I'd witnessed when Larry left his dressing room and headed toward the lobby. A few minutes later, Phil did too. Finally! Now it was time to call in the Posse and prepare for the showdown at the puppet corral.

I retrieved Kate and Carl, and as we headed for the loading dock, I texted Liz, Surya, and Anupa that the coast was clear. At the dock, we handed Carl over to the security team and let the Posse into the building.

"Who are these people?" Carl was no fool. "What's going on?"

"Nothing for you to lose sleep over," I said. "Public relations matters. Good night."

Security escorted Carl to a waiting SUV. Before they could bundle him inside, he gave us one last appraising look. Yeah, he was no fool.

We made our way back to the old studio with me going first

and texting the Posse when the coast was clear. I didn't know who might still be around, for legitimate reasons or to kill Carl, and we needed to get into position before any action began. We met up with the PA Posse in the puppet room. There was no time for pleasantries, but we didn't need them.

"Is everyone still clear on the plan? Speak now if you have questions."

"What happens if no one shows up to kill Carl?" asked Julia.

"Then we're no worse off than we are now," said Kate pragmatically.

"What happens if things get out of hand?" asked Tameasha.

"Then we'll call 911," I replied. "Everyone, make sure your phones are handy, but silence them."

"And Jill's got a gun in her purse," said Anupa excitedly. I think she meant to be reassuring, but four sets of wide eyes indicated the opposite.

"I'm not planning to fire it," I quickly reassured the PAs. "I could always use it to threaten someone if I have to."

Their eyes were still wide.

"Completely last resort."

Eyes like saucers.

"And it's not even loaded," I lied.

They finally relaxed.

With question and answer time over, Tameasha handed out wireless headsets to everyone. They would allow us to communicate wherever we were on the set. Then she and Anupa headed to the control room to get the cameras running and recording so we could have a record of whatever went down tonight.

Meanwhile, Liz and Surya were stuffing Carl's costume with whatever they could find in the puppet room to create a decoy Carl lying on the sofa in the Gingerbread Cottage living room, an open bottle of O'Sullivan's on the table next to him, and an extra crate of the stuff standing by for good measure.

Chuck, Madison, and Julia took positions under the set with puppets. Once the Snickle-decoy was done, Liz and Surya joined Anupa in the control room. Then Tameasha took her place with her puppet under the set, and Kate hid near the main door. Her job was to let us know over the headset if anyone entered the set from that direction and who it was. Once everyone was in position, I joined my Posse in the control room where I had a good view of the door leading to the dressing rooms, so I could inform the team who had entered.

Anupa had things well in hand in the control room, no surprise, thanks in part to her time in secret recording studios and to Tameasha, who seemed to know how to do everything. That was the way to stay employed in this business, I was learning. Anupa had music cued should we need it, the puppeteer mics were hot, and the cameras were running and recording to the hard drive. She dimmed the lights in the studio to the point that the Snickle-decoy looked real to the untrained eye. With Anupa, Liz, and Surya monitoring the different systems and everyone in place, we were ready to go. Now all we could do was wait.

CHAPTER 20

"Carl? It's Patty. Can we talk?"

We didn't have to wait long. Patricia entered the studio so quietly that we almost didn't notice her. She moved slowly and tentatively, and there was a tear in her voice. I could tell she was more than nervous about approaching Carl. She seemed downright scared.

"Chuck," I said into my mic. "Make some Carl noises. Keep her talking."

Chuck grunted, which seemed to satisfy Patricia.

"I know you've never been fond of me. But the truth is, I made a huge sacrifice for you and Marcus many years ago. It cost me my job and my reputation, but I did it for you and for him. And this is how you repay me?"

"It's going down," said Surya. "Should I call 911?"

"I don't think so," said Liz. "She doesn't have a weapon."

"That we can see," countered Surya.

"Just hold off," I ordered. "Let's hear what she says."

"I thought you would mention it in an interview, how the show wasn't as educational as we claimed, how I padded the report, and how you used my expertise as a shield. Because you did use me, Carl. You both did. I thought there might be an article, a segment on *Hollywood Report,* but we could weather that. When the next celebrity scandal hit, we would be old news.

"But a book! Book tours, talk shows, radio interviews, lots of quotable material for article after article. We'll be dragged through the mud, but you'll make a mint. How can you live with yourself knowing you'll profit off the misery of your friends and colleagues?"

Whoa! Our fictitious tell-all book was lighter fluid, and the smoldering tensions in the Carl-Marcus-Patricia triangle were becoming a four-alarm fire.

"I was worried about my marriage. I know Marcus only married me out of a sense of obligation, but I thought my love would be enough for both of us. But this is so much bigger now than just my marriage. Can't you see that?"

"Chuck! Sounds!" I whispered into my mic.

"Humph!" managed Chuck.

"Oh, Carl!" Patricia dissolved into tears. "How can you be so cruel? It would have been better if someone had killed you! You're hateful!"

With that, she ran from the studio. Everyone let out the collective breath we were holding, which wasn't really pleasant to hear through the headset.

"So can we mark Patricia off the suspect list?" Tameasha asked.

"Looks that way," I replied.

"I'm so glad I didn't dial 911," breathed Surya.

"She could always come back with a flamethrower," countered Anupa.

"Quiet!" whispered Kate. "Marcus just entered the studio.

Marcus strode into the middle of the space and paused when he saw "Carl" lying on the sofa.

"I just saw Patricia. She was hysterical. Thanks for that."

"Humph," grunted Chuck.

"You're a cold bastard, Carl, but I didn't come here to fight. I thought maybe we could sit and have a drink together. It's been a long time since we did that." He waited for a reply, but there was no sound from Chuck. What could he say? He couldn't encourage Marcus to come have a drink. That would be suicide.

"No? Okay, then I have something to say."

Marcus began pacing and gathered his thoughts for a moment before he spoke.

"I think you're making a big mistake with this book. You haven't thought it through. It could destroy everything we've done. Yes, people already know about your women and your drinking. You've been in the news enough that it's not going to be a surprise. But to come right out and tell people—that's different from hearing it second hand from a reporter. If you own it, you can never go back."

Marcus was making great sense from a PR perspective. If the book had been real, I would have counseled Carl to take his advice.

"It's the legacy of the show I'm more concerned with. Yeah, we fudged the analysis to get the network to pick us up. So what? We were still a good show, an entertaining show. And it was just those first couple of years. We made changes. We found our way. Why do we have to destroy our legacy over something that happened so long ago? As much as I'd like to say it's water under the bridge, I know that it will cast doubt over everything we've done since then. Don't you care about that? Don't you?"

Marcus suddenly switched direction, mounting the set and heading straight for Carl.

"Puppets up!" I hissed into the mic, but we were too late.

"Answer me, Carl!" He shook the Snickle-decoy and recoiled in horror when he met only stuffing.

"Wha-? Wha-?" Not only had the cat got Marcus's tongue, but he was near to apoplexy.

Then the puppets popped up.

"It's not really Carl," said Moose.

Marcus clutched his chest, staggered backward, and fell off the raised set onto the studio floor. Luckily, he landed on his butt. I was out of the control room in a flash. Kate and I both rushed to Marcus.

"Are you okay?" I asked.

"What were you going to do to Carl?" demanded Kate.

"What did I just see? What's going on?" I don't think the pain of falling on a concrete floor had even registered. Marcus was pale as a sheet and breathing funny.

"Can you walk?" asked Kate.

I felt Marcus's legs for any breaks, but I didn't find any.

"I think he's okay."

"I hope he didn't break a hip."

"We'll find out in a moment."

We managed to haul the stunned Marcus to his feet

"I'm getting back in position," said Kate. "We don't know who could show up next."

I talked soothingly to a babbling Marcus as I walked him to the control room.

"It's okay. I'll explain everything. Don't worry. Everything's fine."

When we got to the control room, Liz took charge.

"You've had a nasty shock. I'm just going to apply this lavender essential oil to your temples. Breathe in and out slowly, and it should help calm your nerves."

"What have you done to Carl?" he squeaked.

"That's our decoy. Carl is safe and sound at home. Now breathe in nice and deep."

Marcus did as he was told because it was hard to refuse Liz, and soon his reason returned.

"So this is a trap?"

I nodded. "For Bryce's killer. For whoever is trying to kill Carl."

Kate's voice crackled over the headsets.

"Flavia has just entered the studio. Repeat. Flavia has entered the studio."

That was unexpected. She certainly had a motive to kill Bryce, but I had dismissed her when we found out that Carl was the real target. What was Flavia doing here? I watched as the floor director came into view and stopped a few feet from the set.

"I didn't want to believe it." Her voice trembled with rage. "When I heard about your plan to get wasted 'for old times sake,' I couldn't believe my ears. I thought, 'He can't be that stupid.' I never thought you'd put the show in jeopardy AGAIN, not after everything that's happened. Are you listening to me, Carl?"

Chuck made a dismissive noise that enraged Flavia.

"You're playing with people's lives, you imbecile! If you go back to your old ways, NetPix will never pick up the show! We'll be out on our ears! I may be directing a show right now that no one will ever see! Do you have any idea how that feels? Can't you think about someone else for a change?"

Flavia clenched her fists, and her body tensed until she was vibrating. For a moment, I thought she was going to charge the set. But then the vibrating changed to sobs. Flavia's shoulder slumped as the fight went out of her.

"I hope you drink yourself to death, you piece of scum." With that parting shot, Flavia ran from the studio.

We were silent in the control room, processing the emotion we had just witnessed.

"We had better catch a killer tonight," whispered Liz. "Our trap is causing a lot of heartache."

My sweet and sensitive friend was right, and I felt awful. If

Bryce's killer didn't show, we would need to come clean about the rumors we'd spread. I'd hoped the plan would fix everything, but now I could see a different outcome that filled me with regret. If we didn't catch the murderer and clear Chuck's name, we would have done a lot of damage for nothing. And who did I think I was? A detective? Hardly. Owning a gun and being too nosy for my own good didn't make me a private investigator. More like a nuisance. Yes, I had good intentions, but clearly I didn't have the skills needed to close this case. I was making things worse.

I was on the verge of bringing the whole operation to a swift end when Kate's voice crackled on the headset.

"Jill, do you have eyes on the other entrance? I think I saw movement."

"Hell's bells!" I ran to the window, and sure enough, we had another visitor.

"Larry has entered the studio from the dressing rooms," I informed the team.

We watched Larry approach the set with heavy steps, like a man marching reluctantly to the gallows. I wondered what emotional bombshell he would drop. How had our lies affected him? I braced myself to hear how else I had wrecked someone's life.

Then I noticed he was dragging something behind him, but the dim light made it difficult to see. When one of the studio lights glinted off polished steel, I got goosebumps.

"He has a sword. I repeat, he has a sword."

"Not the Morgul blade?" whispered Madison.

"Yes, the very same."

"Frodo never fully recovered from its dark magic."

"That's not relevant right now. Reality people. Now is not the time to fly our nerd flags. Madison, we need Joe. Can you reposition near the grandfather clock?"

Larry had paused near the far left part of the set, which

included the front door and foyer of Gingerbread Cottage. If we could keep him there, he might not realize that Carl was a dummy.

"Roger that. On the move."

"Good. We considered this possibility. Don't deviate from the plan. If it doesn't work, get out of there. Don't risk your life for a Snickle-decoy."

"I should go out there and reason with him before he does anything stupid," said Marcus.

"Don't you dare!" Surya put a hand on his chest to keep him in his seat. "If he's the killer, we need to know it. Don't ruin everything!" Marcus stayed put, but I could tell he didn't like it.

Out on the studio floor, Larry began to mount the hidden steps that led up onto the set, putting him right by the open front door and facing the grandfather clock. When Squirrelly-Joe popped up in front of him, he dropped the sword, which clanged to the floor.

"Whatcha doin', Larry?"

The only sign that Larry was confused was a hand raised briefly to his temple.

"J-Joe, you know what I'm doing. We talked about this. You said we should do it."

"*Weeell,* now I'm not so sure."

"But, Joe, we have to save the show. You said it yourself. We'll never get another job. You've been a very bad squirrel."

"I'm not bad. I'm just misunderstood. No one gets me." Madison was improvising well.

"That's right. No one gets us...except Princess Gretel."

"Get him to talk about Princess Gretel," I whispered furiously into the mic.

"Uh, yeah, Princess Gretel. Beautiful Princess Gretel. What does she understand...about us...exactly?"

"That we're handsome and funny and talented. That we're her soulmate."

"But what about Mr.—"

"PG just entered the studio," Kate whispered frantically.

"Abort Joe!" I commanded. Immediately, Squirrelly-Joe vanished into the bowels of the set. Larry swayed a bit and clutched his head. The collision of reality and imagination was taking a toll and keeping him off balance. Good, I thought.

Britney moved cautiously toward the set, taking in the tableau before her.

"What are you doing, Larry?" she asked as she moved slowly, catlike toward the set. She climbed the stairs silently until she was standing right behind him.

"I was just talking to Joe."

"Joe knows what has to be done, baby," she soothed and ran her hand gently through his hair. Larry shivered and then relaxed, closing his eyes.

"Joe isn't so sure anymore," he breathed.

Britney continued to stroke his hair, leaning in close and pressing her body against him.

"Of course he's sure," she breathed into his ear. "He wants you to be successful. He wants me to be successful. And he wants us all to be together. I love you, Larry, and I love Joe. Haven't I proven it to both of you?"

I didn't want to know what that meant.

"Yes." Larry sighed contentedly. He was putty in her hands.

"Then finish him. When he's gone, the show will go on. You and Joe and I will keep our home here in Gingerbread Cottage. We'll be happy here, forever. If you don't, he'll just toss me aside like he did all the others. Is that what you want?"

"No!"

"Don't you love me?"

"You know I do."

Never breaking contact, she slid around to face Larry and ran her hand sensuously across his chest as she leaned in and brushed his lips with her own.

"Then finish this so we can be together."

"Together," he breathed and opened his eyes. Then he picked up the sword and advanced towards "Carl." Behind him, Britney crossed her arms and cocked a hip. Her body language said it all. She was in control and about to get exactly what she wanted.

Larry stopped at the sofa and raised the Morgul Blade high above his head.

"What are you doing?" Carl Biersdorf rushed onto the set from the left. Captivated by the scene before me, I hadn't been keeping watch. Britney and Larry spun around, and for a moment, their minds failed to make sense of what they were seeing. Two Carls?

My mind was either working overtime or not at all.

"Cue the music!" I commanded.

The studio was instantly filled with strains of "The Booger Song." The puppets all popped up and began to sing, this time with Julia on disembodied nose. Now Britney and Larry were really caught off guard. Britney recovered first and tried to make a break for it past Carl, but he caught her in his arms where she struggled furiously. I didn't know how long he could hold on to a woman forty years his junior. Larry, thoroughly spooked, began slashing at the air with his Morgul blade. He was aiming for the puppets, but they had retreated behind the sofa. Larry, in a feat of daring or desperation, leaped onto the sofa right on top of the Snickle-decoy and began hacking away at the boogery nose. I heard Julia squeal as her puppet came under attack. Lucky for her, the nose was mounted on a pole. If her arm had been in it, it would already have been broken for sure. That's when I knew somebody was going to get hurt.

"Abort! Abort!" I yelled into the mic as I rummaged through my bag for my pistol. When my hand clasped cold steel, I took off running out of the control room.

"Jill, wait!" cried Marcus, but I was committed. There was

no other way. As I flew down the stairs to the studio floor, Britney broke free of Carl and ran towards the dressing rooms.

"Leave her alone!" snarled Chuck. He was trying to come between Larry and Julia, whose once ample nose puppet now resembled a rhinoplasty gone wrong.

"My son!" roared Carl, and he rampaged towards Larry, who turned away from the puppets, shifted the sword in his hands for a better grip, and prepared to fight.

Carl was unarmed. Larry had a Morgul blade. Death was imminent. I did the only thing I could. I fired.

CHAPTER 21

The bullet hit Larry's sword arm, and both the blade and Larry fell to the ground.

I told you I could shoot.

Before I could get to Larry to render first aid, Carl's security team arrived from one corridor with Britney in tow while Donato and a significant portion of the NYPD arrived from the other. Immediately I put my gun down and held up my arms. A uniform stepped behind me, grabbed one of my arms, and started to cuff me. That's when all hell really broke loose.

"Get your hands off her!" bellowed Carl. "She saved my life!"

"She did!" hollered Marcus as he staggered out of the control room. "She's a hero!"

"Yeah, a hero!"

Puppets came out of nowhere, joined by my PR Posse. Everyone was yelling. Eventually, it turned into a chant: "Let her go! Let her go! Let her go!" The other cops converged. I thought there was going to be a riot.

Thankfully, Donato stepped in.

"We can do without the cuffs!" he yelled.

The officer attempting to cuff me, who was now cornered by some very scary-looking puppets, thanks to Larry hacking off some of their bits and pieces, was very grateful.

"You and your mother," snarked Donato with a massive eye roll. Mama had a history of discharging firearms in the City of New York. She was going to be so proud.

"I have a permit."

Donato sighed in relief.

"Thank heaven for small favors."

Finally, someone stopped "The Booger Song." Yes, it had been playing the whole time and has since shown up regularly in my nightmares. With blessed silence restored and the NYPD hauling Britney to the slammer and Larry to the hospital, we all hastened to tell the story, taking it in turns to explain the plan and how it had gone down.

"It was all Jill's idea," boasted Kate proudly

"I have no doubt," Donato responded dryly.

"It took all of us!" I asserted. "There were so many variables because we didn't know who was going to turn up. And we didn't want to put Carl in any danger. That's why we lied to get him away." I shot a critical look at Mr. Snicklefritz.

"I knew you were up to something," said Carl unapologetically. "So I called Detective Donato to ask about the threat on my life. He didn't know what I was talking about. That's when I snuck out of the house."

"Luckily, we saw him climbing out the bathroom window and gave chase," added the head security guard.

"We knew Larry was worried about his job security," I continued, "what with the PR nightmare that was Carl Biersdorf. No offense Carl."

"That was the old Carl, so none taken."

"But we thought he might have been working with Phil, who co-authored the letter of complaint against Carl. We had no idea he was working with Britney."

"In reality, she's been working him, convincing him to kill Carl to save his job and hers," put in Surya.

"She didn't want to go the way of all the other Princess Gretels," remarked Liz.

"No Princess Gretel lasts more than two years," I explained. "She was past her expiration date." I remembered the round-table when the others had teased her about it. "Tick tock" they had said. At any moment she expected to lose her relationship and her job. How desperate must she have felt to resort to murder?

"But how did she and Larry get together?" asked Anupa.

"I think I can answer that," said Carl. "Larry always had a little crush on Britney. She said she thought it was sweet."

"An isolated loner with a crush on her. Britney couldn't have chosen a better patsy to manipulate. I feel bad for him," offered Liz sympathetically.

"Don't!" exclaimed Madison, Tameasha, Julia, and I all at the same time. Normally that would have made us giggle, but not this time.

"But Britney could have gotten another job," said Kate. "She's young and beautiful. Losing your job isn't the end of the world. I don't get the need to kill."

"She and Larry both worried about being hired," explained Carl. "Britney, like many of us, made some, er, questionable choices in her youth."

Her youth? Like last week?

Then two more pieces of the puzzle clicked together for me.

"Detective, I think you may find some evidence of those poor choices in a stack of DVDs in Larry's dressing room. It would also reinforce the link between Larry and Britney and somewhat explain his devotion to her." Imagine if the subject of your fantasies showed up one day and became a fixture in your world. A healthy person would be thrown temporarily.

Someone on the edge of madness might lose their grip on reality altogether.

Girls Gone Crazy? The title was prophetic.

"Oh! Those kinds of choices," said Julia knowingly once the penny dropped.

I looked at the PAs, four beautiful, talented young people, and I hoped they were learning some lessons from all of this. I was tempted to hold a class later just to make sure.

Then I looked at my Posse. In our late twenties, we were just six or seven years older than the PAs, but those few years held a lifetime of experience that made all the difference. I offered up a silent prayer of thanks that we had navigated our twenties, our youth, without too much disaster.

"Okay," said Donato, cutting off our explanations. "I have the basic rundown, but we're gonna have to go through it all again."

A variety of moans and groans filled the air.

"I have a better idea," said Anupa with a wicked grin.

Ten minutes later, we were all crowded into the control room. The PAs had wrangled more chairs from the production offices, and the Posse and I had raided the craft services closet with Marcus's blessing. On a row of monitors in front of us, the evening played from start to finish and from three different angles.

"Ooh! Ooh! I love this part. Wait for it!" crowed Tameasha.

"I thought maybe we could sit and have a drink together. It's been a long time since we did that," said Marcus to the Snickle-decoy. He paused for a reply. "No? Okay, then I have something to say."

The control room burst into laughter.

"You totally thought that was really Carl!" hooted Tameasha.

"I can't breathe!" gasped Julia between belly laughs.

"I can't believe how funny this is!" chortled Marcus. Carl slapped him good-naturedly on the back.

One of the uniforms stepped forward to speak to Donato.

"Sir, this is highly unorthodox."

"Just go with it," he said without looking away from the monitor. Just then Martin popped up, scared Marcus, and he fell off the set and onto his butt on three different screens. We all screamed with laughter, Donato included.

"This has to go in the blooper reel!" Madison exclaimed.

I held a bowl under Donato's nose.

"Peanut butter cup?"

"Oh yeah!" He grabbed a handful, and, wonder of wonders, he smiled at me. "Thank you. Really."

Well, hush my mouth!

"You're very welcome."

CHAPTER 22

The butterflies in my stomach were starting to resemble a swarm of bees as I stood outside the front door. Stars and garters! How had I come to this place? Was this really happening? I reached up and adjusted my crown, which was much heavier than expected. Then I took a deep breath to steady my nerves.

I could hear Mr. Snicklefritz talking to Martin, Moose, and Joe. My cue was coming up.

I watched Tameasha carefully. She raised her finger, held it in place for a moment, then pointed at me. I knocked on the door to Gingerbread Cottage. It opened to reveal Mr. Snicklefritz surrounded by his forest companions.

"It's Princess Gretel!" exclaimed Mr. Snicklefritz, and he doffed his woodcutter's cap and bowed to me. Gathering my skirts, I sailed through the doorway and into television history.

Three days ago, I had been plain old Jill Cooksey hatching a plot to catch a killer that, amazingly, worked. The PR Posse and the PA Posse had joined forces with incredible results, delivering the two killers to Detective Donato with a minimum of bloodshed, no further deaths, and a whole lot of laughs. That had to be a first for a murder investigation. And while Britney had denied everything, even in the face of video evidence, Larry had broken down almost immediately and spilled his guts. Larry's confession and the video would no doubt assure two convictions.

Despite Anupa's brilliant idea to replay the entire incident for Donato and the NYPD, it hadn't completely forestalled questioning. We still had to give statements, yada yada yada, and it was nearly midnight by the time Donato let us go. Still, we were hopped up on success and peanut butter cups, so instead of heading home, we migrated around the corner to the Irish pub where we pushed a bunch of tables together.

"Drinks are on the show!" announced Marcus, and we all roared our approval.

By the time the first round was delivered to our banqueting table, Dominique and Patricia had joined us. Patricia, or Patty as she was now telling us to call her, was so relieved that there was no tell-all book in the offing that she burst into tears. She and Dominique sat at one end of the table with Marcus and Carl, and I could imagine that it was a bit like old times for them. The four people who had begun a children's TV classic, completely unaware of the impact it would have on millions of kids and adults for decades to come. At one point, Dominique caught my eye and gestured to the bar. We met there a moment later.

"I owe you a debt. You saved Carl and you exonerated his son." She raised her glass to me and took a sip.

"When did you know?"

"That Charles was Carl's son? The moment I saw him. I couldn't believe Carl himself hadn't seen it, or Marcus or Phil. It was like being transported back in time."

"Carl seems thoroughly taken with Chuck." He was holding forth for his son, recounting some story, and when Chuck laughed, Carl's face lit up like a candle.

"Carl is his old self when Chuck is around. Again, I have you to thank for that."

"I think Britney may be more deserving of your thanks. It took someone trying to kill him to make Carl take stock of his life. I'm just surprised it took thirty years."

"You and me both. But you're too modest."

"I heard you when you offered Britney advice about Carl. Why?"

"Because I want him to be happy."

"Because you still love him."

Dominique smiled sadly and studied her drink.

"I love who he used to be. If he can be that person again…"

"What happened all those years ago?"

For a moment she didn't answer, and I was afraid I had overstepped.

"I think you figured out that Patty fudged the educational assessment of the show."

I nodded.

"I was furious. I saw how in love she was with Marcus. He was using her, and Carl was standing by and letting it happen."

"But why not just change the show? Why lie?"

"Because the episodes were already written. Some footage was already in the can. To change the show would have meant delaying a season and possibly being dropped by the network. All their dreams were about to come true. They weren't going to give up just because the FCC had grown a conscience."

"Sounds like you've had a change of heart."

"Not really. It was wrong, but time gives you greater understanding and more compassion for people's bad choices. We all make them to various degrees. We should never forget that. Anyway, I gave Carl an ultimatum, and the rest is history. I left, and he spiraled."

"You don't blame yourself? For his choices?"

"Oh yes," she smiled bitterly at me. "That's something else

time gives you, a greater understanding of the impact you've had on the people around you, for good or for ill."

I wanted to absorb her words because they felt like wisdom. The PAs weren't the only people who could learn. I looked at my old friends and new friends sitting at the table and hoped that my impact on them would be half as positive as theirs had been on me. And then I thought of Bryce, and I hoped that I had earned my redemption.

"Well, perhaps you have a second chance now." I motioned to Carl, who was fist-bumping with Chuck over some shared joke. Dominique smiled, a real smile without bitterness.

"Maybe." She squeezed my hand and headed back to the table.

We closed the bar at two after loudly singing several Snicklefritz classics, the PAs in full puppet voice.

"You guys are incredible!" said Marcus for about the fifteenth time. "Did you know we had such talent in The Pen, Carl?"

"I had no idea! But I do take credit for one of them. Biersdorf genes are strong!"

Chuck rolled his eyes, but he laughed too.

"Bryce knew," I said. "He was mentoring Chuck."

"That sounds like Bryce," said Carl.

"Devon knows too," piped up Tameasha. "He's my mentor."

Then Carl raised his glass.

"To Bryce and Devon and the next generation!"

~

THE NEXT MORNING WAS ROUGH, but I was out of bed soon after the alarm sounded because I couldn't wait to find out what the day would bring. It was my last day on *The Mr. Snicklefritz Show,* and we had brought Bryce's killer to justice. But had we saved the show? I roused my PR Posse, who had spent the night crammed into my place. Bleary-eyed but excited, we continually bumped into each other as we poured coffee, grabbed showers, and raided my closet.

Despite the late night, everyone was on time at *The Mr. Snicklefritz Show*. They must have been feeling just as anxious as I was about what the future would hold. We found everyone in the cafeteria, and after loading up our trays, we joined the PA Posse at their table.

"Long time, no see," joked Chuck, who was positively chipper. Already the future was looking brighter.

Then Marcus entered with Detective Donato.

"Attention, everyone! Attention!" Marcus began. "No doubt stories are running rampant about what took place here last night. So to begin, I have asked Detective Donato to give us the official word from the NYPD."

"Thank you. Last night, Larry Stubbins and Britney Spiers were apprehended and charged with the death of Bryce Camplen and three counts of attempted murder against Carl Biersdorf. No one else is under suspicion for Bryce's death or the attempts on Carl."

The cheers were so loud that I flinched, causing everyone at the table to laugh. It took Donato and Marcus several minutes to calm everyone down.

"As we make our case against the suspects," continued Donato, "I will be questioning some of you again, but no one else is under suspicion."

"Let's give Detective Donato and the NYPD a round of applause for their hard work on this case," urged Marcus, and the applause was thunderous.

"We have more people to thank," continued Marcus once the applause had died down to a low roar. "As you've no doubt heard, last night a group of our own risked their lives and were directly responsible for apprehending Larry and Britney, and luckily they're all sitting at the same table. Tameasha, Chuck,

Julia, Madison, Jill, Kate, Liz, Anupa, and Surya, you have our deepest gratitude."

The cast and crew were on their feet to give us a standing ovation. Tears filled my eyes, and I wasn't alone. The whole Posse, PA and PR, was a hot mess.

"I feel like Elrond just called us 'The Fellowship of the Ring,'" sobbed Madison.

"Is that a good thing?" asked Surya.

"The best!" Madison hiccoughed and buried her face in Chuck's shoulder.

I thought that would be the end of it, but when the applause finally died down and everyone sat, Marcus really got down to business.

"As you know, with the departure of Larry and Britney, we are left with some holes in our cast. But there's another hole, as well. After thirty years, Carl has decided to step down from his role as Mr. Snicklefritz."

There were gasps and murmurs around the room. Carl stood, and silence fell once more.

"If I have learned anything the last couple of weeks, it's that I alone am not Mr. Snicklefritz. It takes everyone in this room to make *The Mr. Snicklefritz Show,* and I know it's in good hands. I also know that there comes a time to make room for new talent, to pass on the opportunities so others may benefit as well. To that end, I would like to announce that my successor will be…" Carl looked at Chuck, who nodded firmly back at him. "Devon Cauthorne." With that, Carl strode over to a very stunned Devon and offered him his hand. Devon stood, and the two men shook hands and grinned at one another. Thus the woodcutter's cap was passed to the next generation.

"Oh snap!" I cried. "I wish I had a—"

"On it!" cried Kate as she captured the moment with her phone.

When the third round of applause finally died down, we all looked to Marcus and braced for the next surprise.

"Devon's move to the lead role will necessitate further staffing adjustments, so now I'd like to read a list of changes to cast and crew that will be effective immediately. First, Flavia Gomez will direct the remaining episodes of this season. As a result, Tameasha Horton is promoted to Floor Director. The role of Squirrelly-Joe will be played by Madison Klemper, and the role of Martin the Marten will be played by Chuck Cameron. And Julia Osgood will be our new right hand."

For a moment, the PAs were too stunned to react. More tears trickled down my face as I watched my friends' dreams come true. The moment it finally hit them was a thing of beauty. With a scream of delight, they collapsed in a group hug. Their joy was infectious, and soon people all around the room were grinning and surreptitiously wiping the corners of their eyes. My Posse and I were full-on ugly crying with joy. We didn't care who saw. The moment was perfect.

And then Dominique was there, and she was handing me something, a wand, a silver wand crusted with gemstones. And Flavia was placing a tall silver crown on my head. And Marcus was speaking again.

"And then there's the matter of Princess Gretel. She's supposed to be a role model, brave and kind, a true friend. You, Jill, have been a true friend, the best friend, to this production. Will you be our Princess Gretel?"

Thank the good Lord for waterproof mascara.

And that's how I found myself gliding into Gingerbread Cottage to read a story to my childhood pals. I don't think I was very good, but I enjoyed every minute of it. Everyone was very gracious and very patient, and they let me live out my childhood fantasy in the gown I had coveted since I was two. They had even moved back to the old set (for continuity reasons, according to Marcus), so it was like coming home. Life didn't get any better.

When the scene was done, everyone burst into applause, and I looked up to find my Posse beaming at me. As I carefully descended the set in my gargantuan confection of silver tulle, Flavia rushed towards me.

"That was fantastic! You're a natural. Do you think you could finish out the season as Princess Gretel? It's only one day a week."

Holy hoop skirts! Life could get better! But then I thought about my vacation days, all used up. I'd even called in sick on what was supposed to be my first day back at Waverly Communications so I could live my Snickle-fantasy. I couldn't see a way forward, and I was fixing to say thanks but no thanks when Kate answered for me.

"Of course she will!"

"We'll make sure of it!" added Surya firmly.

"It's what we do," murmured Liz as she pulled me in for a hug.

Anupa piled on. "We're her Posse."

A short time later, I found myself at the craft services table looking for bottled water. The peanut butter cups were calling to me, but since I'd barely been able to zip the zipper on the Princess Gretel gown, the cries of chocolate and peanut butter landed on deaf ears. Now that I was an actress, I was going to have to starve myself.

I was still chuckling at my own joke when Donato turned up trying very hard to look nonchalant.

"Really good job, Jill," he said with a smile as he reached for a peanut butter cup.

"The case or the acting?" I laughed.

"Both actually."

"Thank you."

Then he surprised me by leaning in conspiratorially.

"You know, Jill. You've never asked about…him."

Him. He meant Mike.

"Just know, you can ask about him. It's okay."

I gave Donato a long, hard look. He meant well.

"I don't know who you're talking about," I quipped. Then with a wink and a smile, I flounced off in the dress to rule all dresses with Donato chuckling in my wake.

Jill Cooksey is an island.

Part of an archipelago, actually, with lots of friendly neighbors who looked out for each other. Jill Cooksey was doing just fine.

EPILOGUE

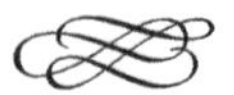

"Well, you already received—and used—your big present from me," said my mother with great satisfaction. I quelled an eye roll because it was Christmas and eye rolls didn't feel in keeping with the spirit of the holiday.

We were both sitting on the floor in front of the Christmas tree in the living room of my childhood home. Every surface as far as the eye could see was covered in Christmas decorations, from elaborate Santa dolls to bowls of clove-studded oranges. I could see at least three manger scenes without turning my head. A fire crackled in the hearth behind elaborately embroidered stockings. The air smelled of cloves and ham. I was in heaven.

Mom and I had been opening presents, but we had reached the end of the stack.

"Well, I guess that was the last one for this year," I said as I leaned over to kiss her cheek. "Thank you, Mama."

Mom had graced me with two work outfits, the next book (hardcover!) in the time travel romance series to which I was now addicted, and an enormous black concealed-carry purse with a special pocket for my .22—a Behemoth Black Bag with a bang.

Thanks to *The Mr. Snicklefritz Show,* I hadn't had to sell my hair to purchase presents for my mother, and I had gifted her with several new cruise-wear outfits with matching accessories. A shorter version of me, with the same blonde hair and blue eyes, she looked great in capris and boatneck shirts in shades of blue. I had also purchased some madras plaid boat shoes with a matching fanny pack that had her vowing to start researching her next cruise after Christmas dinner. For the joy of gift-giving alone, it was great to be back in the black.

"You're quite welcome, my dear." She kissed me back, licked her thumb, and scrubbed lipstick off my cheek. "I'm just going to go check on the ham. Can you start clearing up this wrapping?" She headed for the kitchen.

"I thought you said we were having chateaubriand for Christmas this year," I called to her as I crumpled festive paper.

Mom poked her head back into the living room.

"Now Jill, I said no such thing. Don't put words in my mouth." She popped out again.

"Okay, sure. My bad," I said while remembering distinctly that she had decided on Chateaubriand. "Whatever."

I finished gathering the wrapping paper and ribbons into a giant ball and carried it into the kitchen to put in the garbage. As I entered the room, the back door closed, and Santa Claus strolled past the kitchen window. I looked at my mother to find her looking slightly alarmed. And was her lipstick smudged?

"If I didn't know better, I'd say I just caught Mommy kissing Santa Claus."

"Don't be ridiculous, Jilly."

"Well, then who was that?"

"Just the mailman. He dresses like Santa on Christmas and makes the rounds."

"I didn't recognize him."

"He's new."

"I see you gave him some of our ham." I pointed to the succulent piece of glazed pork now resting on top of the stove, which was missing a chunk.

"Just being neighborly."

"Uh-huh."

"Don't take that tone with me, or I'll take back your Christmas presents!"

I chuckled. "Okay, Mama. Have your secret."

"Oh, pshaw!"

I opened the door to the utility room and tossed the wrapping in the garbage can. Between the can and the washing machine, I saw a cardboard tube with my name on it.

"What's this?" I held it up to show my mother.

"Oh, I forgot about that! It came a few days ago. It wasn't wrapped, so I didn't put it under the tree. I assume it's a Christmas present."

I examined the tube as I carried it into the living room. There was no return address, and my name and address had been written in block letters. The postmark, however, was from New York. Curiouser and curiouser.

Gathering scissors from the secretary in the corner, I plopped down in front of the fire and began cutting through layers of packing tape. Soon I had one end open, and I was sliding out a roll of heavy paper. I shook the tube for a card or something identifying the sender, but there wasn't one. Slowly, I unrolled the paper, but I knew exactly what it was before I had gone a quarter of the way. It was a movie poster and not for just any movie.

With great care not to tear the edges, I unrolled the poster and then placed nearby books and knickknacks at the corners to prevent it from rolling back up. Then I took a good look at the original movie poster for *Citizen Kane*. It was certainly a reproduction with bright colors unfaded by time, but it was beautiful.

And I knew who had sent it. I had no idea why, after two months and the incident in the park, he felt the need to send me a Christmas present, but it was undoubtedly from him.

I don't know how long I looked at the poster while my mother puttered in the kitchen. I wasn't aware of any conscious thought, but at some point, I must have made up my mind. Removing my makeshift paperweights, I rolled the poster up and began to lay it, like Rosebud, on the fire. Just before the flames could lick the edge of the paper…

I changed my mind and snatched it back.

Jill Cooksey will return in *Cruising Toward Death*.

ACKNOWLEDGMENTS

I'm so grateful to everyone—family, friends, and fans—who reached out to tell me how much they enjoyed *The Sweet Scent of Death* and who gave me so much support during its launch. Your love and enthusiasm was overwhelming, and I will forever treasure it. That encouragement helped me to believe the world would like to see another Jill Cooksey adventure and propelled me onward to finishing this book.

Thank you!

As always, I want to thank my alpha reader, Melissa Carothers, and my beta readers, Sarah Seager Stewart and Stephanie Thames, for their eagle eyes and honest feedback, and my cozy crew, Scarlett Moss and Molly Burton, for their sound advice. A second shout-out goes to Molly for another splendid cover. It's good to have a Posse.

Many moons ago, I worked in children's television with incredibly talented casts and crews, including some downright amazing puppeteers. I'm forever grateful that I got to be part of that world. Unlike Jill, I always felt at home in the puppet realm, but it was very amusing to see how some people reacted to the puppets. I'll admit that I channeled some of their discomfort into this book. Why wouldn't I? If you've ever seen a grown man brought low by a bright pink, towheaded puppet with ping-pong-ball eyes, then you'll know what I mean. Priceless! (Love you, Suzie.)

I owe the biggest debt of gratitude to my husband, Matthew. Not only does he give expert advice about weapons, he taught me to shoot last summer so I can write from experience. Most importantly, he's my biggest supporter who has never wavered during this past year of publishing highs and lows. I simply couldn't have done it without him.

Ephesians 5:20

ABOUT THE AUTHOR

Lesley St. James began her career in film and television before moving to public relations and then to education. A devoted, lifelong reader of mysteries, she always knew the kind of books she would write. When she's not writing or teaching writing, Lesley enjoys traveling, movies, and genealogy. She resides in Virginia with her husband, Matthew.

For more books, newsletters, and information,
please visit www.lesleystjames.com.

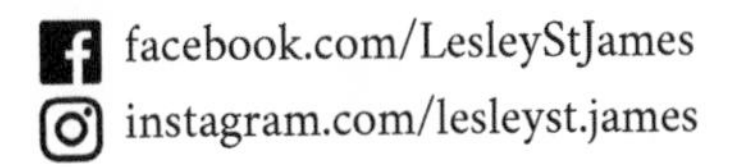

CPSIA information can be obtained
at www.ICGtesting.com
Printed in the USA
LVHW042312220621
690927LV00004B/172

9 781736 185551